Unbroken Silence

Henrik Ekström

www.henrikekstrom.com

Acknowledgements

A sincere thank you to the people that have put their time and effort into this book. To my wife, Nicole, who read it but also put up with me while I wrote it.

A big thank you to the main contributors. This book would still be a dust-collecting draft if it were not for you. My father Ulf, Helena M Linge, Andreas Häglund, John Emmanuel and the McCoy's, Darren, Nathan and Liam. Not to be forgotten the people who inspired the start and continued momentum of the project. Dave Scollon, Matt Gower, Simon Wood, Kieran Kelly.

Introduction

The extent of intrusions by foreign submerged vessels deep into Swedish waters is unknown to this day, at least to the general public. Navy personnel and civilian investigators have spent decades debating what took place without any firm conclusion.

The sixties and seventies held increasing sightings of underwater activity. In the early eighties, sightings increased rapidly, coinciding with a significant Soviet operation in the Baltic Sea. This led members of the Swedish Navy to believe these were submarines and underwater vessels originating from the Soviet Union.

On October 27th, 1981, these events culminated when the Soviet submarine *U-137* ran aground in the archipelago close to the Swedish naval base in Karlskrona. Witnesses aboard *U-137* stated faulty navigation equipment as the reason, while some Swedish naval officers believe the submarine was present to collect Soviet special forces practicing infiltration.

Severe tension between the countries

followed. After the grounding, and as the Soviet Navy looked to draw closer to Swedish waters, the Prime minister of Sweden, Thorbjörn Fälldin, famously uttered the order "Håll gränsen" (hold the border) to the Swedish Armed Forces.

U-137 was designated a Whiskey-class submarine by NATO, hence the event is jokingly referred to as "Whiskey on the rocks." In this particular case, there was little doubt about the facts. For many other sightings, debate about the legitimacy of the sighting and the nationality of the intruder is endless. At one point, the discussion was intense enough that even the Swedish Army allegedly accused the Swedish Navy of making up sightings to get their hands on a more significant part of the Swedish defense budget.

The largest operation occurred in 1982 in Hårsfjärden, close to the Swedish Naval Base Berga, south of Stockholm. Reports of contact with underwater vessels caused a flurry of activity, including the release of live weapons. By some, this was considered decisive action to drive an intruder away. Others deemed it a choreographed ruse for the benefit of international media.

Throughout this period, many events triggered discussion around a cover-up, and the four investigations that have followed have not cast any light on what could or could not have happened. Perhaps we will find out at the end of the seventy-year confidentiality stamp. Today, what happened beneath the surface of the Baltic Sea in the 80s remains unclear.

Visby, Sweden 2021
Henrik Ekstrom

Chapter 1 – Contacts

Baltic Sea, April 13th, 1982, 0745hrs

It could be nothing. Carl Lindberg reached forward and polished the screen with a small cloth. At the same time, he wiped the sweat from his other hand before rolling a finger across the tracker ball next to his keyboard. Referred to as an "ape skull" in Swedish Navy slang, the tracker ball allowed him to move the sonar's directional microphone.

The sonar would cover most of the 360 degrees around them, but this microphone would provide additional sound quality and relay it directly to his headphones. It would help him evaluate the contact, if he could find it again. Slowly, he moved the ape skull, sweeping the microphone back and forth across the bearing where he thought he had heard something. Blank. Nothing at all.

He cleaned his screen again and blinked his eyes a few times before looking back at it. Still nothing. The yellow line, which would indicate a contact, moved slightly with the ocean's background noise but with no indication of anything real. He looked up at the BTR, the printer that would continuously print the contact bearings on a paper roll as the minutes passed. The screen in front of him would tell him the bearing to the contact just now. The printer would tell him where it had been and how it was moving.

Squinting while running his index finger across it, he looked for anything that would mark the sound he thought he had heard. Not a thing. He reached for a pen to make a note of the time. That would help him rewind the tape later to see if he could find anything interesting.

Before he found his pen, another bulge appeared on the sonar screen and he immediately tracked the microphone toward it. The contact was weak but had appeared very suddenly. Lindberg looked at the time. *That makes sense*, he thought. He was confident that it must be the ferry from Visby.

"Con, Sonar. New contact bearing 175, weak. Bearing stable."

"Understood," the torpedo officer answered. "Is it the ferry?"

"Very likely, sir," Lindberg replied. "Give me a minute to confirm."

Lindberg closed his eyes and listened to the contact. It was an easy job when you knew what to listen for. *M/S Visby* would depart Visby Harbor at

0730, pass the rim of the pier 10–15 minutes later, which would remove all barriers for the sound of her engines and propellers to travel far out into the Baltic Sea. Twin screws, making only ninety RPM, would give her a speed of 8–10 knots. Cavitation was less than many ships her size but still considerable. It would increase as she accelerated to full cruising speed toward her destination, the Port of Nynäshamn south of Stockholm.

Cavitation was the lifeline of a Navy sonar operator. Often referred to as "cold-boiling" of the water, the change in pressure from the front and the back of a turning propeller blade generated millions of bubbles, like opening a bottle of champagne. As the bubbles collapsed, they made a noise that their sonar would pick up.

Lindberg pulled out a binder and checked the ferry timetable before listening for another thirty seconds. Then, he looked in the Navy ship library, which hosted characteristics of thousands of ships. M/S Visby had a bent propeller axle, which meant it would give off a squeak with every turn.

It was easy to find. Lindberg smiled to himself. Someone was stepping on a squeaky toy ninety times per minute.

"Con, Sonar. Contact bearing 175, now bearing 176. 90 RPM, twin screws, heavy cavitation, axle noise, on time according to the ferry schedule. Contact identified as *Gotland Ferry M/S Visby*."

That was the end of his report, but given the ferry and its destination, he added, "Contact likely to turn north shortly and increase speed to eighteen knots. She's coming right at us. The bearing will be stable and increase in strength over the next few hours."

"Understood, young man," the torpedo officer replied, already aware of what Lindberg just told him.

Lindberg's mind had been distracted by the ferry, but his body hadn't relaxed. He wiped his hands again before moving the microphone across the bearing of his phantom contact. The lack of sound was worse than anything he had ever heard.

* * *

Military headquarters, April 13th, 1982, 0800hrs
How are you able to be the highest-ranking officer in the Swedish Navy and still be subjected to shit coffee? Klas Nylund, vice admiral and head of the Swedish Navy, wasn't impressed with his reception. He hadn't been to this part of the military headquarters before and was unsure of the reason for having a briefing here. Undoubtedly, this was the work of the self-proclaimed know-it-alls in intelligence. He took a second to grin at his

4

thoughts. Judgment about coffee took priority over thinking about why he was here, along with a handful of senior commanders in the early morning hours.

He was interrupted by the Military intelligence commander who walked up to him, did not salute him as they were indoors, but did stand ramrod straight in front of him. Commander Ola Löfgren had started in the Navy but spent most of his career in military intelligence. He didn't think much of Nylund, but it came with the job to act in an old-fashioned military manner to please this relic. Nylund was older than his Army and Airforce counterparts, but all three possessed the same high-flying view of themselves.

Without further pleasantries, Ola Löfgren turned on his heel, walked a few steps to the large oak table, and dropped a folder, landing with a thud. *That caught their attention all right*, he thought as he sat down.

"Gentlemen, I know you're wondering why I've asked you here this morning." There was a grunt of agreement among the officers, now all sitting around the oak table. It looked to weigh as much as a small car. Löfgren was happy he hadn't been the one to move it into place for the briefing. His herniated disc wouldn't have done well with that.

"There's something we need to talk about."

Nylund sat at the end of the table, looking at the intelligence officer with ill-concealed disdain. He had an impulse to reproach Löfgren to show who was boss in this room, but he was also keen to get to the content of this session. He had lived through the shit coffee, and hopefully, that wouldn't have been in vain. Nylund couldn't help himself from letting out a sigh and whispering, "Well, let's get on with it then, Commander."

In response, Löfgren shot Nylund a short look of defiance.

"Well, then," he said as he stood up, walked a lap around his chair for effect, and then looked at his audience. "On April 11th, 0945 to 0953, a submarine was sighted in Danziger Gatt."

Löfgren took a breath to continue, but Nylund, already underwhelmed, interjected, "Why are you trying to brief the Navy on a sighting? That runs through our operational office. I haven't seen anything about Danziger Gatt."

He was pleased when he got a nod from the commander of the fourth surface fleet and what he felt was silent agreement from the rest. It wasn't the place of intelligence to tell the Navy what happened in their waters. Fueled by the audience's response, he continued, "You haven't spoken to the lady who saw the last three periscopes, have you? She's so lonely out there in her cabin, she looks for company wherever she can find it." The crowd was warming up, and Nylund was contemplating continuing his rant.

Löfgren looked at the group with no hint of a smile and continued with a stern voice. "It did run through your operational office, and you ignored it."

The crowd turned silent, waiting for the response of the Navy chief before daring to commit to a reaction. Nylund shot Löfgren an angry look but didn't find suitable words to go along with it.

"It was on the surface, and it is not, I repeat, it is not one of ours," Löfgren continued.

"How can you be so sure?" asked Nylund, whose brain just caught up with the news, only realizing after the fact that this was the wrong question to ask. What did Löfgren mean the Navy had ignored it? Before he got his thoughts straight, Löfgren was well into his explanation.

"One, our submarines are accounted for, and none of them were in Danziger Gatt. Two, one of the witnesses sketched it and sent the picture to us."

Löfgren pulled a few pieces of paper from a binder and handed them out. "As you can tell, the shape of the conning tower is completely at odds with a Swedish submarine. I trust this doesn't look like Sjöormen or Näcken to you, gentlemen?"

Nylund said nothing for a few seconds, as his mind was still working out what to do next. He decided to interrupt Löfgren and get some clarity on this. "When was this sighting reported, and why have I not been made aware of this?"

Löfgren flicked through some notes on the table.

"First report was called in on the 11th at 1010. Naval operations requested a visual scan from the crew at Mällsten. There was also a flyover by a Coast Guard airplane that happened to be in the area. Both searches came back blank, and it seems the Navy took no further action."

This was bad news. Nylund would have to get to the bottom of it. He could sense the uneasiness among his commanders in the room on being called out like this. Technically, it wasn't their job to report a sighting, but somewhere along the way, naval routine had broken down.

The number of sightings since last year made it difficult to cope, but if this leaked, it would be an embarrassment for the Navy, another one to add to the pile. Nylund decided to change tactics and go on the offensive.

He spoke to Löfgren in a harsh tone. "So, you've had information on this for two days, and this is the first we hear of it? What the hell have you people been doing? Why were we not informed immediately?"

Löfgren was sure he had their attention, as well as the psychological advantage. "Gentlemen," he said with a softer tone than necessary, acting like the adult in the room. "As you know, there are many of these sightings every year, and before the sketch landed on my desk later in the day, we didn't know more than you did. Once we saw the sketch and questioned the witnesses, it took us a fair bit to confirm that this wasn't one of our own." Löfgren paused. "It's not."

Nylund now struggled to keep himself under control. "Why would a sketch like this end up on your desk and not with Navy operations?"

"I don't know, Admiral. It seems a man handed it to the Navy personnel in the guard booth, and it stayed there for hours until someone finally brought it upon themselves to walk it up to the main building. Major confusion if you ask me."

An intense discussion followed among the commanders in the room. More than one thing had gone wrong in the Navy that day. They mentioned the lack of resources. Also mentioned were the many budget cuts the socialists had carried out through the past decade.

"The nationality of the boat?" Löfgren interrupted, bringing them back to the matter at hand.

Before he could answer his rhetorical question, Commander Melker Nilsson from the first submarine division at Berga interrupted him.

"There's no way we can be certain based on this sketch. It could be anything. However, if the

sketch is correct, it can't be a Swedish submarine."
He continued, "We can speculate as to why it's here
and who it is. The main question to me is, why the
hell is it running on the surface? Except for a
catastrophic mechanical failure, nobody in their
right mind would run on the surface in foreign
waters." Commander Nilsson leaned back in his
chair as if to signal the end of his contribution,
leaving a gaping hole in the conversation.

* * *

Baltic Sea, April 13th, 1982, 1130hrs

What the hell is going on here? Lindberg frowned as
he heard it again. What is that? Most contacts had
some rhythm to them. That was the effect of being
propelled by machinery. A diesel engine turning
over, a propeller churning through the water. It all
produced a rhythm you could dance to. Fishing
vessels with their smaller, usually three-bladed
propellers would give out the standard Waltz-like
one-two-three, one-two-three, but at an RPM that
was fast enough to make it hard to count, let alone
dance to. 130–150 maybe, more than two
revolutions per second. The larger tankers and
cargo vessels typically had four-bladed propellers,
larger with a lower RPM, 70–80—easy to count.
One-two-three-four, one-two-three-four. Slow
foxtrot.

There was something there. Diffuse and with no hint of a rhythm. Like someone taking a piss on the stone floor of a cathedral. The Swedish submarine made forty RPM, giving it a speed of about four knots. This meant they were nothing but a hole in the water, almost impossible to detect. The bearing to the contact wasn't moving much, so whatever it was, it also moved slowly. He heard it at bearing 301 a few hours ago and now estimated it to be at its strongest, if you could call it that, at 290. Whoever was relieving himself in the cathedral was almost standing still—probably trying not to piss on his shoes.

Lindberg snapped out of his thoughts. "What is that?" The torpedo officer had the con and was moving around the command center. Now he was leaning over Lindberg's shoulder, looking at the screen.

"What?" was all that Lindberg managed to get out.

"That," said the torpedo officer with a stern voice, pointing to a slight bulge in the yellow line on the screen.

"Damn, Lindberg, stop daydreaming and focus on your fucking job, or I'll personally rip your head off. You know the first paragraph of the submarine rulebook, right? So, follow it."

The torpedo officer took a few steps back toward his regular pacing area next to the periscope, before turning around and gesturing angrily at Lindberg to get on with his job.

The first paragraph of the Swedish Navy submarine regulation stated that *one man's failure to perform his duty might endanger the ship and all of its crew.* It was a call to teamwork in this unique environment, where failed collaboration could have fatal consequences.

Lindberg looked at his screen. "Con, Sonar. New contact bearing 126, weak." He looked at the BTR waterfall. "Bearing moving right, slowly."

"Yes, I already know that," answered the torpedo officer, aggression lingering in his voice. "So, what is it?"

Lindberg listened to the contact for thirty seconds and then moved on to his second report. "Con, Sonar. Contact bearing 126, now bearing 127, 85 RPM. Single screw. Heavy cavitation. Turbodiesel. Contact classified as a large merchant, moving toward us."

Need to sort my shit out, Lindberg thought.

As the contact bearing 127 continued to move right and the BTR plotted its movements, he picked up the sliding ruler and estimated the plot's angles. He spent thirty seconds calculating the movements of the contact.

"Con, Sonar. Contact reported 126, now bearing 136, estimated course 220, estimated speed, 12 knots, Calculated distance 111

12

hectometers."

"Understood," the torpedo officer responded, still pissed off.

The captain entered the command center, casually walking around overlooking the ongoing activities. He walked past the radio room and glanced over Lindberg's shoulder at the sonar screen and BTR. "Clean plot," he stated but kept moving without waiting for a response. He disappeared, moving toward the galley, and returned a minute later with a cup of coffee. The smell quickly filled the small compartment, spreading an intense feeling of home.

As Lindberg drew a full breath of the aroma, he froze in his chair. There it was again. Bearing 285. Barely distinguishable from regular background noise. *I'm probably just hearing ghosts here*, he thought while moving the ape skull back and forth to find the best signal. *Highly questionable whether that's anything*, he thought, but he couldn't convince himself. He looked at his watch, which read 1143. He was due to hand over his shift in seventeen minutes. *To hell with it,* he thought. Corporal Wikingsson from the port watch, who would likely replace him, was useless anyway. He wouldn't pick it up if it ran him over. Looking at the screen and not letting himself drift into thoughts again reminded him of the torpedo officer scolding him just a few minutes earlier.

The submarine rulebook also stated that he needed to report every possible contact. *Possible is a relative term*, Lindberg thought, knowing that if he reported it, the sonar chief would come rushing. He was on the port watch and would be having lunch now.

The captain's voice echoed through the room. "Coming up on 1200hrs. We need to report our position."

He turned to the helmsman. "Forward sixty RPM; make your depth two-five meters."

"Forward sixty RPM. Make my depth two-five meters. Aye, sir," the helmsman answered, punching the new orders into the steering console.

Lindberg's mind started racing, and he could feel his heart rate pick up. Twenty-five meters meant they would pass through the temperature layer and get closer to the background noise on the surface. If he was to report anything, it would have to happen this second—this very second. As he felt his heart rate throbbing in his temples, he took a deep breath.

"Con, Sonar. New contact bearing 285, weak, bearing stable."

Chapter 2 – Rising Stakes

Stockholm, April 13th, 1130hrs

Löfgren had left the others in the meeting room after the briefing. It had taken some doing to get the Navy out of disbelief about the submarine. Even more to engage them with the important questions of who, why, and how. Those were their real concern. Especially the question of how a foreign submarine could run on the surface in Swedish waters without being detected. *Bold bastard*, Löfgren thought, allowing his mind to wander, soon settling upon the submarine's captain. Surfacing his boat in foreign waters. Bold indeed.

Löfgren didn't care about the sighting. This event would undoubtedly create the right effect within the ranks of the Navy, high command, and the government. Now it was a case of making this stick. He had seen it before and was confident he could predict the Navy's next moves.

The Navy receiving this sighting and doing nothing but call someone to have a look through binoculars was an embarrassment for them. They would likely first interrogate every detail of the sighting to see if they could make it go away. If they failed to do so they would come up with some plausible, but probably halfway-false, explanation to make themselves look better. They would start throwing rocks his way to see if they could label this whole thing as misinformation and confusion based on incompetence in the intelligence community.

In one way, he felt for them. The Swedish military suffered greatly through the seventies due to continuous budget cuts. The Navy struggled with the mission to control over three thousand kilometers of coastline while it saw its resources diminish. It wasn't an easy task. That was why this sighting needed to get further up the chain. It started last year with *U-137*, but they needed to fuel fire to get the politicians moving.

Löfgren looked at his watch. Once he arrived back to his office, maybe it was time to place that call to his contact at the Ministry of Defense. Just to make sure they were ready for the Navy. The sailor boys would come knocking once they got their act together.

* * *

Military Headquarters, April 13th, 1140hrs
Back in the room, Klas Nylund sat at the oak table's end. Sunk into his chair, he wore a tired expression on his face.

"One sighting," he said out loud. "A few people claim to have seen a submarine. This happens to us forty times per year. This one we miss, and of course, it happens to land with military intelligence. This makes us look even worse than last year. Then we didn't see it. This time we saw it and didn't do anything."

Nylund was in a foul mood after the embarrassment of being schooled by intelligence. They should keep doing what they were supposed to and stay out of naval operations.

"How can the rats in intelligence find this claim more believable than the regular ones? The old lady on the island sees a new periscope every month."

"The statement from the observer is quite detailed," the head of the fourth surface fleet started. "The sketch—"

"The sketch is a thermos with a square on top," Nylund interrupted. "Some six-year-old could draw that." He stood up and wandered around the room's far end for a minute. Then, he turned to the group. "I don't buy this. Where was this guy again? The one who did the sketch."

Melker Nilsson looked through some papers in front of him. "He was in his boat, heading back toward Nynäshamn."

"So, he saw a submarine on the surface running through Danziger Gatt, without anyone else getting a good look at it. You tell me how that's possible. The place is swarming with people. You could see that thing from the ferry running to Gotland." He paced around the room again, wishing his wife hadn't made him throw out his cigarettes before she decided to leave him altogether. He could use one now.

* * *

Baltic Sea, April 13th, 1155hrs
Both the captain and the torpedo officer stood in the middle of the command center, staring straight at Lindberg—the question written across their faces. They were waiting for more information about the contact that he just reported. Lindberg felt their eyes on the back of his head as he moved the microphone across bearing 285.

The submarine changed its trim as the helmsman pulled back on his steering wheel to take it to the ordered depth. A minute passed before the helmsman called out, "current depth two-five meters, balanced."

"Understood," the captain said without taking his eyes off the back of Lindberg's head. Then he decided he didn't want to wait any longer.

"Sonar, 285, what's going on?"

Lindberg had to say something. He couldn't pick up anything in 285 now and wasn't sure what to say. "I heard some noise at 285, but it's gone now."

"Some noise?" the torpedo officer said, surprised. "Was it a contact or not?"

"It was, I think, very faint, and I couldn't make out what it was. Not anything I have heard before. No rhythm."

The captain walked over to him and looked at the BTR. "I can't see any contact at 285, son."

"I know. It was fast and faint and . . ." Lindberg sweated profusely as he stuttered the last words under his breath. "Like pissing on a stone floor in a cathedral."

The torpedo officer grinned. "Okay, I've heard enough of this. I'm going to have lunch. Get your shit together, Lindberg. First, you're daydreaming, and now you're pissing in a church."

He turned toward the mess hall as he called for Wikingsson to come in and relieve Lindberg in sonar.

The captain looked at Lindberg. "Contact or no contact, Petty Officer Lindberg?"

"Contact, sir"

The captain frowned. He knew better than anyone that ignoring contacts, especially those that disappeared as you moved above a layer, wasn't the right thing to do. Besides that, the young sonar operator looked like he had seen a ghost. The captain turned toward the door to the mess hall.

"Sonar Chief."

Sonar Chief Edward Sandberg stuck his head inside. "Yes, sir?"

"Lindberg has a possible contact we need to verify. Get your butt in here. Hook up to console two."

"Right away, sir."

Sandberg was too tall to be a submariner, but years of experience had taught him where to duck. He expertly navigated his way to his seat at the second sonar console. Lindberg liked him. He was a calm, quiet man. Mid-thirties. He must have been overlooked for promotion or further training at least once, as he was still a chief petty officer. He was a nerd with no drive to command a submarine but was more interested in perfecting his sonar skills. Sonars and chopping wood in his uncle's cabin; that was Sandberg in a nutshell.

Either way, Lindberg had seen nobody like him. He could take indistinguishable clutter and turn it into something sensible, while the rest were still simply guessing. He wasn't the Sonar Chief for no reason.

"What are we looking at?" Sandberg said as he sat down and put on his headphones. Lindberg gave him the rundown of only the last brief contact and, before he finished, Sandberg hit rewind on one of the tape recorders next to them.

The captain looked at his watch. It was time

for them to report their position to base.

"Ahead forty RPM. Take us to periscope depth."

The signal officer walked up to the captain. "Position is ready to be sent. You want to include anything on this contact?"

The captain scratched his stubbled chin while thinking for a while.

"No, no need. Just the regular things."

As the helmsman reported the submarine balance at one-three meters, the captain simply nodded to the signal officer, who quickly disappeared into his little cabin. They could still hear his voice as he instructed the enlisted radioman. "Up antenna."

"Antenna going up," the radioman answered. While responding, he would hold the switch that raised the antenna above the surface.

"Antenna is up. Ready to transmit."

"Transmit message. Lower the antenna."

Only a few seconds later, the radioman confirmed.

"Message transmitted. Antenna coming down."

* * *

Stockholm, April 13th, 1220hrs

Nylund walked out into the spring sun. He was hungry. The early start and the need to find a new corner of the facility had prevented breakfast. This intelligence clown Löfgren thought he could ambush the chief of the Navy. He should know his place.

The discussion had progressed well after Löfgren left, though. Melker Nilsson of the first submarine division couldn't care less about this sighting. He was constantly busy confirming the exact whereabouts of his boats to rule them out, as people were calling in "sightings." Someone saw the Loch Ness monster, and he had to start radioing his boats on the low frequencies and spend his time waiting for them to report in. Bloody nuisance. The head of the fourth surface fleet was keener to go out and check the observation. Per Bergwall was an obsessive bastard but an excellent commander.

Ultimately, Nylund convinced them that this report needed to go away. The Navy had been discredited enough. Beaten down by budget cuts and lack of training to then be ridiculed for not managing its mission. This would not be the final nail in his coffin. There was no submarine in Danziger Gatt, and that was it. Melker Nilsson was right in his initial question. A submarine running on the surface in foreign waters. A foolish and unlikely idea.

The previous year, *U-137* had hit a rock in the Swedish archipelago outside Karlskrona. That was true. But that would only deter them from running around Swedish waters again, Nylund figured. If the submarine had enough mechanical troubles to surface, it would still be on the surface. It was not. Tons of ships running in and out of Nynäshamn port would have seen it.

They would add it as a sighting to the thick binder of people seeing floating logs and fishing equipment. He probably wouldn't even have to bring this up with high command at their regular briefings. It would all go away if Löfgren, the ambitious bastard, kept his mind focused on better things.

Maybe he could get one of his counterparts in Poland to send a coded message to be picked up by the Swedish spy ships. That should keep Löfgren busy for a few months, trying to figure out what the Warsaw pact was up to. Brilliant. It might be worth giving Slawek a call.

* * *

Baltic Sea, April 13th, 1230hrs
Sandberg spent fifteen minutes rewinding the tape—probably thirty times. He exchanged the roll of paper in the BTR to rip the other one out and examine it in detail. Sandberg took a lot longer than

23

both Lindberg and the Captain expected. He regularly identified things in thirty seconds or less but was struggling this time. Sandberg grimaced to himself while listening to the tape for what felt like the fiftieth time. Eventually, he took off his headphones.

"Very hard to tell, could be some compression noise. Very faint. The soft thud could be rudder hydraulics, but I wouldn't bet my car on it."

The captain interrupted. "So, if what you just said is right, you're thinking submerged contact?"

Sandberg looked uneasy in his chair. He wasn't used to being uncertain. "Unlikely it's a surface vessel, sir, if I could add some complete guesswork."

"Vague contact that disappears as we pass above the layer. Now you're saying an unlikely surface vessel."

The captain didn't hesitate for long. "We'll take a look on the surface to rule out that option. Up periscope."

* * *

Stockholm, April 13th, 1430hrs

Löfgren left the café after finishing his lunch. He had spoken to his contact at the Ministry of Defense. If his judgment didn't play any tricks on him, the Navy might try to make this sighting go away. Pretend to have done some follow-up work before sticking it in an archive in some damp basement. There, it would be forgotten with the other submarine sightings they received every year. He couldn't let that happen this time around. He needed to inform high command and the government about this. The Navy desperately needed the funds that would come its way following another intrusion.

He made a right at the end of Västerlånggatan and followed Järntorgsgatan toward Slussplan. He made a 180-degree turn at the end, crossed the street, and doubled back. He wanted to see who might be interested in following him. He walked northbound up to Tullgränd before he pivoted again and walked back the same stretch for the third time, scanning all the people on the street to see if anyone suddenly seemed extra interested in the shop windows. When satisfied with the people's behavior on the street, he turned left onto Norra Dryckesgränd and continued down Skeppsbron. He had one more personal appointment today.

Stockholm, April 13th, 1430hrs

Damn snake, Nylund thought after slamming the phone down hard. One of the aides from the office of the high command had just phoned him and asked questions about the possible sighting of a submarine. A sighting in Danziger Gatt that the Navy had reported. There was only one way this information could have reached high command, Ola Löfgren.

Löfgren was hard to get to. He had been consorting with the Supreme Commander for years and had undeniably been appointed to his current role directly by Rosenfeldt himself.

His aide carefully opened the door, but was met by a hiss from Nylund.

"Get out."

The aide immediately closed the door and disappeared down the corridor. Nylund regretted his behavior, but there was no time to think about that now. High command would meet tomorrow at 0800hrs, and he would need to brief them on this.

Things are falling apart quickly, he thought. If they know about the sighting, they would know the Navy had withheld this information without any attempts to present it. This is out of the bag already. He would need to have a plausible scenario that explained both the sighting and his behavior. That will have to be the priority, but I'll find a way to get the upper hand on this bastard Löfgren, once that's done.

Chapter 3 – Confirmation

Baltic sea, April 13th, 1330hrs

Lindberg's vessel had been running close to the surface for almost an hour. The end of his watch had come and gone, and he rubbed his eyes to try to get them to give him a clearer picture of the sonar screen. The rubbing didn't help.

The captain wanted to verify Sandberg's suspicion that this wasn't a surface contact. As this was peacetime, he had even spent most of the hour steaming west toward the potential contact. They used both visual and electronic search to see what was out there.

The ESM operator, whose job it was to track radar signals, had picked up a lot of radar traffic in the area throughout the last hour. It all seemed to be from known models of civilian radars, and there was nothing close to 285 where Lindberg had reported the contact. Their own radar confirmed what the ESM operator reported. Nothing at 285.

The captain was tired, and though he had shown great determination to follow up on Lindberg's report an hour ago, his resolve seemed to soften as time passed. Stefan Lindholm was an experienced submarine captain with most of his time on the Swedish submarines *Nordkaparen* and *Sjöhunden.*

He was likely on the verge of retirement from active duty over the next year or two to leave room for the executive officers next in line to take up their commands. He was tired, and it was clear that he had hoped for a swift and straightforward resolution to this predicament Lindberg had put him in. The man was a professional, though, and it would be uncharacteristic for him to do the wrong thing.

"Okay, I've seen enough," Lindholm said, not directing the words toward anyone in particular. "We'll get below the layer and see if there's anything there to have a look at. Then, we move on northbound toward Berga." He spoke with weariness, going through the motions without conviction that this would lead anywhere.

"Ahead sixty RPM. Port twenty degrees rudder. Make your course 180." The submarine leaned to port as they initiated the turn.

The helmsman confirmed the new course and speed. "Sixty RPM, running, 180, on course."

"Understood," the captain responded. "Nice and easy now. Make your depth four-five meters. That should leave us some room below the keel still." As if to confirm what he just said, he took one step and leaned over the chart laid out on the navigator's table. The depth at this location was 65 meters, with a deep trench of 112 meters coming up in front of them.

Sandberg was at his station at the second console while Lindberg was still sitting in console one. He was tired after the long and somewhat eventful watch. Similar to the captain, he looked forward to completing this so they could head home. If he was lucky, he wouldn't be up for pulling watch on the weekend. Then he could see Jenny.

Once at the designated depth, they let a few minutes pass. Except for some merchant traffic, there was no sign of any contact. Sandberg was so focused on his screen that Lindberg wasn't sure if he ever blinked. The captain walked by, had a look at their screens, and just gave Sandberg a questioning look.

"Nothing," said Sandberg. "Regular merchant traffic but nothing out of the ordinary."

The captain walked back to his regular pacing area next to the navigator's table. "Let's check our back."

The nose-mounted sonar theoretically had 360-degree capabilities, but the hull of the submarine and the sound of its own propeller would compromise its efficiency straight aft. Submarines routinely made changes to their course to make sure that nothing could sneak up behind them.

Sandberg straightened up in his seat and almost shouted, "Con, Sonar. New contact bearing 344, medium."

The entire command center snapped to attention in their seats. Suddenly, the belief that this was a wild goose chase disappeared, and they all inadvertently turned their heads away from their panels and toward Sandberg.

Without waiting for the regular confirmation reply from whoever had the con, Sandberg continued, "Compressed cavitation. Not sure of the range, but it must be close."

Lindberg was listening to the bearing as well but was hopelessly behind Sandberg in dealing with this sound. It was the same as he had heard before but more evident this time. The movement in bearing seemed to be increasing. It was close.

Sandberg's voice came through the command center again. "Contact 344, five-bladed propeller, forty RPM and increasing. It's a submarine. It's a submarine for sure."

Lindberg's mind raced. It couldn't be one of theirs. Swedish submarines always operated alone in peacetime due to the risk of misunderstandings or collisions. It had to be someone else.

"We came down right in front of it." The captain swore under his breath before he continued. "Ahead eighty RPM. Left full rudder. Go to battle stations."

A siren sounded on board, and the torpedo officer's voice came over the intercom. "Battle stations, battle stations."

The siren sounded again. Within seconds, hatches to different compartments opened, and people hurried through the boat to their respective battle stations. Once the crew had made it to the correct compartment, the heavy watertight hatches were closed again. The tables in the mess hall were covered in green cloth, while all the medical instruments were hung on the wall, all within reach of the ship's medical officer. Each section reported in, and when they were all ready, the torpedo officer confirmed the ship's status.

"Ship is at battle stations, Captain."

Lindberg was almost shaking in his seat, and it took considerable effort not to panic. The prospect of actual underwater combat made his heartbeat to levels where it was hard to think. The captain, visibly tense but vigilant, turned toward Sandberg but didn't have to give the order to start attack protocol on the contact. Sandberg was already ahead of him and knew perfectly well what he needed to do.

"Submarine bearing 344, now bearing 342, contact marked, designated target Alpha. Sending to fire control."

The torpedo officer answered while still

struggling to get into his seat, "Got it, got it, target Alpha, bearing 342. SESUB is working on it."

SESUB was the fire control computer that now continuously received sonar data from console two and worked to determine the course, speed, and most importantly, the range to the contact.

Lindberg sat in his chair, frozen solid, unable to do anything. He shook his head and eventually reached for his ruler and the Q-plot paper he needed to start his paper plot.

It was Navy standard operating procedure once they initiated attack protocol. While SESUB chewed on the data, a Sonar Petty Officer, using pen and paper, would work on it as well. Computers were faster and better at calculating, but they had no common sense or judgment. If there was a glitch between the sonar console and SESUB, a human would spot the error while the computer mostly kept going, ending up with the wrong result.

It was too late to start a meaningful Q-plot. It would take five to ten minutes to get a good picture and who knew for how long this could go on?

For all its excitement and action in the movie theatre, most submarine combat was long, slow, and very drawn out. This situation was different, as they had stumbled on the contact, and it was already at close range. How close was unclear. Due to the sonar regulating the contact's sound level automatically, either enhancing a weak contact or pulling back on something substantial, it was impossible to hear how far away something was. The fast and initially increasing change in bearing, however, told them that this was close. He might be dead before he managed to get his first calculations in order. Maybe he would never see Jenny again.

"We'll lose Alpha in our wake," Sandberg announced. "We need to keep turning before she disappears behind us.

"All ahead full, left full rudder," the captain responded immediately. Now with a calmer demeanor than a moment earlier.

"Any change in course on Alpha? Is she turning?"

"No, sir. RPM is increasing still, and she's on a straight course.

"SESUB has a range," the torpedo officer stated. "Target Alpha, now bearing 265, distance twenty-two hectometers. Not sure on that one but feels reasonable given the movements in bearing."

The torpedo compartment reported tubes five and six now flooded, and they were ready to open the hatches on command. Once the front torpedo hatch was open, they would be ready to fire.

Sandberg's voice again. "She's doing well over 150 RPM now and turning her back to us. I have clear propeller noise. Single screw, confirmed five blades."

"She's still on course?" the captain asked, half-expecting the answer to be no. Turning your back on a threat and running was an excellent option in some situations where you could outrun a torpedo. At this range, there was no way the target would be able to escape fast enough to escape their weapon. By turning tail and running, the targets propeller would interfere with its own sonar and it would lose contact with the Swedish submarine. It could even be hard to hear a torpedo while running at that speed.

That makes no sense, Lindberg thought. The target just tried to put as much distance as possible between itself and Lindberg's boat, with complete disregard for anything else.

"What's our exact position?" the captain asked.

A second later, the navigator read out the position. Confirming what the captain really wanted to know, the navigator continued, "We're in Swedish waters, Captain."

They were in Swedish waters, and this wasn't a Swedish submarine. That would mean they were authorized to release a live weapon at the target.

The captain knew better than anyone, the risk that the navigator was wrong was almost nonexistent. They had a position-fix from running close to the surface less than two hours old and had been on a westerly course toward the Swedish mainland since then. That position put them more than two nautical miles inside Swedish territorial waters. There was no doubt to be had, but the Captain still wanted absolute certainty before firing the weapon.

"Double-check that position. This isn't the time or place to get our position wrong."

The navigator let out a sharp snort at this doubt of his expertise, but he followed the order and spent a few seconds bent over his chart.

"Position is good, Captain. We're in Sweden, all right."

Captain Lindholm decided to disengage from what looked like an underwater hi-speed chase. Firing at high speed would increase the risk of having a wire failure and losing control of the weapon. Besides, the torpedo would be able to make up any lost distance.

"Ahead forty RPM. Make your heading 190."

The submarine had come almost full circle and was coming up behind the target. As their speed decreased, the captain ordered the torpedo crew to open the hatches, which would mean the torpedo officer could fire the torpedoes from SESUB.

"Contact is weakening. Target is passing up through the layer," Sandberg said.

"Make your depth two-five meters," answered the captain. "We'll stay right on her in case she slows down again and tries to disappear."

Lindberg wasn't sure what to do besides doing his best with the Q-plot, but there was something odd about this. He wasn't as experienced as most of the other officers in the command center, but it seemed like the target wasn't behaving as you would expect.

Like running into an enemy soldier in the woods, and what you do is turn your back and run, making it easy for him to shoot you in the back. Why would you do that? Why would you desperately put distance between yourself and your enemy like that? Because you knew that you needed to be out of the way. Out of the way of what?

Sandberg's voice brought him out of his thoughts, "Alarm, torpedo bearing 134, port 56, torpedo moving left."

Lindberg finished his thought from before. The target ran away because he desperately needed to make sure his friend knew who was who, and he needed to get out of the way in case the torpedo's guidance wire broke. Without thinking, Lindberg blurted out his conclusion. "There's two of them."

Sandberg shot him a quick glance that told Lindberg he was stating the obvious.

The captain responded with surprising calm. "Fire tube five."

The torpedo officer pushed the safety catch on his console and proclaimed, "Limit maneuvering, tube five, firing in three, two, one, fire."

Limiting the maneuvering when firing the torpedo was another precaution to minimize the risk of the guidance wire breaking. Once the torpedo officer had pushed the button, the captain interrupted and continued, "Close the torpedo doors. All ahead flank, right full rudder." The helmsman responded and turned the boat away from the incoming torpedo.

"Get a noisemaker ready aft," the captain ordered, "and stand ready at the air release."

Sandberg continued, "Torpedo moving left. Port fifty-nine, port sixty-five, port eighty." To make it easier for the captain to determine where the torpedo was, he didn't express it as a bearing. Instead, the sonar operators would convey on which side the torpedo was as well as the angle. The torpedo was moving left on its own, which was now compounded by the Swedish submarine turning sharply.

It wasn't unexpected, given the captain's order to shut the torpedo hatch, but the torpedo officer reported it anyway, "Lost the wire on fish five. It will continue for the last known position."

As the guiding wire for the torpedo was cut, they'd lost the ability to control the weapon and wouldn't get any information from its seeker-head. The fish was on its own. Best case, they would hear the explosion. If there was no hit, the torpedo would search for a target until it ran out of fuel and then sink to the bottom.

"Port 115, port 150, port 165." The incoming torpedo was now on their rear, and they were running at twenty knots away from it. The question was if the distance between them and the torpedo would be enough or whether it would catch up with them before it ran out of fuel.

The captain wasn't going to wait and see. Still at a depth of twenty-five meters, there was water below them to play with, not to mention the temperature layer at about thirty to thirty-five meters.

"Chief, launch the noisemaker, stand ready for air release."

The chief engineer pushed a button on his console to eject a small canister through the aft release chamber of the submarine. A few seconds after ejecting, it would create millions of bubbles in the water, something that would be picked up as an echo by the torpedo's active search sonar and that would block their submarine's noise from any passive sensors that were in play.

"Okay, helm, nine-zero meters. Quickly."

The boat immediately started to tilt forward. The helmsman needed no additional motivation to push the rudders to their max and dive as fast as possible. *Just make sure you pull up in time*, Lindberg thought as he checked his seatbelt.

The captain had his eyes glued at the depth gauge. "Air release in three, two, one, now."

The engineer twisted a valve. Compressed air flowed through small tubes installed alongside the conning tower's outside and spread millions of bubbles that stayed above the layer and rose toward the surface. As they created chaos in the water, the submarine dove deeper in an attempt to disappear. The helmsman read out the depth as the submarine descended. "Three-zero meters, four-zero meters, five-zero meters."

"All stop," the captain ordered. The helmsman repeated the command, but the tension in his voice was clear as he realized he would come out of his dive with no propulsion. It didn't sound like a big problem in theory, but it would require a skilled helmsman to deal with what he was up against.

As the submarine slowed down, the rudders would be utterly useless in controlling the submarine's depth. All that was left was to balance it by controlling the amount of water in the main tank, much like a scuba diver inflating or deflating their diving vest. If a submarine was sluggish using rudders, balancing it by pumping water in and out was considerably more difficult. Losing control of the boat and missing the depth by ten meters wouldn't be uncommon.

The helmsman started to pull the submarine out of its dive. "Eight-zero meters, nine-zero meters."

That was terrible. Once at reported depth, the helmsman should follow up the statement with the word *balanced* to report that he had the boat under control at the ordered depth. A second later, things were getting worse.

"Sinking through," said the helmsman.

The captain darted over to him, looking over his shoulder. "How much?"

"Nine-four meters, nine-seven meters. Turning, the boat is turning. Depth under keel fourteen meters."

They all let out a sigh of relief, as it was clear they wouldn't plow a furrow into the seabed. At least not yet. Just as Lindberg started breathing again, Sandberg's voice reminded him of the original threat.

"Torpedo actively transmitting, port 175, port 177, starboard 179."

Lindberg's second of relief was replaced by gripping fear as he realized the torpedo was still tracking them.

Chapter 4 – Submarine Late

Stockholm, April 13th, 2030hrs

Löfgren took a long sip of his drink. *Not bad,* he thought as he savored the taste of juniper and lime. Not bad at all. He checked his watch and noticed that his colleague was late. It was as common in the intelligence community as in regular corporations to arrive late to show who was boss. My time is more important than your time, so you can sit here and wait for me. Löfgren had done it himself many times and was too experienced in this game to give a damn. *You can think whatever you want about yourself, and your ego can agree,* he thought. In the meantime, I may have time for a glass of water. One drink was enough while discussing the matters that would undoubtedly be on the agenda for this meeting.

Twenty minutes late, a man walked up to Löfgren and politely asked whether he could join him. As the man sat down, Löfgren could feel his heart rate increasing to a level that was getting uncomfortable. *Maybe a second drink wouldn't have been a bad idea,* he thought, but it was too late for that now.

As much as Löfgren considered himself an experienced spy, he was not. He had spent most of his time working desk in military intelligence, and though a very skilled intelligence officer, he wasn't a field operative.

The man smiled briefly at him before turning to get the attention of the waitress. Lack of field experience notwithstanding, Löfgren had both a keen eye for detail and a suspicious mind to go along with it. The man was of average build—Fit but not overly muscular, with a shaved head and three-day stubble.

Löfgren noted that the man was speaking excellent Swedish to the waitress, with only a hint of an accent, which he couldn't place. Whenever you can't place an accent, they're always South African. Part joke but halfway true based on his experience. His heart rate was coming down somewhat, and he shifted slightly in his chair to get comfortable as the man turned his attention back his way.

"Commander, I trust you've been well?"

"Yes, very well, thank you. How about yourself?"

"Very well, thank you," the man said before continuing. "I also trust that you passed on the necessary information to, let's say, the proper authorities?"

"Yes, high command and the government is pushing the Navy to come up with the facts and explanations about the sighting. The briefing will take place tomorrow morning. The Navy is still skeptical, but they can't ignore the sighting reports that have come in. The Nynäshamn area has enough inhabitants to keep them coming for another few days potentially, I would think."

The man turned and accepted his drink from the waitress with a smile, then turned back to Löfgren. "Beautiful girl, as you would expect at a place like this in Sweden. Blonde even."

Löfgren didn't care much for the comment, but was annoyed he wouldn't have been able to describe the waitress. Being preoccupied with thinking about the upcoming conversation, he had barely looked around the room. *Strong attention to detail indeed, but not much of a multitasker*, he thought to himself while suppressing his anger.

The man's eyes changed and seemed to penetrate Löfgren's mind.

"Any problems at all?"

Löfgren hesitated while making his final decision on what to pass on.

"Only a minor one, but it's handled."

"Let me be the judge of what's minor and what isn't," the man said harshly. "What happened?"

"As expected, most of the sightings are from

people onshore around the Nynäshamn area. They were close enough to tell it's a submarine without being able to notice any details. One fisherman was coming in with his boat at the time. The sub must have missed it before surfacing. He had a good look at the profile and sent us a sketch of it."

"That's what you call a minor problem?"

"Well, unfortunately, there were quite a few people made aware of the sketch. We couldn't make it disappear, as that could have raised some suspicion, but trust me, the drawing is generic enough not to cause any issues."

"And who else would have seen it in detail?"

"That's a nobody, administrational staff sorting through files and preparing briefings. Mrs. Falk couldn't care less about actual intelligence. She makes coffee and prepares materials."

"So, you're confident that there is no risk of identification? You know that this whole thing hinges on that?" It sounded like a question but, in reality, was a stern reminder for Löfgren not to mess this up.

"Positive, there is no sighting coming in with any more detail than saying it's a submarine. Round hull close to the waterline, conning tower. That's all. And you don't have to remind me that this is crucial. You're the ones who gave this operation the green light."

You've got some nerve, he thought, *to take a*

risk and then offload it to me.

The man opposite him sipped casually on his drink while looking around the room. Then, suddenly, he finished it in one go and stood up.

"Was a pleasure, Commander. I'll see you shortly." The man spun on his heel, smiled at the waitress, and left the bar.

* * *

Stockholm, April 14ᵗʰ, 1000hrs

Klas Nylund sat at the far corner of the table with his chair at an angle to face the others. "The others" consisted of Swedish high command, which meant his peers from the Airforce and the Army as well as the Supreme Commander himself, General Fredrik Rosenfeldt. Their aides and two representatives from the Ministry of Defense were also present.

That bastard Löfgren must have talked this situation up quite a bit to make these two clowns show up. It wasn't typical for civilians from the Ministry to attend regular hearings of this sort.

General Rosenfeldt, with his background in the armored corps of the Army, scanned the room before looking in Nylund's direction and gesturing for him to start.

"So, what do you have for us, Klasse?" he said, using the casual version of the Navy Chief's first name.

Nylund went through some of the paperwork he had in front of him. High command used to be a well-functioning leadership group, like any corporate leadership group in a civilian company. A group of people that worked together toward a common goal. That all changed when *U-137* hit the rock in Karlskrona. It deteriorated quickly. Nylund was blamed for the Navy not responding fast enough, while on the other end, he was told he exaggerated the naval threat to get more of the defense budget. Since then, he was tired of chasing phantom periscopes while the Army chief, who never dealt with any of this, sat around and made comments about what others were doing. The shorter these meetings were, the better.

He got his papers in order and started the briefing.

"Gentlemen, as the briefing note from yesterday states, we're here to run through some of the facts about the possible sighting of a submarine in Danziger Gatt."

"Possible?" the Army chief interrupted. "As far as I can tell from the document, several people sighted it, including one who sketched it. Where is the sketch, by the way?"

"Let me rephrase," Nylund responded acidly. "The definite sighting of something that could possibly be a submarine. Is that close enough for you, General?" He directed his questions straight at the head of the Army.

Without waiting for an answer, he continued. "At the current time, there are nine separate people who have reported seeing what they suspect could be a submarine. Most of these observations are from a far distance and what seems to be from behind. They report no details; in fact, they cannot say why it would be a submarine, only that it looked like a submarine to them at the time."

"And our submarines are all accounted for?" the head of the Army interrupted again.

Nylund ignored him. He would have to answer that question but not just yet. "The sighting took place on April 11th in the morning. Reports coming in are stating times between 0945 and 0953, so within eight minutes of one another. They only witnessed the object for a few minutes, and let me remind you that April 11th had weather conditions that would make good visual observations difficult."

Anders Didriksson, head of the Swedish Airforce, cleared his throat carefully. He was a quiet and thoughtful man, not anything like his Army counterpart. Didriksson would never interrupt, but now as he had created a pause in the conversation, he spoke slowly, like most people from the far north of Sweden.

"To me, there is just one question here. I

know I'm a layman in terms of naval warfare, but why would a submarine run on the surface?"

This was the opportunity Nylund had been waiting for. With a bit of luck, he could shut this down right here without even getting to the sketch.

"It wouldn't. A submarine is vulnerable and clumsy on the surface. A severe mechanical issue could force a submarine to the surface, but it would be severe enough to keep it there for more than a few minutes if that happened."

"And our submarines?" the head of Army went on. "Certainly, the main reason for a sighting of a submarine would be that it is one of ours?"

As much as Nylund wanted to leave this one hanging, he had no choice but to answer a direct question regarding the matter. Not having checked positions of their own fleet of subs would come across as highly negligent.

"No Swedish submarines are operating in this area. The closest one we have is operating at least ten to fifteen nautical miles south of Landsort. Nowhere near Danziger Gatt. It reported in as per regular procedure at 1200hrs that day, and it was in its assigned area of operations."

I need to shut down this damn meeting, Nylund thought.

"To summarize, gentlemen, we have a few people who have seen something in poor visibility that they suspect could be a submarine, but they can't say for sure. To add to that, a submarine in foreign waters would never surface unless they had a critical mechanical issue, in which case it would likely have to stay surfaced for a while. We have searched the area and found nothing. We judge the chances of this being a real sighting as highly unlikely."

He turned to the supreme commander to try to force a decision so they could end this. General Rosenfeldt moved somewhat uncomfortably in his chair and was about to speak when one of the Ministry of Defense observers wrecked Nylund's plans to end this.

"And the sketch?" he asked, "if someone had a good enough look to make a sketch, I would assume it made it clear what it is?"

Nylund made a dismissive gesture. "A box on top of a bigger box, drawn on a napkin by some fisherman who saw it through the haze."

Rosenfeldt finally pulled the trigger, "Okay, let's leave it there. It seems highly unlikely this is anything serious, but Nylund, I do want to see that sketch, and I do want you to check in with our submarine that was closest to make sure they have seen absolutely nothing out of the ordinary."

"Right away," Nylund said reassuringly as he stood up. *That was that*, he thought. No further investigation needed. Coming up with the sketch that looked like nothing and checking in with the submarine closest to the action would be neither complex nor time-consuming. It was, however, time to deal with that intelligence rat who had made him show up today.

* * *

Stockholm, April 14th, 1245hrs

Nylund got into his car and told the driver to take him back home. The view from his house at Stortorpsvägen and a glass of wine with lunch would help sort the thoughts he had flying around in his head.

He had never liked Löfgren and the feeling was undeniably mutual. Löfgren was younger than him and probably considered Nylund a thing of the past. He deemed Löfgren a careerist pencil pusher wearing a Navy uniform but who would be useless at sea.

Löfgren had pulled similar things before, making people look bad before he waltzed in with his intelligence, looking like he was the most competent officer around. It had been minor things on the commander level, though. Never before had he put Nylund himself in front of the high command against his will like this.

He got out of his car and asked the corporal behind the wheel to pick him up at 1430hrs for the next meeting. Nylund quickly walked inside and locked the door behind him.

The house had an empty feel to it—as if the place had been enshrouded in a damp cloth since Christina decided they were no longer meant to be together. The naval service and more extended periods away from home had been challenging at times, but it wasn't until later, when he was a vice-admiral with a desk job, that she had decided to leave.

He sensed that things weren't great the last year or two, but the abrupt decision still came as a shock to him. Christina told him she was moving out. A few days later, she moved out and never came back. Thirty-five years married, and she walked straight out the door without so much as a glance over her shoulder.

He hadn't spoken to her in a few months, but she seemed fine last time they met, brought together by their daughter's visit back to Sweden. Cecilia now lived in London, working some bank job that seemed horrendous to him. Fixed-income trading, buying or selling something, whatever she called it. As far as he was concerned, she wasn't actually doing anything at all. That couldn't be true, though, because she made at least as much money as he did. Maybe one day, one of the women in his family would come to their senses and return.

He pushed the thought of the empty house aside and poured himself a glass of Bordeaux red.

A minor dose of alcohol would help him think. He looked at his watch, 1245, potentially a bit early for wine. He walked into his study and looked out the window at the water. It wasn't the sea, but water was water, and it always calmed him down to look at it. Returning to his previous thoughts of Löfgren, this did seem like a bit much, even by Löfgren's standards.

The intelligence bunch always considered themselves unique but they wouldn't be a match for the head of the Navy under normal circumstances. Now, Löfgren wasn't a regular intelligence rat, given his pre-existing relationship with the Supreme Commander. He was still in intelligence, not in the operational arm of the armed forces, though. If this proved Nylund incompetent and got him replaced, Löfgren would hardly be up for the job. Would he be helping someone else to get to it? A few people he knew would be interested if the job came up, but he had served with these men for decades, and he figured none of them would try to get to it this way.

Could there be another reason for all this? Was it at all possible that Löfgren knew something that he didn't? Something that made this a more significant issue than it appeared to be? He had a swig of wine and looked out the window again. A foreign submarine operating on the surface was remarkable. He had to admit that. The whole thing started to give him a strange feeling; he almost felt sick to his stomach. If there was something more to this, he needed to know. He put his wine glass down and walked over to his desk. Somewhere there would be a card with some details for people he had used before. He searched his desk for a minute before he found what he was looking for. Right, that was her name. Frida Wikström. Former police investigator, nowadays self-employed.

The telephone on his desk rang.

"Yes, Admiral Nylund speaking."

"Admiral, this is watch commander at the first submarine division, Berga. I got the word you were at home."

"Yes. What's this about, Commander?"

"Admiral, one of our boats is missing."

Chapter 5 – Delays

Berga Naval Base, April 14th, 1337hrs

What's going on? Where is the watch commander?" Nylund shouted as he burst through the door at the first submarine division at Berga Naval Base.

"That's me," answered a small, skinny man. "Captain Rolf Eriksson, Admiral."

"So spit it out, man. What's going on?"

"She missed her window, Admiral. We've executed protocol for a late submarine, and . . ." Eriksson paused to look at his watch. "We are twenty-three minutes away from declaring the submarine missing."

Nylund swore loudly as he waved the captain into one of the briefing rooms. "We need to find her, NOW! In here, in here. Give me the rundown of what we know. And get the salvage crew in here too."

As he burst through the door, he found the salvage team already there. They were standing in a corner bent over a chart of the area where the submarine was last reported.

"As you were," Nylund shouted before anyone had the chance to bring the room to attention. "Everybody sit down. Eriksson, you need to bring us all up to speed on what's going on here. And where's the commander of first division, by the way? Where is Melker?"

"He's on his way here, Admiral. I'd guess it'll be about fifteen minutes before he gets here."

"We don't have fifteen minutes, now Eriksson, now."

Captain Eriksson was already tense, and the presence of an angry Admiral didn't improve the situation. He took a moment to gather his thoughts and then started his briefing.

"Admiral, last verified position is from 1200hrs on the 13th. That is when they reported their position according to the procedure. The report stated position as N 58°32'10" E 18°04'22", course 350, speed 6 knots. As you can see on this chart, this is just on the verge of their operating area. The reason for this is that they were ordered to move from one area to another. The order was later belayed, and they were on their way back to their original area again."

"Why was the order belayed, or wait, why was there an order to swap areas in the first place? I've seen no planned order for a change like that."

Eriksson hesitated. "I don't know, Admiral. There's no such switch in their original orders, and

I haven't had time to find out the details about this. We're trying to work out where they are now."

"Yes, yes, I get that, but this switch and belay have never happened to one of our boats in my forty years in the Navy. Once the division commander gets here, you'll find out, and that's today." Nylund took a deep breath and gestured for Eriksson to continue.

"Admiral, we don't know more than this for sure. Up until 1200hrs today, there was no indication that anything was wrong. They had their reporting window at mid-day today, and once they missed it, we executed protocol and started to transmit on the low frequency. If they're below fifty or sixty meters, they won't get it, though."

"I know. What else?"

"We've been transmitting for more than an hour with no response. There's a missile cruiser, *HMS Halmstad*, close by. We diverted it toward the area, but they have no underwater search capability. They can only look for traces on the surface."

"What did you tell the cruiser?"

"Nothing, we just gave them a new course and a position to get to and wait for further instructions. They're at full speed, but it will still take them a good hour and a half to get there."

"Good. Who else knows about this?"

"The people in this room, two conscript radio

operators, division's signal officer, and the division commander. That's it."

"Good. Keep it that way." Nylund felt his head throbbing, and his thoughts were spinning out of control. Sighting a submarine, Löfgren adamant it needed to get reported to high command, and just after that, one of their own submarines in the area goes missing. What a damn disaster. He needed time to think this through. What was it that Löfgren knew that he didn't?

"Admiral."

Someone touched his shoulder. It was the head of the submarine salvage team, a bulky young lieutenant.

"With all due respect, Admiral. If she's on the bottom and in bad shape, there's no time to waste. We need the order to get the whole Navy on this, Admiral; we need to get the URF on board and get Belos steaming toward their last known location. My men and I can stay here and work on the planning and transfer to the Belos by helicopter when it's time."

Belos was the Navy's largest salvage vessel, commonly used for diving operations, designed and equipped for precisely this eventuality. It was the mothership of the URF, which was essentially a tiny submarine specifically built for submarine rescue. The URF could dock with all Swedish and most NATO submarines, transfer the crew, pressurize them if need be, and bring them to the surface, moving them into the main pressure chamber on board the Belos.

The submarine crews practiced this many times a year. If the submarine was upright and one of the deck hatches was undamaged, it had a very high success rate.

"No word of this leaves this room until we know what's going on."

The salvage lieutenant's jaw dropped as he looked at the admiral, stunned. "But, Admiral—"

"No buts. Not one word leaves this room." Nylund gave the lieutenant a stern look and spoke with a tone that wasn't to be argued with. That was all a façade, as on the inside, he felt like he was about to have a nervous breakdown. *I've just marginalized the sighting to high command. If I sound the alarm, the whole world will know about this within the hour. The sighting, Löfgren's behavior, and now this. There is something here I'm not seeing.*

The commander of the first submarine division burst through the door, one of the division's radio operators following right behind him. The commander's face was white as a sheet. He stopped abruptly and almost screamed as he read from a clipboard.

"From *M/S Taurus*, registered in Valetta. Position N 58°27'05" E 18°01'07." Course 012, speed 14 knots. Major underwater explosion witnessed at about 1355hrs, bearing 325. It's from bloody yesterday."

"That isn't far from the position where our boat checked in yesterday," Rolf Eriksson said in a low voice.

Melker Nilsson leaned on a chair and bent over at the waist; it was clear he had been sprinting to get here. A few seconds later, he stood up again. He didn't look any better, but at least he was upright.

"Stay in here, all of you," Nylund commanded and darted out the door, missing the puzzled looks he got as he left. He went up the stairs to the office of the division commander, slammed the door shut, and sat down at the desk. What the hell is going on? He felt around his pocket and came up with the note he had found at home.

He needed to make some phone calls. Fast. He looked at his watch. Fourteen minutes before the protocol would turn the corner and officially move them to the status of submarine missing, which happened ninety minutes after the submarine was supposed to have reported its position.

Rolf Eriksson was the watch commander and technically didn't need Nylund's approval to sound the alarm, spread the news to every naval unit in the country, and get them steaming toward the area. He hoped he had been clear enough in the room that they would do nothing before his return. *I hope the salvage Lieutenant stays in check,* he thought. That short little monster could rip them all in half if he wanted to.

Sounding the alarm would let the whole world know about this, and he would completely lose control of the situation. High command, government, and foreign press would eat him alive. He would be tied up explaining the problem rather than trying to solve it. On the other hand, if it got out that he was aware and didn't blow the whistle, the outcome would be the same. I need more time, he thought. I need to come up with an excuse to delay this just a little bit longer. I need to know what's going on before the world jumps me.

He dialed the number on the note. It rang three times before a voice answered on the other side.

"Frida speaking."

"It's Admiral Klas Nylund. I need your help. Today. I'll call you tonight. We need to meet." He cut the call with his index finger before there was even a response from the other side. She was a professional. She would understand.

He lifted his index finger again and got the dial tone. He dialed zero for the Navy switchboard.

"Commander Löfgren," he shouted at the switchboard operator. The line went dead for a second.

"Commander Löfgren."

"What the hell is going on?" shouted Nylund.

The other side remained silent. Löfgren was trying to understand who this was and what this was about.

"Nylund?"

"Yes, Nylund, and the time for games is over. We got a damn submarine missing south of the area of the sighting. You better tell me what the hell is going on, and you tell me right now, Commander."

"What do you mean missing?"

Nylund stared angrily at the phone, "How hard is it to understand? It's missing, as in not reported in on time. Missing! We need to release the submarine missing status in four minutes unless you can enlighten me on a good reason why not. And this is two days after the sighting you so dearly wanted to be escalated to high command. Well, what is it? What do you know?"

Löfgren was entirely caught off balance and wasn't sure what to say. Had the visitor run into a patrolling Swedish submarine? For sure, the plan would take that into account and make sure it didn't happen. No bloodshed. That was the plan.

He felt a chill sweep over his body as he tried to come up with a plausible answer. There would be thirty men on that submarine. After another second, he found his footing again and decided that this was a situation where an attack would be the best form of defense.

"I had reports of a submarine. Reports that the Navy ignored, by the way. I called a briefing with you and your little kindergarten of commanders and gave you the facts. If you have chosen to do nothing about this, that's on you." *That should teach the old bastard to shut up.*

Nylund had a different idea.

"You listen to me, Commander. You know more than you've told us, and you will tell me what it is. I will walk downstairs now and tell them to hold off on sounding the alarm due to a confidential intelligence operation that probably has caused a delay. Someone will probably ask you about it at some point, and you will agree with it."

"But there are no filed documents for any form of—"

"So, make them appear then. You and I will talk later."

Nylund slammed the phone down, stood up, and snorted angrily like an old horse. He stood still in place for a few seconds, gathering himself, and then opened the door to walk back downstairs.

The room was at boiling point when he walked in again. Submarine missing should have taken effect one minute earlier. The entire salvage crew was up in arms about not being allowed to do their job. The division commander was sitting down looking even worse than before, while Eriksson tried to calm everyone down.

As he slammed the door shut, everyone froze in place and looked at him. He took a few steps into the room and stood tall between them all. *This is it, Klasse*, he thought to himself. *You need to keep it together now.* The salvage team lieutenant was shaking with anger, and for a second, a spike of fear ran through Nylund's body.

"Gentlemen," he said in his calmest voice, "I have spoken to military intelligence. Our boat has conducted some confidential tests related to our ability to navigate in mined waters. It is of great concern that the report is late. However, from the intelligence branch's point of view, this was not unexpected, given the nature of their mission."

Everyone in the room looked at him with doubt in their eyes, but nobody said anything. Nylund continued. "I'm genuinely concerned about this, but we'll delay a full-blown search mission until tomorrow morning due to the extraordinary circumstances. That is all, gentlemen. Report back to your regular stations."

Without meeting anyone's eye, Nylund spun on his heel and calmly walked out the door. He hoped it wouldn't show that his knees were weak and barely carried him.

Stockholm, April 14ᵗʰ, 1420hrs

Löfgren held the phone so hard, his knuckles went white. He knew it was a breach of protocol, but he had to know what Nylund was talking about. Submarine missing hadn't been declared in Sweden since the loss of *HMS Ulven*, almost forty years ago. *Ulven* was involved in an extensive exercise on the west coast of Sweden. The same protocols had been in place back then. When nobody was able to establish contact with *Ulven*, transmission on the low-frequency submarine communications channels had begun but didn't result in anything, just like now.

Ulven had hit a German mine and likely sunk immediately with all hands. This had been wartime, though, and even if Sweden wasn't actively engaged in the war, there was an awful lot of naval warfare going on in the waters where *Ulven* had made its final dive.

Löfgren shook his head in disgust. These days amounted to wartime too. *Let us not forget that,* he thought. Different enemy and a vastly different war, but Sweden had been periodically weakened in its military power and acted unacceptably with regards to global politics.

The election would be up later this year, and with the social democrats likely to regain power, this wouldn't get better anytime soon. On the contrary, Sweden was likely to become more friendly with the East and make even further budget cuts to its military. *U-137* had provided a small break in the budget matter but was unlikely to be sustained. This deterioration had to come to an end.

"Watch Commander Eriksson, first submarine division."

"Rolf, it's Ola. How are things?"

"How are things? You already know that, don't you? One of our boats is missing, and we're not doing a damned thing about it. Admiral's orders."

So Nylund hadn't tricked him. The submarine was missing, and Nylund had held back the order to declare the submarine as formally missing. He shifted in his seat to get comfortable, but comfort eluded him. *No bloodshed*, he thought. No bloodshed was supposed to come from this. Nylund knew that Löfgren was behind the hearing with high command and Ministry of Defense, and now one of their submarines was lost at sea in an area not far from the sighting.

"Yes, I know. The situation is a bit complicated with the mission they're on. I'm sure they'll report in soon", Löfgren said, hoping that his doubt wouldn't carry over the phone to the watch commander.

"I damn well hope so. If it turns out we have broken protocol and done nothing in terms of search and rescue, I don't want to know what will happen to all of us if there's no happy ending to this."

Eriksson sounded worn out. Löfgren looked at his watch, the man must be overdue to get off his shift, but that was unlikely to happen before they solved this situation.

"Hang in there, Roffe. I'm sure this will all resolve itself soon."

Rolf Eriksson looked at the telephone that had gone dead without warning. He knew Ola Löfgren well from the naval academy. Early on, Löfgren joined the intelligence ranks and propelled his career upward by leaps and bounds, avoiding anything Eriksson considered real work. Real Navy work. *Pencil-pushing intelligence clown*, Eriksson thought, as one of the division's radio operators knocked on his door.

Chapter 6 – Insubordination

"Enter," Eriksson shouted. The enlisted man opened the door, carefully closed it behind him, and stood straight at Eriksson's desk.

"Sir, we got three new messages relating to the explosions reported earlier." He looked down at his clipboard. "Three different cargo ships have reported position, time, and bearings to a large underwater explosion, or explosions."

"Explosions? Is there more than one?" Eriksson's mind worked on this information while he awaited the reply. *What would it mean if there was more than one?*

"I'm not sure, sir. W plotted the positions as reported, and it turns out there's some discrepancy in the exact location. About two nautical miles apart. Also, the timing reported differs by a few minutes. The signal officer is confirming the reports now, sir."

Several explosions at different times and locations. Eriksson signed for the messages and then looked out the window. It wasn't uncommon for submarines to carry out intelligence missions. The submarine was the ideal tool for covert intelligence gathering. Inserting attack divers for reconnaissance, tracking foreign military exercises, listening in on radio traffic. All these things were part of the regular duties of the Navy submarines and always involved people from military intelligence.

Navigating in mined waters was a different matter. Why would Löfgren and intelligence have any interest in that? It sounded like an operational Navy item run by the commanders that wrote and evaluated Navy operating procedures. He had seen nothing of this on the boards lately. Several explosions, only a few minutes apart but still as far as two nautical miles from each other. If the submarine hit a mine, it sure as hell wouldn't hit another one a full two miles from there a few minutes later.

He rested his face in his hands. *We need to find our boat.*

* * *

N 58°31'50" E 17°56'25", April 14th, 1510hrs
"All stop."

The helmsman aboard missile cruiser *HMS Halmstad* repeated the order and pulled back the speed setting to zero. Seconds later, the engine room responded. The crew heard the noise of the three Bristol Proteus gas turbines decrease as the vessel quickly lost speed.

A few minutes later, the vessel was entirely still in the water. Its lookouts scanned the horizon with powerful binoculars while the combat center personnel looked carefully at both radar and electronic survey consoles.

HMS Halmstad was designed for surface warfare and didn't have any underwater search capability. Its mission in a time of war was simple. It carried up to eight RBS-15 anti-ship missiles after its early 1982 refit, and it could still fit two torpedo launchers. They could storm out of the archipelago and deliver a hard blow to any incoming enemy surface fleet, then disappear between the islands again.

The watch officer called all stations on board, one by one, to interrogate what they had found. Radar reported a few echoes that were identified as slow-moving cargo vessels. Electronic survey measurement picked up only known civilian radar traffic. Nothing. The lookouts could confirm a few of the radar echoes and nothing else. After ten minutes of intense attention, they could only conclude that there was nothing of interest to report.

"Did they say why we needed to come here?" the watch officer asked.

The captain shook his head. "No. Set course for this position, proceed at maximum speed, and report all vessels and activity."

"Well, there isn't anything here, apart from a few merchants. We've been in contact with them all to confirm. Nothing is out of the ordinary. No unusual radio-chatter either."

"That's a mission accomplished then, I suppose. Send the report. Keep everyone alert and on task. We'll stay around here until told to leave."

"Yes, Captain. At least the weather is reasonable. Sitting still in this tin cup in rough seas would be a challenge for some of the youngsters."

The captain smiled, "You think so? I bet you a beer that one of them is still going to lose their lunch. There's always one sensitive soul around. Two beers if it's Corporal Axelsson. His sea-legs are terrible."

"No deal. Axelsson always pukes. Too easy for you."

* * *

Stockholm, April 14th, 1630hrs

"Have a seat," Nylund gestured with his hand against the chair opposite him. "Can I get you something to drink?"

"Water," was all the answer he got out of Frida Wikström. She looked around. The restaurant on Stora Nygatan was only half full at this hour. It would probably get busier later in the evening. She had spent almost two hours walking around the area. That way, she could keep an eye on this place to see if any people seemed to be hanging around for no reason. *Paranoid doesn't begin to explain it,* she thought, smiling to herself.

When the head of the Navy needed the services of a freelance investigator, it was better to take precautions.

"Your message today was short."

"Yes, my apologies. I was in a rush."

"No shit," she said with an exaggerated tone of surprise in her voice.

"What can I do for you, Admiral? What's going on in the great world of the Navy that makes you need the services of someone like me?"

She certainly wastes no time on pleasantries, Nylund thought.

Frida Wikström was younger than the admiral. Considerably so. He would estimate her to be in her late thirties, average height and weight. She had brown hair with a hint of ginger, tied up in a high ponytail. She looked like she would have been athletic but had softened a little bit with age. A lot of late-night work with bad food choices, Nylund figured.

She had been a good police officer at the start of her career. Her way of thinking like a criminal and relentless work ethic had quickly got her out of the uniform and into investigating drug-related crime. Her work ethic had relented some as she had discovered the losing battle they were fighting.

Following all the rules and collecting evidence beyond reasonable doubt was tough when dealing with people who followed no laws and didn't hesitate to do whatever it took to get what they wanted. Along with bad hours and worse pay, she had given up on the noble purpose of making a difference in society.

She usually worked short and intense jobs for people that paid well to have some police work done without the hassle of involving the actual police or any other authorities. It gave her a good life, the ability to tell customers to get lost, and a lot of free time to spend on what she would rather do.

"Well, it is quite simple. I received some very loose information suggesting a foreign vessel was seen in Swedish waters. Several people have made this claim. Let's just say I would need some unofficial help to confirm this. Time, place, and some other details, but mainly I would need some of that famous female intuition to tell me whether people are honest. Whether they have actually seen something or if I'm looking at a bunch of people seeing a fishing vessel. People sometimes see a lot of things at sea on a hazy day, you know."

"You want me to do some driving around and talk to some people and see whether they are reliable witnesses? That's all?"

"Essentially, yes, and see whether any of them have any details to add to their statements. You still have your police ID, don't you?"

Frida smiled. "I may have an old one somewhere."

"See, it should be easy then. I will finish my drink now and leave you, but there is an envelope in the bag on the floor. I'll leave it there."

"And my fee for this easy work?"

"Same rate card?"

"Same rate card."

"Well, something to get you started is in the bag already. Once you have something, we can figure out what the final amount looks like."

Drive around and play police eyewitness interviewer for a few hours. Not like she hadn't done work like that before. It should be easy enough.

"When do you need the results? Tomorrow?"

"As soon as possible. Tomorrow would be ideal."

Nylund examined his empty glass for a while, considering whether to have another drink. No, it would have to wait. He looked at Frida. She would do a good job. She always had, and he had no reason to doubt her this time. He stood up, glanced toward the floor quickly to mark the location of the bag. Then he shook her hand like it was an official business meeting before leaving the restaurant.

* * *

Stockholm, April 14th, 1730hrs

Löfgren was walking down the street, running through the last few days' events in his mind. *No bloodshed*, he repeated to himself. What the hell had happened out there?

It was a cold evening, even for this time of year. He had placed the call earlier to the agreed number and they confirmed a new meeting time. He assumed the same man with the shaved head would meet him again.

A car pulled up next to him and crept alongside. He briefly looked and could see the man in the driver's seat. It was the same man as before, and as the car pulled over, Löfgren got in. The man pulled out into traffic again. He kept looking straight ahead and seemed like he was out on a regular drive around. After a few seconds of silence, Löfgren could not stay quiet anymore.

"What the hell happened? You haven't sunk one of our damn submarines, have you? No bloodshed, remember?"

The man glanced at him and then kept

looking forward, "I'm not sure. We're still waiting for the final report from our vessel. There was a complication with one of your submarines turning up where it wasn't supposed to be, but I'm not sure of the outcome yet."

"Well, then you need to find the hell out. If one of our submarines is lost, it's only a matter of time before the Navy will sound the alarm. Once that happens, this will be all over the news."

"Yes, we didn't plan it that way, but it wouldn't be a bad thing considering the overall objective, would it?"

"If you have killed thirty Swedish sailors to get headlines, that is a price we are not willing to pay."

"You may have already paid it. Remember, Commander. You're in this up to your neck, so you'll have to play along whether you like it or not. Besides, the poor bastard Nylund will have to take the fall for a missing submarine."

"At first, yes, but I've stuck my damn neck out to make sure this sighting got reported to high command, and Nylund knows that. If he gets cornered by the government or the press, there's no telling what he might say or do. I know he seems like a tired old-timer, but he's showing more initiative by the hour. This could quickly get out of control."

"You'll need to calm down. You have no

choice but to finish the game now."

Game? Löfgren thought. *It was a game until you morons decided to sink one of our submarines.* This matter had a body count to it now. Real lives lost. That changed everything.

He needed to find the least terrible way out of this. The only way he could think of was to play along with Nylund and make sure the obscure mission of the submarine seemed official. That way, he could stand behind what he had told Eriksson. Things were complicated due to intelligence necessities.

The sighting was Nylund's problem, and the connection between them was just speculations that he could refute. It would all be suspicious but not decisively so.

"You need to let me know the second you have word from your vessel."

"We'll let you know what happened when we see fit." The man's voice was calm but there was no ignoring the aggressive undertone.

"I believe this is your stop?" The man gestured toward the corner in front of them and pulled over to let Löfgren out.

Löfgren started walking toward the subway sign, which was only a block away. He would have to call Nylund. As much as he hated it, they would need to stick together to ride this storm out.

* * *

Stockholm, April 14th, 1830hrs

Frida Wikström was going through the materials from the bag that Nylund had left her. *First things first*, she thought and reached for the thick brown envelope. She looked inside and quickly counted what was there. About twenty thousand Swedish crowns. She didn't know where the Admiral drew these funds without anyone noticing, but it didn't matter.

She started digging through the materials that were in the larger envelopes. Names and contact details for witnesses who had reported the sighting. In addition, there were some notes from the interviewer.

She found a sketch among the notes. Alvar Segerfors was the name on the file. It had the most notes in it, and it seemed clear he was the one who had the best look at this thing. Frida held the sketch up at arm's length. *A bit rough but looks like a submarine, all right,* she thought. Maybe the Navy types could figure out what kind of submarine it was. She would leave that up to them. *Best to talk to these witnesses in person,* she thought. Segerfors was the most relevant one, but a few others lived on the way to him. She would get to it first thing in the morning.

Berga Naval Base, April 14th, 2000hrs

Eriksson looked at his watch. Submarine missing was over six hours overdue at this point, and he was the watch commander. He had heard the orders from the admiral loud and clear, but he also knew it was his responsibility to sound the alarm. This was the reason the protocol existed—to not make it someone's judgment call whether to look for a missing submarine or not. It was a rule, not something optional.

Eriksson paced back and forth in his small office. A mine explosion was likely to sink a submarine in one go, but what if she was only damaged? What if the crew was still alive, and he was sitting around in his office not doing a damn thing about it? Once this came to light, someone would ask him why he hadn't followed protocol. All Eriksson would be able to answer was, *because Nylund said so.*

That's how the military works, he thought. Someone with more gold on their sleeve tells people with less gold on their sleeve what to do. *And we follow orders no matter what?* He stopped pacing and stood in place, his hands on the backrest of his office chair. Outside, the sun was just setting, casting long shadows along the pier where they docked the submarines while in port. How do you live with thirty men dying while you do nothing? He froze for a second. You don't.

Chapter 7 – Casting off

Berga Naval Base, April 14th, 2100hrs

Rarely had anyone seen Berga Naval Base at this level of activity. It happened now and then during major exercises, but they were few and far between these days. Eriksson's phone call had awoken a sleeping giant. Submarine missing protocol would get the message to every available military unit in the country.

Pilots were rushing to their aircraft at the twelfth helicopter division, located next to Berga. They were fast and agile and carried powerful dipping sonars. They would be their best chance to locate the submarine quickly.

Black smoke was showing above the Belos. The URF was being loaded and tied down by able seamen while her engines were ready to push her to se. She was a slower ship but would be in the area in three hours.

Looking toward the surface fleet, even *J20*, *HMS Östergötland*, set to be taken out of service, was leaving its berth to steam out into Hårsfjärden.

Eriksson looked at his watch again. With

some luck, the reconnaissance aircraft or helicopters would be able to find a lead quickly. They had lost eight hours due to indecision from naval command, including himself, and time was of the essence.

* * *

N 58°33'41" E 18°19'14", April 14th, 2130hrs

The pilot had just started thinking about getting some sleep when she received the call. The feeling of being tired had disappeared in a second as she learned this wasn't an untimely exercise but a response to submarine missing protocol.

Suddenly wide awake, she met up with her crew twenty minutes later and started the pre-flight checks while a communications officer had handed them the details regarding position and timing.

A missile cruiser had made a pass at the position, but the CASA aircraft would be the first unit to arrive with any underwater search capability. From what she heard, the rest of the Navy wouldn't be far behind.

She brought the plane around in a wide arch while her co-pilot examined the surface with his low-light binoculars. The sun had set a fair while ago, and it was hard to make out just about anything on the surface.

After a few minutes of searching, her co-pilot

lowered his binoculars and shook his head at her. "I can't see a damn thing other than a few merchants running along their regular routes."

The pilot toggled the microphone on her headset. "Jimmy, I'll bring her out wide for a minute, and then we come in low for a MAD run. Is the gear calibrated and ready?"

She got a double click from Jimmy's microphone switch in return. Magnetic Anomaly Detection (MAD) was used to measure disturbance in magnetic fields. A large amount of metal, like a submarine in the Earth's magnetic field, could be measurable. This had been commonly used ever since World War two to find submarines on shallow depths.

"If she's lying still on the bottom here at seventy or eighty meters, I'm not sure what our chances are of getting a reading," the co-pilot stated.

"Not good, but we need to try every option."

The modified CASA C212 made a wide turn away from the position, and the pilot then lined it up with the last known location and brought the plane down close to the surface. She flew it in a straight line for two minutes before toggling her microphone again. "Jimmy?"

"Nothing," was all she got in response from the technician in the back.

"Okay, we'll stay on this course for another

minute, and then I'll turn her around, and we work our way south from here. Keep an eye on the radar too."

The plane kept straight for a while before starting on a long lazy turn so the pilot could line her up again. Flying search patterns wasn't an easy thing, even on a sunny day. At night, it would be a significant challenge to make sure they efficiently covered the area.

* * *

Berga Naval Base, April 14th, 2144hrs

Eriksson nervously shifted the telephone from hand to hand wiped each one on his uniform. He had initiated submarine missing protocol ninety minutes prior, and the first ships and aircraft were on the way to the submarine's last known location. It wouldn't take them long to reach the destination and start searching. It was ringing on the other end.

Eriksson had deliberately waited to tell the admiral about his decision. He didn't want to give Nylund any chance to reverse this decision. The salvage crew hadn't objected when he told them to start preparing for diving operations but to stay a little subtle about it until it was all up and running.

The decision reached the commander of the first submarine division, per the reporting structure, once the order came through. Melker Nilsson had then called Eriksson and reminded him of the admiral's orders. *This was only to protect his own sad rear*, Eriksson thought. In case of any problems, the commander would say he had reminded the captain of his orders but that the captain had chosen to disobey them. Always politics. Always politics and very little space for straightforward, old-fashioned courage to do something. If this was the last decision he ever made as a naval officer, so be it.

"Nylund speaking."

"Admiral, Captain Eriksson, watch commander Berga. I apologize for the hour. I'm calling to inform you that submarine missing protocol is in force."

The other side was quiet for a few seconds. "I must not have heard you quite right, Captain. You're telling me that you have declared submarine missing despite my order to wait until morning?"

"Admiral, that's correct. I believe that if our crew is in danger, we need to try our best to find them and—"

"Were my orders not clear to you, Captain? Missing protocol waits until I say so. This involves highly classified intelligence."

Before Nylund could continue, Eriksson cut him off. "The order is almost two hours old, Admiral. I expect the aircraft to have already done its first MAD pass, and a large number of ships are already on their way."

Eriksson got nothing but silence from the other end. "Admiral?"

Nylund had hung up the phone.

* * *

Stockholm, April 14th, 2150hrs

Nylund slammed the phone down so hard on his desk, he knocked over the wedding photo that was standing there for twenty years. Now it was a pile of broken glass on the floor. *Fitting end for it*, he thought.

With that last phone call coming in, he had a feeling that most good things in his life were coming to an end. With no family left around here and a house that was too big for him alone, the only real fear he had was that someone would take the Navy away from him. Forty years of service would all be forgotten as the high command, the government, or God forbid, the press got ahold of him.

Nylund walked downstairs to pour himself a drink. He found a bottle of gin and looked around in the kitchen for some tonic. Finding none, he walked back and poured himself a sizeable shot of whiskey instead. Nylund sat down in one of his lounge chairs and looked out the window. This was it, wasn't it?

He dismissed a threat. He did it again even after intelligence had briefed him on it. That, in itself, was probably ground for dismissal. Not sending the fleet for search and rescue after his missing, and possibly sunken, comrades. That would be an inexcusable crime in the mind of every man and woman serving in uniform.

Maybe Löfgren was right. Perhaps he was too old for this. Raised in the era where the enemy was well defined and Navies fought with blazing guns within sight of each other, this cloak and dagger intelligence game was too hard for him to get his head around. Confused and overwhelmed, he had hesitated when confronted with all this information. Löfgren was up to something, but he probably would never find out what it was.

Nylund sipped his whiskey and laughed at the next thought that entered his mind. If this was a movie, there would only be one suitable way of ending this—his career and his marriage all in one go. Dress up in his parade uniform, similar to the one that he had been wearing in the wedding photo upstairs. Then end this with a shot of the revolver he kept in a locked box in his desk upstairs.

He could write a note, of course, and let them know his thoughts on the matter. A final desperate attempt to explain why he had been too tired to deal with the sighting and why he wanted to avoid submarine missing at all costs. Thirty men. They were possibly lost because he couldn't keep up with modern warfare and the confusion that accompanied it.

Nylund looked at his watch. He was amazed that high command hadn't called him yet. Of course, they were focused on what was going on. They weren't yet clear that an old, tired admiral delayed the missing status of their submarine. Once they caught up, he would lose the Navy too.

Wife, daughter, and now the Navy. It had all slipped through his fingers. On the wall was an old photo of Cecilia. She must have been about four or five in that picture. Blond plats, smiling in the sun, sitting on the side of a sandbox in the garden. *I wonder how she'll react to all this*, he thought. Reading about her father failing miserably at the thing he seemed to have cared more about than he did for her. No wonder she had left the country as soon as she was old enough. Maybe she wouldn't care about it at all.

The revolver came back into his mind. The coward's way out from this situation. You could call him many things, but *coward* wasn't one of them. His rise through the ranks in his early years had come from pushing ship and crew to the max, staying just inside the rules. Some of his superiors had hated him for it, but everyone, including them, had been impressed. He was daring but level-headed.   *Daring but level-headed*, he thought to himself again.

Nylund stood up and dashed up the stairs. Walking past his broken wedding day portrait and over to his closet where he kept his uniforms. He changed his clothes and then walked over to the desk, unlocked the box, and picked up the revolver. I'll be damned if they get me this way, like a politician being outmaneuvered in some debate. And regardless of what Cecilia thought of him, she wouldn't see him go down like this. He pocketed the revolver and walked out the door. He would get there faster in his own car.

* * *

Stockholm, April 15th, 1030hrs
Frida waited in a black Volvo 142, parked at the side of the road in Trångsund. She spoke to the third witness without finding out much more than what was already in the file. They were sure of two things. One, the vessel was real. Two, it was a submarine. That was it. In terms of how they could tell it was a submarine, all three had answered something about knowing a submarine when you see one. She understood what they meant. Submarines did have a very distinct profile, and when you saw one, there was no mistaking it for anything else. On the other hand, it didn't make for

compelling evidence.

Her feelings were clear. All three of them were honest and convinced they had seen a submarine on that day. Easy money, even if Nylund would probably be unhappy with the result. He seemed to prefer that the sighting went away, so finding some doubt among the witnesses would be preferred. *Well, you can't always get what you want,* she thought. *He pays for thirteen years of experience and some female intuition in addition to that. Instinct tells me these people have seen a submarine.*

She started her car and drove toward the most promising witness, Alvar Segerfors. He was the witness who'd been in his boat at the time of the sighting. He had been very close and was the only one who seemed to have seen the vessel in profile. He was even able to sketch it, and later handed it to the Navy.

Driving up the street, she reflected on the current state of the Swedish Navy. *Somebody claims to have seen a submarine. The sharpest intelligence minds in the country trawl through the testimonies and come up with a conclusion. Then, the admiral hands this over to a non-official private investigator who works for no other purpose than money. The military must be in a sad state. Either Nylund thinks they're incompetent, or he feels he cannot trust them.* Neither was a great scenario, given the amount of taxpayer's money that went into maintaining this beast of an organization.

* * *

Stockholm, April 15th, 1100hrs

Nylund had been pacing restlessly back and forth during the late evening yesterday and almost felt close to collapse at some point. The morning sun and likely the three cups of coffee he drank this morning helped him regain his wits and energy levels. He stood at the end of a long table, watching the markers for the different units move as they were moving around the submarine's last known position.

He had burst in through the doors late last night. Wearing his combat uniform—the one worn while on duty on the ships in the Navy. He had stormed right into Rolf Eriksson's office, given the man an aggressive look, but then slapped him on the shoulder and muttered that it was time. He had then turned and disappeared into the central control room, where they were keeping contact with all naval units involved in the operation.

His daughter might still read about him failing at his job, but if so, she would see him go down with his ship, not crawl away in shame. He had tried to teach her to stand up for herself. Apparently, she had been listening, as she then elbowed her way into what seemed like a harsh, male-dominated work environment. It was his turn now to show her what he was made of.

The sighting was a mistake. The delayed submarine missing was a critical error in judgment, but they wouldn't get him like this. *You want to fight, whoever you are? Let's fight.*

He still had his revolver in his pocket, and though useless in this situation, he felt good having it there. The commander of the fourth surface fleet was still in command of the operation, but Nylund followed his every move. He tried not to interfere but knew that the commander got nervous from his presence. Nylund didn't care. It was his Navy, and if he made the wrong call, he would be on deck when they fixed it.

The CASA had been flying search patterns most of the night, searching for a MAD contact. All without so much as a twitch of the gauges. The helicopters of the twelfth helicopter division outside Berga had been second on the scene, starting to search the waters with their powerful active sonars.

A helicopter was one of the best tools to find a submarine. They could move positions fast and were very hard to detect from a submarine. When the sonar crew would identify a helicopter, it would already be very close and most likely hovering in place. It only took a minute for them to lower the sonar into the water and start transmitting signals.

The Swedish Navy had an annual submarine competition held in November, where the submarines lurked in their operational areas waiting to attack a convoy. It was unusual for the surface fleet to find a submarine and stop an attack, but every time they did a helicopter had been crucial.

A surprising active sonar search from a helicopter would force the submarine to maneuver to get away. This would increase the chances of catching them on passive sonar from other vessels. The night of April 14th, 1982, however, the helicopters failed to find anything.

Chapter 8 – Vantage Point

Nynäshamn, April 15th, 1200hrs

Wikström walked along the waterfront in Nynäshamn. She had visited Segerfors' block of flats a bit further from the coastline. A non-inspiring, yellow block of three-story flats. He wasn't there, but a friendly neighbor told her he spent most of his time in his fishing cabin. She had been unable to be much more specific than that. There weren't many of them in this area, though, and it shouldn't be hard to find him with a bit of luck.

She could see a floating jetty with two white cabins on it. There wasn't much activity, but she could see a few people moving around.

"Alvar Segerfors?" she asked the first man she could find, who was sorting through a box of lures and other fishing equipment.

"No, but I saw him just a few minutes ago, probably back there in his cabin," the man said and pointed.

She kept walking, and as she turned the corner, she saw a man sitting on a foldable chair outside the cabin. The cabin was in a poor state and didn't look anything like what you would imagine when you thought about a Swedish archipelago fishing cabin. It was more of a poorly maintained shed. White with peeling paint and a dark gray door. Ropes, nets, and cables laid around in piles on the jetty.

Alvar looked up at her with a hint of surprise in his eyes. He held a can of beer, and Wikström couldn't help but glance at her watch briefly.

"I know, I know. Not quite time for that yet, is it?"

"You'll get no judgment from me," she said. "You are Alvar Segerfors, I take it?"

He nodded almost invisibly, and she continued while flashing her fake Police ID. "I apologize for interrupting. I'm Maria Wennergren, from the police."

She had used this ID many times before but had still taken the time to practice her introduction a few times, making sure she could casually state who she was without raising any suspicion. She knew it was all in her head. If you were dealing with people in general who had no reason to be suspicious in their everyday lives, you would have to fumble badly to make them doubt a police ID.

Alvar threw his hands into the air, still holding the beer can.

"I confess, I should have waited until after

lunch to open this beer."

Wikström laughed out loud and then smiled. "Not to worry. I'm not that kind of cop. I am just here to confirm some details about a sighting you reported a few days ago, here in Danziger Gatt."

Alvar gave her a puzzled look but motioned toward an empty seat next to him. "There's coffee in the cabin if you want some."

Wikström figured that was as good as any excuse to look inside. She smiled and nodded, "I'll grab some."

The inside looked like the outside of the cabin. It needed some serious time and effort to be brought back to a representable state. Most of it was old fishing gear, life vests, and other nautical goods. One tiny corner was cleaned out and had a new shelf put in. It had neatly stacked and labeled things on it. As she returned with the coffee and sat down, Alvar started.

"As you can see, some work to be done still. I neglected this place for years, as my wife was ill. I've just started to pull myself back together again after her passing. Sorting this place out is good therapy, if you see what I mean?"

He caught her looking at her watch again. "So, you're here to verify my story about the submarine, are you? I understand the Navy people's interest, but why would the police be involved in this? You haven't started hunting submarines as well, have you?"

"No, we haven't," she said with a laugh.

"It's just a routine check. There are problems with things being smuggled by boat, both people and drugs. Unlikely they would have a real submarine in the Baltic Sea, but since it was a vague sighting on a hazy morning, I'd like to verify what you saw, to exclude that it was any other form of a vessel."

She paused and lifted her coffee cup but never let her eyes leave Alvar. His reaction would tell her better than anything how solid the sighting was.

"Vague? What the hell do you mean by vague?"

"The report I read said potentially a submarine. That's why I wanted to hear for myself."

"You can tell whoever writes your reports that they're full of shit. I have lived by the sea my whole life. I served in the Navy myself back in 1930 and 1931. Not on a submarine, but I know what a damn submarine looks like when I see one. There is no doubt it was a submarine running on the surface. I even drew the idiots a sketch of it."

"Yes, I saw it. But the sketch wasn't all that clear as I can recall." She dug around in her inner pocket and unfolded a piece of paper.

"Here's the sketch. I can see that it could be interpreted as a submarine. All I'm saying is, we can't completely exclude the possibility that it was something else."

Alvar untangled his reading glasses from his white, somewhat curly hair and looked at the piece of paper.

"That's not my sketch."

"No, It's a copy, but what I mean is—"

He aggressively interrupted her, "I know what a copy is. What I'm telling you is, that isn't what I drew."

She looked at him, somewhat dumbfounded. It was a strange turn of events. "You mean this sketch is different from the one you drew before?"

"Yes, that's what I'm saying. Give it to me."

He snatched the piece of paper from her hand, and as he looked around for a pen, he grunted at her, "I was in the damn Navy, you know. I know what a submarine looks like, and I also know this isn't one of ours."

"Whose was it?"

"I don't know . . . but not one of ours. Both Sjöormen and Näcken have the conning tower further in the front than this, and they're a different shape. Look here."

Alvar spun the paper around. He had started to draw a second sketch just below the original one. He continued the work upside down for a few seconds and then lifted his head and looked at her. "See, that's what I saw. I'm not exactly Rembrandt, but for sure, that is enough details to tell it's a submarine?"

Frida looked at the picture. The sketch was rough, but it was undoubtedly the silhouette of a submarine. Anyone who ever saw a submarine would agree. The conning tower was much further aft than on the sketch she brought, and it had a different shape. Someone had altered the drawing. His reaction had been strong when she referred to his testimony as vague. His words, tone, and facial expression would all witness that he was telling the truth. *Not an old, lonely crazy man seeing periscopes.*

"Who took your statement?"

"Some Navy guy called me and took the statement over the phone. I never met anyone. Later that evening, I drew the sketch, and as I figured it was important, I put it in an envelope, and I drove up to the Muskö Naval Base and handed it to the youngsters in the guard booth. I wrote the guy's name on the envelope, but I can't remember what it was. He was polite enough but sounded like he was about twelve years old. But everyone is young to me, you know."

Wikström used all her willpower to keep looking relaxed. She didn't want to seem like this was anything groundbreaking and raise more questions than necessary. But if it turned out that Nylund had received altered information, there

99

could be some major drama in the naval ranks soon. Did someone want this to either not be a submarine or be a submarine that was impossible to identify?

She finished the last of her coffee.

"Well, I guess this is why we make these visits to verify things," she said and used one of her best fake smiles. She was good at it but knew very well that smiling when you didn't mean it was one of the most challenging lies to get away with. "I'm sorry I bothered you today but very good to get this sorted out. I hope you get your gear in order here."

"And thanks for the coffee," she called over her shoulder as she walked away. As she got out of sight from the cabins, she sprinted toward her car. This news needed to get back to Nylund.

Chapter 9 – Press Release

Muskö Naval Base, April 15th, 1220hrs

Intelligence mission. That's what the man had said. Then intelligence mission is what it would have to be. It made sense. Intelligence orders could be handed to a naval vessel outside the regular order process under certain circumstances. It had its own process to go through, but Löfgren would have to circumvent that somehow.

If the orders were archived among the original one's, the result would be correct, even if the process wasn't. The archive would stand up to scrutiny as long as nobody went through the painstakingly demanding job of backtracking the process and sign-offs. There were hundreds of documents flying around the naval bases, and the likelihood that someone would try was low.

Löfgren wasn't a frequent visitor to the archive himself but did request items to be placed in there from time to time. He gave some thought to how he would get the orders in there. If they saw him in the archive, it would look out of the ordinary to many people, and there would be a trail from him swiping his pass to get in there. If he asked one of the secretaries to do it, they might question it, but it seemed unlikely. It was worth the risk.

Mrs. Falk and her colleagues were responsible for handling the hundreds of orders. The risk that she would take any notice was slim to none. He decided to hand it to her after lunch to ensure it ended up in the right place.

* * *

Stockholm, April 15th, 1230hrs

"Jesper Bergman speaking."

"Mr. Bergman, I assume you've heard that half the Navy cast off late last night?"

"Who is this?"

"There was a sighting of a Soviet submarine a few days back."

"What? Who is this?"

"Check it out. Submarine sighting in Danziger Gatt, and there's been a Swedish submarine missing since yesterday. You should have a look at it."

"Yeah, but—"

"There will be a package for you at reception."

The line went dead, and Jesper Bergman, sitting at his desk at one of the leading Swedish newspapers, was left staring at his phone.

Soviet submarine? What the hell was this about? Reception was only one floor down, and it would take him no more than two minutes to get there. Curiosity quickly got the better of him, and he started down the corridor for the staircase. After speeding down the stairs, he made a conscious effort to walk more casually over to reception.

"I think there should be something here for me, is that right?"

"Good morning," the receptionist answered him with a smile before she turned and looked at some files on the table behind her.

"Yes, a courier dropped it off earlier this morning. There you go."

Jesper grabbed an A4-sized envelope. It felt like it had quite a few pages in it. He started tearing at the envelope while walking back up toward his office. He found his manners halfway to the elevator and shouted a thank you over his shoulder.

Once back in his office, he opened the envelope and spread the contents on his desk. It contained copies of Navy intelligence reports with confidentiality stamps on them. A sketch that looked like it could be a submarine. *Hard to tell*, Bergman thought, but it undoubtedly resembled a submarine.

He spread all the documents on his desk and started to read through them. There were reports on nine people who claimed to have seen a submarine in Danziger Gatt. Nine different people, all thinking they had seen a submarine. That's hard to ignore, he thought.

Leaning back and taking a sip of his one-hour-old coffee, he thought about what to do with this. It could all be a prank, but if it turned out to have something to it, it would make for a damn fine first-page headline. It could be worth spending a bit of time fact-checking some of this. Half an hour later, after calling a few people with Navy ties, he hung up the phone. *I'll be damned.* Half the Navy cast off yesterday. Berga was empty, and planes and helicopters had been passing overhead all night and all morning today. He couldn't remember the Navy ever having an exercise like this in his lifetime. If they did anything significant, they usually announced it beforehand to ensure civilians were out of the way.

He picked up the phone again to see if he could speak to any witnesses on the list. Even if he couldn't get the complete picture, verifying the sighting and half the Navy scrambling to sea would be enough to get started. Whatever the truth was, it would make for one hell of a story.

* * *

Nynäshamn, April 15th, 1230hrs

Wikström reached a pay-phone in Nynäshamn and dialed Nylund's number. When there was no response on his direct line, she called the Navy switchboard and asked for him, only to draw a blank again. The operator told her the admiral was in a meeting with an unknown end time.

The unfriendly operator also informed her that there would be no messages collected for the Admiral unless she could leave a name, number, and the nature of her call—a typical condescending military attitude. *We are so busy with important matters, like war, we cannot be bothered to speak to civilians.* The last time Sweden was at war, Napoleon was still alive. Maybe they should relax a little on the self-importance side of things. Wikström hung up and ran back to her car.

* * *

Stockholm, April 15th, 1230hrs

Didriksson, head of the Swedish Airforce, was late, and the meeting got to order fifteen minutes after the expected start time. Nylund looked around the room. Regular meetings with high command usually only included the leaders of the various military branches, Supreme Commander Roselfeldt, and some less senior officers.

Today, the room was full. Nylund recognized

the two clowns that were there last time, but they had brought their bosses as well this time. The minister of defense, Thomas Nordin, had just sat down in his chair and looked anxiously at his watch before looking around the room to find the person who needed to get things going.

"Can we get started?" Nordin stated straight out at nobody in particular. "We will need some clarity on this situation urgently. It seems the whole Navy is on the move. Soon enough, someone will start asking why. I need some clarity myself, as I can't keep track of whether this concerns our submarine or someone else's."

Nylund stood up as he began to speak. "We're all here, so yes, let's start."

This meeting will likely cost me dearly, Nylund thought. *So be it.* It was the time to stand up and get this done right. *Daring but level-headed.*

"Minister, gentlemen. I will give you a short timeline of what has happened the last few days and then move on to explain what is currently underway in terms of search and rescue operations."

"On Monday, April 11th, between 0945 and 0952, we received several reports of sightings of a submarine in Danziger Gatt, about here." Nylund pointed to a projected image of a sea chart on the wall. "There are no details on what type of submarine this is or where it came from. We

106

discussed it within high command, but we didn't deem the report reliable due to the vague descriptions and the hazy weather conditions."

"People saw a submarine, and you ignored it?" the minister asked.

"Yes, essentially," Nylund said. "Note that we get these types of sightings all the time, mainly from people seeing our own submarines, but also from floating logs, fishing boats, barges, and other traffic in our archipelago. In retrospect, it was a mistake to ignore this, but at the time, there was no indication of it being any more real than the many false sightings we get every year."

He paused and looked around the room.

"This alone was not a cause for major concern, but about seventy-two hours later, one of our submarines operating in this area missed its reporting window, and these two events together become significant."

"Reporting window?" one of the civilians from the Ministry of Defense asked.

"Our submarines have a standing order to report in at regular intervals during peacetime operations. Every twenty-four hours, they will report position, course, and speed as well as any problems they may have." He turned toward the chart on the wall again.

"As you can see here"—he pointed to the last reported position of the submarine—"on April 13th at 1200hrs, the submarine would have reported in as per the regular schedule. Position, course, speed. No issues." As Nylund turned back, he felt something poking into him. Jesus. He hadn't changed clothes for the briefing and was still wearing his sea gear, including the revolver in his pocket. He quickly leaned toward it to get his uniform to sag over that side. The audience probably didn't see the reason, but the distraction on his face was evident.

"Admiral?"

"Yes, apologies, The next reporting window was 1200hrs, mid-day, on April 14th. As the submarine didn't report in on time, the watch commander at Berga raised the status to submarine late within five minutes. A few different things happen when this occurs. Firstly, additional personnel are called on duty in the control center to ensure more people are aware of the latest information. This is so they can relieve each other in a potentially lengthy operation. Secondly, the submarine division salvage crews go on alert. At this time, they were located at Berga by coincidence and could attend in person. Then, we start to transmit messages to the submarine through our low-frequency facility, which means the message can also reach a submerged submarine. The depth it can reach will vary depending on the water conditions, but the submarine won't be able to respond without being at periscope depth or surfaced."

The minister was all over this now. "And for how long does this go on?"

"This goes on for ninety minutes when the protocol states that the status of the submarine should change from submarine late to submarine missing. This is when we launch search and rescue operations."

There it was, the moment of truth. Nylund heard pages turn in the briefing documents around the room. The question would come right at him in a few seconds anyway, so he decided to pre-empt it.

"As you can tell from the timelines, submarine missing was put in force at 2000hrs on the evening of the 14th."

"And I'm sure you will now tell us why that is," admiral.

"Minister, there is no real excuse to this other than confusion in communications."

"You were confused and forgot to report that you lost a submarine?" Nordin's facial expression and skeptical tone said more than his words.

"No, there was some unusual activity surrounding the orders for the submarine where they swapped operating area and were then ordered back again. This has never happened before, and the watch commander is still looking into why this took place. As we were unsure of a few of these items, I decided to hold the submarine missing decision."

"You broke your own protocol? Isn't that insubordination in some way, even for an admiral," Nordin asked rhetorically before continuing. "Essentially, you have ignored intelligence on a submarine sighting, and then you have failed to start looking for your own submarine because you were all confused. Frankly, gentlemen, I'm not impressed."

Nobody in the room said anything. All the military commanders showed clear signs of being uncomfortable, and Nylund was sure they wanted to shout that it was all his mess. *They would be right*, he thought. *I downplayed the sighting, and I did delay the search.* Nylund was going to get these facts out there when the pragmatic minister started talking again.

"This is, however, neither the time nor the place to deal with any shortcomings in the chain of command. Don't get me wrong, this is a major problem and will not go away, but for now, I need to know what else you have so we can respond if this becomes public."

"At 1355hrs on these two positions here, we received reports of explosions that occurred at sea. They're close to each other but not at the same position and also not at exactly the same time. Four minutes apart."

"What would cause a major explosion like that?"

"A torpedo or a mine would do it."

"You're saying that our submarine potentially hit a mine or was struck by a torpedo?"

"We are working on finding that out, minister. If our submarine hit a mine or was hit by a torpedo, she wouldn't be hit again four minutes later, several miles away. It could be two non-related incidents, but we're working on the assumption they are connected. Our fleet has searched the area since late last night. As you are probably aware, finding a submarine in these waters isn't easy."

There was a moment of silence as Nordin seemed to contemplate the implications of a lost Swedish submarine.

"How many men on our vessel?"

"Thirty-one."

"And what's the likelihood that they are still alive if they hit a mine?"

"Almost impossible to tell, but the odds are not good."

Nordin's face took on an expression of genuine concern. Losing a naval vessel with over thirty men on board.

"You've got to find that boat, Admiral. You search for our submarine and find out what's happened. Get the men back home safely. The rest of us will have to start caring about the political implications of this. With the whole Navy at sea, it will only be a matter of time until the first journalist gets a whiff of this and starts to ask questions. I need your Navy crew to sit down with my staff." He gestured to the two clowns that had been in the previous meeting as well. "We need to come up with an official version we can feed the press."

The minister stood up. He picked up his briefcase and jacket and turned to leave but stopped halfway to the door. "Find the sub, Admiral. Tell me it was a broken radio or something. If this gets any other outcome, we're going to have a major international incident on our hands."

Chapter 10 – Resurrection

Stockholm, April 15th, 1300hrs

Jesper Bergman had spent the last thirty minutes calling people to verify as much information as he could from the documents he received. t was a fact that large parts of the Navy was scrambled late last night and were now at sea. The purpose was still unknown, but it was unlikely to be an exercise with no prior communications. The sighting was a fact, as he had called three witnesses, of which two would speak to him. If two people were dead-sure they had seen a submarine, that would be enough to write an initial piece around this.

"Navy Switchboard."

"Jesper Bergman, *Evening Press*. I have some questions and need to speak to someone who can tell me what the Navy is up to, running operations all night."

"I'm sorry. We know nothing about that."

"I know you don't. That's why I need to speak to someone who does. I'm sure you have a communications officer who would be more than willing to have his say before I write up a story of a sunken Swedish submarine."

The operator on the other side hesitated for a second. "I'll patch you through. Lieutenant-commander Edvinsson will answer your questions."

The operator connected the call and heard the click that signaled Edvinsson answering the phone. She turned her head to the woman standing next to her, sorting through a few pieces of paper.

"Some reporter was talking about a sunken Swedish submarine."

Eivor Falk looked up at her, remembering the meeting she had helped prepare for just two days earlier. "What, where?"

"Jesper Bergman, evening press. I was hoping you could help me with a few questions?"

Lieutenant-Commander Edvinsson sighed in his mind but didn't let any air out. *Here we go.* "Mr. Bergman, what can I do for you?"

"I'd like to confirm a sighting of a foreign submarine in Swedish waters in Danziger Gatt on the 11th at 0945. I would also be interested to know what the Navy is up to. Every berth at Berga is empty, and the helicopters are only landing to refuel. We need to know what's going on."

"The Navy is running a major exercise south of Landsort. This does involve a lot of the Baltic Sea fleet. Concerning the sighting, we get tons of these;

they come in all the time. I can't confirm anything surrounding the particular one you mentioned. I would have to check that and get back to you."

"Get back to me. Good answer. Look, there has been nothing communicated about this major exercise. I would think they're looking for the sunken Swedish submarine."

Bergman was bluffing, but what the hell. He didn't have anything riding on this. He might as well try all the tricks.

Edvinsson remained calm on the other side, often having reporters call him to bluff their way to information.

"What the Navy is doing is an exercise. Sudden as it may be, it has nothing to do with any sunken submarine."

"A submarine is sighted in Swedish waters, and a few days later, the entire Navy sets to sea. Come on. This doesn't add up for me, and it won't add up for my readers either."

"Mr. Bergman, the Navy is conducting a major exercise. I can get back to you about the sighting, but as I said, we receive many of these, and I need to confirm the one you are speaking about specifically."

Edvinsson did his best to follow his instructions without sounding like he was reciting something. He was both excellent and experienced at this, so he would think he had done a reasonable job. It would be one hell of an upside if someone told him what was going on for once, rather than handing him scripts with official communications without context.

"Right, so I take it you're happy that we print this, Commander Edvinsson?"

"I can't endorse any of your writing. All I can tell you is that the Navy is conducting a major exercise, and I will have to get back to you about the specific sighting."

Bergman hung up the phone. *Military bullshit*, he thought. Anyway, he had enough to go on for a first, questioning piece about what the Navy was up to. More facts would have to follow. He would need to use his less formal contacts, but that might take some time.

* * *

N 58°29'55" E 17°46'35", April 15th, 1330hrs

They were in service since over twelve hours now. Even with backup crews and the regular sleeping cots in the hangars, they struggled to stay focused. The Navy Helicopter 4, internationally known as the CH-46 Sea Knight, was hovering fifteen nautical miles south of Landsort. It had its dipping sonar at twenty-five meters depth, searching for any submerged vessel.

The search was frequency modulated,

meaning it sent a pulse that changed in frequency. This allowed a better chance of one frequency penetrating a temperature layer and increased the chance of getting the first indication that something was there. Once there was an indication, a better option to evaluate would be to use a continuous wave, a signal sent at one frequency only, which would allow for a Doppler effect. A signal sent at one frequency and coming back at a slightly higher one would indicate the object was moving toward them. Much like the pitch of a Formula 1 car's engine changing drastically once the car passed the point of the spectator.

The lookout and winch operator called out. "Heads up, flare on the surface, three o'clock." He trained his binoculars to his eyes and continued. "Yep, definitely a smoke and flare marker, less than one kilometer away. Must have come from below."

The pilot didn't waste any time.

"Echo 1, Echo 1, this is Yankee 6-4. We got a likely sub-launched flare, one kilometer south of position N 58°29'55" E 17°46'35." Moving in to investigate."

He was just going to order the dipping sonar wheeled in to move the helicopter when his sonar operator called out.

"Contact, contact, bearing 180, distance eight hectometers, must have come through the layer, switching to continuous search."

The sonar operator flicked a switch on his controls, and the sonar started to send a 22KHz signal to evaluate the contact.

"Weak doppler, two to four knots. Heading our way."

"Okay, arm the fish," the pilot ordered, now clearly struggling to keep his excitement under control.

Swedish submarines used these flares to mark their location, and it was much more likely this was their lost sub rather than an intruder. But just to be sure, he would have the torpedo ready to drop.

Seconds later, the entire crew saw the conning tower of a submarine break the surface.

"Echo 1, Echo 1, Yankee 6-4. We got a visual of a submarine. Parts of the conning tower in view. Her masts are coming up. I can see the snorkel, periscope, and radar mast. The orange light on the snorkel is blinking. We'll move in to confirm, but it looks like our missing boat to me."

As the submarine continued to surface, the pilot and lookout continued to examine her through their binoculars. They retrieved the sonar and moved the helicopter to get a clear view from the side. Once in position, identifying her was a small matter.

"Echo 1, Yankee 6-4, it's our missing boat, repeat it's our missing boat. She's on the surface and slowly moving north. Looks undamaged from here."

The pilot followed up by nodding the helicopter to the submarine, showing her they recognized a friendly vessel. He let out a long sigh of relief as it registered with him, he finally would get some rest.

* * *

N 58°29'30" E 17°46'35", April 15th, 1330hrs

The captain was looking through the periscope as the submarine surfaced. As the helicopter suddenly had appeared and they had picked up the active transmission from its sonar, he decided it was better to mark the position and surface than to stay submerged and risk being mistaken for an intruder.

Good decision, he thought, as he could see the torpedo hanging in its rack on the side of the helicopter. Outmaneuvering that thing when dropped from a helicopter at close range would be close to impossible.

A few moments earlier, he saw what he interpreted as a bow from the helicopter. He instinctively felt the helicopter had recognized them, and a visible sign of relief swept across his face.

Definitely visible, as he heard the entire

command center simultaneously exhale behind him and then start to breathe again. The first relaxed breaths they had drawn in more than twenty-four hours.

The captain left the periscope up and walked over to the radio room. The message was ready, and all he had to do was nod to the signal officer, and the details of their activities were sent off to headquarters.

All hell must have broken loose when they didn't report in as planned. Potentially, he would get into trouble for it, but it seemed unlikely. During wartime operations, the regular reporting schedule wasn't in place. The submarine might not be able to abandon operations to report in. It would report in when the captain saw fit. Being on the receiving end of a torpedo was maybe not quite a declaration of war but could not be far from it.

After the detonation of both torpedoes, he figured a cold opponent would stay above the layer and wait for them to come up and report. Hence, he had chosen to stay as deep as possible and work their way toward their previous contact to evaluate.

This brought them outside their operating area, but again, he figured the Navy would forgive him under current circumstances. His boat was still in one piece, and his crew, including himself, was still alive. He could live with that, despite potential consequences.

Lindberg was off duty but was standing in the door between the mess and the command center. He too had held his breath for a minute when the helicopter must have caught them on sonar. All he could do was hope they were identified before the helicopter crew decided to launch a weapon at them.

All the tension he had stored in his neck and shoulders the last day was released. His shoulders sank back to their regular position, and he felt tired enough to sleep for a month. The madness was over. He felt desperate to go home and leave this behind. The officers had signed up for this. He was just a conscript.

Two days before, when they ran into the contact, they heard the explosion of the incoming torpedo somewhere aft of them, rolling in like thunder across the hull of the submarine. None of them had heard anything like it before. Lindberg had almost lost it at that point, sweating profusely as a feeling of panic crept into his brain. It had taken all his mental efforts to simply stay in his seat. The torpedo must have detonated chasing the noisemaker. They couldn't be sure of what exactly had happened, but any outcome where they were still alive was a good one.

The captain had calmly ordered the helmsman to balance the boat and carefully put it down on the bottom. With no machinery noise at all, she would be impossible to detect on passive sonar. An active sonar, sending out the famous ping known from submarine movies, could find her if it got very close, but submarines rarely used them. Sending sound pulses into the sea was an effective way of finding out what was out there, but it also revealed the sender's position.

They had heard their own torpedo detonate a few minutes later but heard no other sounds from the bearing at which their initial contact had raced off. If it had been damaged or sunk, there would likely have been some noise from it. More likely was that it got away and then did the same thing they had done. Slowed down and disappeared.

The officers had discussed going to periscope depth to report what had happened, but the captain decided against it. They spent four hours on the bottom—Sonar Chief Sandberg glued to his console. The captain had then took them off the bottom and started to move south toward the direction of their last known contact. They were creeping along the bottom at no more than two knots, using the drift of the current to move them in the right direction.

To cover their rear, they frequently made ninety-degree turns to open the sea behind them to their nose-mounted sonar. Methodically, they swept the area for any noise relating to the previous contact but there was nothing out there.

Lindberg had been busy making copies of the recording from the encounter, which would be helpful for later analysis. It wasn't easy to determine the origin of the submarine, but they had good data on the runner, and someone like Sandberg would be able to work it out once he could take his focus off the current operation.

They had heard the Swedish Navy steaming at high speed out of the archipelago, but had expected it to be sooner as submarine missing protocol should be initiated ninety minutes after their reporting window. Though concerned that nothing happened, they could do nothing else but assume some other information was in play. Maybe the Navy had heard the explosions and suspended peace time protocol.

The Navy could have been searching for anything submerged, but as they seemed to be moving mainly in the assigned operational area of Lindberg's boat, they were likely looking for them. The Navy had moved south, closing in on their position, and suddenly the helicopter showed up out of nowhere.

The frequency modulated signal had partially penetrated the thermal layer. It was hard to tell whether enough of the signal would bounce off the submarine to give the helicopter crew an echo, but at this point, the captain had found it too risky to stay hidden. He had decided to launch the flare and surface the boat.

Chapter 11 – News Value

Berga Naval Base, April 15th, 1335hrs

Nylund leaned over the back of a radio operator in the command central at Berga Naval Base. As the news broke their submarine had been found and seemed undamaged, he joined everyone else in a sigh of relief. It had been trying times for his nerves the last couple of days, and even though Nylund still knew this would likely be the end of his career in the Navy, he wouldn't go out as the admiral that lost a submarine. He had made a mistake. He had made a few of them, but then marched into his naval base and been part of the search that had now ended well.

There would still be plenty of work to figure out what had happened out there, but there would be no Swedish lives lost on his watch. He suddenly remembered the explosions involved and looked over toward the radio operators that manned the regular radio station. The signal officer stood behind his conscript operators with a grim look on his face while he scanned a message form. He looked around the room and, once he caught

Nylund's eyes, gestured for the admiral to join him.

As Nylund walked to the other side of the room, one of the secretaries touched his arm and handed him a phone. He shook his head, but she held it out again and whispered to him that the woman had been calling several times the last hour, and they didn't know what to tell her anymore. Nylund reluctantly grabbed the phone.

"Hello"

"Klas, it's me, Frida."

"I'm busy. We'll have to—"

"Not too busy for this," she said. "I spoke to the main witness, Alvar Segerfors, in Nynäshamn—the man who drew the sketch."

"And? I really need to go."

"The sketch you have in your files isn't the original sketch."

"What are you saying?" Nylund's jaw dropped for a second before he found himself again and put on a straight face for the crew in the command center.

"I showed him the sketch and questioned how he could be so sure it was a submarine. He basically shouted at me that this wasn't his sketch. He drew one next to it that looks quite different. Much more detail. The conning tower is in a different place. I don't know anything about submarines, but I guess this means the sketch was changed at some point between leaving Segerfors and reaching yourself."

Nylund felt a chill crawl up his spine. Löfgren. It must be Löfgren that was playing him for a fool again. Was it one of their own boats? Löfgren would then have changed the sketch so we couldn't identify it. We would launch a major operation and look like fools when it was clear we were chasing ourselves. That would be a major fiasco for the Navy.

No, they had verified the positions of their boats. Melker Nilsson had them call in. It wouldn't have been one of theirs—not unless Nilsson was in on it, of course.

"What does it look like?"

"As I said, I don't know anything about submarines, and I haven't had time to look it up. Alvar was apparently in the Navy back in the day, and he was adamant it wasn't a Swedish vessel. I've asked for a background check on him to verify. They just take a bit longer when you're not an actual police officer anymore."'

Not a Swedish submarine. Still a legit sighting of a foreign vessel then? A sighting of a foreign ship, explosions, a submarine that disappears but then re-appears. He lifted his gaze and looked at the signal officer, face pale, waving the message form at him in urgency.

"Find Segerfors and bring him in. Call the real police if you must. We need to get to the bottom of this mess." He hung up the phone and walked over to the signal officer.

The signal officer handed him the form and nervously nodded for him to read it. It was a relatively long report sent from the re-appearing submarine. Nylund started scanning it but didn't get far before his heart rate elevated. Contact report, at least two submerged contacts, certain submarines. One torpedo fired and another one evaded. Explosions. It read like some damn war novel. What the hell? This was Sweden under peace conditions. He continued reading and got to the part he was looking for. Identity of the intruder, unknown. But they had all of it on tape and as well as copies ready for analysis.

Someone has shot a torpedo at my Navy, he thought. In Swedish waters and during peacetime. I think we just got our international incident that the minister of defense had been talking about. This needs to be confirmed and get up the chain. He waved at the signal officer, who had taken a step back.

"Get a boat or helicopter or something out there to get the tapes, and get that sub tied up as soon as possible. We need to debrief the crew."

* * *

One of the Navy's small transport crafts came roaring along to meet the submarine. It pulled up alongside, and one man looked like he was getting ready to jump to the submarine.

"He's not going to try to do what I think he is?" The captain mumbled more to himself than anyone in particular.

Before anyone could answer, the man jumped. He fell short but got a hold of the footing support around the conning tower and pulled himself up on top of the hull.

"Have they lost their damn mind?" the captain said out loud and bent down to reprimand that man, but he got distracted by the radio.

The submarine's giant propeller was churning the water only thirty meters behind where the man had landed. Had he missed, he would have been chewed up just seconds later with no chance for the submarine to evade him.

The young lieutenant climbed down the main hatch and entered the command center.

"Orders from high command. I need all the tapes of the contact report, now. They need to get to military intelligence as soon as possible."

He handed over a piece of paper to the torpedo officer.

Arrogant prick, Lindberg thought. *You weren't the one who almost got blown to pieces in this thermos.* He packed up all the tapes and put them in a small box. He checked that all recorders had new tapes in them and were running. It was unlikely the sonar would pick up much at this speed while on the surface, but standing orders said they should always run.

It was stupid they needed to hand it all over. Someone like Sandberg would be the most likely person to make sense of it all anyway, and now they were passing it on to some land animals who sat in their offices theorizing over what this might be. Bullshit. He handed the box over to the Lieutenant.

"Don't drop them, Lieutenant. I made them myself."

The lieutenant shot him an angry look and turned and disappeared up the ladder.

"Fine, have no sense of humor," Lindberg muttered.

* * *

Muskö Naval Base, April 15th, 1410hrs

Löfgren received the message of the submarine appearing again, and his first reaction was a sigh of relief. That meant no loss of Swedish life for this operation. Not that he was faint-hearted when it came to fighting the secret war they were now in, but a whole submarine and crew would have been a high price to pay for a sighting.

A few seconds later, he remembered the evidence that he had told Mrs. Falk to file. The materials point to an intelligence instruction that nobody on board the submarine would have ever heard of. Before they returned and were being debriefed, these orders would need to disappear from the archive again, or he would potentially have a lot of explaining to do.

* * *

Berga Naval Base, April 15th, 1420hrs

The signal officer waved Nylund over again, not looking any happier than before. Nylund was there in a few seconds and read through the message. He shot the signal officer a puzzled look. All he got in return was a shrug.

"We told them we were sending a craft to collect all the tapes, and this is their response. A few minutes ago, they handed all the tapes over to a Navy lieutenant who boarded the boat from a small Navy craft. The craft was official Navy. They were in uniform and had a signed order that looked legit. The captain had no reason to believe this wasn't official. We're looking for the source of the order in the logs. Nothing yet."

"When did they hand over the tapes?"

"Just a few minutes ago, Admiral."

Nylund marched straight over to the chart

table. This is the last damn time they messes with him. He checked the positions of the Navy units. One benefit of the search mission was that the Navy was already operating in the area with every unit available. *Now we'll see who's going to be in trouble.*

"Confirm where the boat disappeared. How many helicopters do we have operating?"

"Four Helicopter 4 sub hunters and three smaller ones for visual search."

"Get them all into this area and find that craft. And send the whole damn fleet in after them. Find them. Now! Get the word out and get Navy base security to get ready to intercept anything and anyone that makes it onto land. This stops here."

The signal officer hesitated for a second.

"Now," Nylund shouted at him.

Base security was the Navy land units with the specific purpose to protect Navy ships while docked. Consisting of small units—usually four men and a dog—they would search large areas around the Navy installations. Small and mobile, their main job was to track and report contacts to coordinate larger forces. However, heavily armed, the group packed a punch that would surprise any enemy.

A few minutes later, Nylund saw the radar blips moving toward new positions. The helicopters moved quickly into the search areas as they were briefed on what to look for. Slower blips consisting of Navy patrol boats turned toward the position and were steaming at full speed. The entire Navy had every available form of radar in use, and they could almost feel the energy flowing through the air. The Petty Officer at the ESM console tasked to track radar signals looked overwhelmed. He had reverted to simply looking for outliers—anything out of the ordinary. The signal officer also confirmed that eight base security groups had left by road, deploying around the Nynäshamn area, where they hoped to intercept the craft.

Nylund clenched his teeth as he looked at the screen. "Here we go," he whispered to himself, then thought better of verbalizing anything. *I'll get you now, whoever you are.*

* * *

Stockholm, April 15th, 1430hrs

Call the real police. Frida Wikström frowned to herself. *If anyone is the real police, it's me. As real as they come. I'm better because I don't have to spend half my time writing reports and follow a thousand rules that apply to everything.* During her time on the force, she had seen more than her fair share of people slipping through the cracks of the legal system. Most due to meaningless technicalities. Eventually, she just wasn't able to watch it anymore.

Toward the end, it almost made her feel physically ill. Everybody knew they were guilty. The police knew; the accused knew; the court knew. Worst of all, the damn defense attorney knew as well—something that unfortunately didn't stop them from helping criminal after criminal walk free. Maybe the police broke protocol by having an officer and not a trained lab technician collect evidence. Perhaps they failed to file the correct paperwork in the correct order and at the right time, which caused a dismissal of the case. Anyway, she was done with that garbage.

She turned the corner and stopped close to Segerfors' fishing cabin. She guessed he would still be there. Keeping one eye at the surroundings, she walked down to the cabin. There was nobody around anymore. *Maybe they got tired of untangling nets and just went fishing instead.*

She reached his cabin and walked around to the front, and immediately froze mid-step. Something wasn't right here. The table was knocked over, and the coffee cup she had used a few hours earlier was broken on the ground.

She took a few steps back around the corner to make sure the wall shielded her from the entrance to the cabin. She stopped and listened for any noise and scanned the surroundings for anything out of the ordinary. There was nobody around and nothing she could see or hear raised any suspicion.

She pulled out her weapon. It was no longer technically a service weapon, but there were ways to get a hold of them. Walther PPK was the preferred weapon of Her Majesty's Secret Service but also of the Swedish police department. She stretched the weapon out in front of her and stepped away from the wall of the cabin. Slowly she sidestepped and sliced the angle to the front door. She moved up to stand next to the entryway. There was a window on that side, but it was on the far side of the door. Nobody could see her from inside, but they could have heard her.

If they were ready on the inside with anything heavier than a pistol, they could probably shoot her straight through the wall. Not to mention what could happen as she opened the door.

If she burst inside, it would be impossible to react in time if anyone was waiting for her. Instead, she decided to open the door, inch by inch, seeing if there was a reaction. As she had a bit of a gap and nothing had happened, she crouched, had a quick look, and pulled her head back immediately. Doing it at waist height might be confusing for the person on the other side.

She saw nobody inside. Heard nothing. No movement, no breathing, nothing. Stepping away from the door, she continued to move until she had a good view of the inside. Not seeing anyone, she took four quick steps inside and swept the room. It was empty.

She let out the lungful of air she had kept in before going through the door, and let her weapon drop. She held it by her side while drawing some long breaths, trying to calm her heartbeat down so she could think straight.

The corner he had cleaned up had items fallen out of the shelf, and it looked like there was blood on the floor. She knelt down and looked closely at it, careful not to touch anything. Some of the police rules were still functioning by default. It was blood. Not enough to suspect a shooting or stabbing. More likely someone took a punch to the nose.

She found out someone had altered the sketch and, hours later, the witness is gone with blood left in his cabin. *The timing of this is too close to be coincidental*, she thought as she looked at her watch. She left Segerfors sitting in front of his cabin about three hours earlier. No way. Someone except Nylund must have known what she was up to. She hadn't told anyone.

Her heart rate refused to come down as she stood in the middle of Segerfors' cabin. The remaining options were that Nylund had disclosed it to someone or that some communication had been intercepted. She spoke to Nylund on her home phone and called the Navy switchboard when she got no answer at his office. Would the Navy line be monitored?

* * *

Stockholm. April 15th, 1600hrs

The first papers rolled off the truck. Breaking news.

Sighting of Possible Soviet Submarine at Danziger Gatt.

Navy Reticent about Significant Operation.

What Is the Navy Hiding?

Once Bergman confirmed the actual sighting and spoke to the naval communications man, who was less than cooperative, convincing his editor was no big task. The Soviet bit was a tad loose on the facts, but if it was a possible submarine, it could possibly be a Soviet submarine as far as Bergman was concerned. That's what the voice on the phone said, and with the word *possible* in there, he wasn't spreading any untruths. Bergman needed to get a hold of more information about this. He had the upper hand against the other newspapers, but they soon would be swarming like flies on a dead fish. He had materials somewhere in the office from a previous story on the military. If not mistaken, Admiral Klas Nylund's home address was in there somewhere.

Chapter 12 – Engagement

Stockholm, April 15th, 1600hrs

Wikström was driving back toward her apartment, mentally reviewing what had happened. She had spent half an hour looking through the shed for anything that could help her find out. Except for the minor signs of struggle, there was nothing. At least nothing she would find without a real forensic review. She left it all untouched and closed the door behind her. To not draw attention from any of Segerfor's neighbors, she had put the table back in its place and brought her coffee cup with her. Her prints were on it, and it was hard to wipe all the broken parts.

She would need to speak to Nylund but wasn't yet sure how to approach this. He was the one who handed her the clearly classified files with Alvar Segerfors' name and address. Was it possible he wanted traces of this out of the way? He used her to find out who knew enough to call whatever bluff the Navy was running? Once she had called in to tell him about the sketch, he could have organized for someone to come and grab Segerfors.

It was a plausible scenario, but she had known Nylund for a long time. Did he have it in him to behave like this? The other possibility was someone knew what Nylund was up to and tailed her here. That felt like a complicated option but not impossible. But who?

Fully alert to the fact that something wasn't right, she was constantly checking her rear-view mirror, trying to keep track of the traffic behind her. Twice, she turned off the main road, continued for a few kilometers, to then suddenly turn back again.

I'm getting paranoid, she thought. Maybe she shouldn't go home at all, but she needed to get a hold of Nylund.

* * *

N 58°47'00" E 17°48'25", April 15th, 1630hrs

"Echo 1, Echo 1, this is Yankee 6-7. We got a visual on a small craft, Navy type, tied up at a jetty south end of Torö. We'll move in for a closer look. Navy craft, nobody around. Can see a road leading from the jetty up through the forest."

Got you, Nylund thought.

"Tell them to follow the road and see what they can find."

The signal officer relayed the command, and Yankee 6-7 started a slow search up the road, radioing in directions and distance as they went on.

"One kilometer, the road is still northbound, no sight of any vehicles."

This will make some people very unhappy, the pilot thought as his twin rotary helicopter roared along the road at low altitude. Someone will call the complaints department for sure. He glanced at his co-pilot and the smile he got in return told him they both were thinking the same thing. Both men continued to smile as they kept searching the road. This was more fun than their regular day.

* * *

Woods North of Oxnö, April 15th, 1730hrs

The dog's ears perked up several times during the last few minutes. They heard helicopters in the distance, and Zetterberg wondered whether that would be the reason. The corporal that handled the dog and knew it best shook his head. There was someone out there. Zetterberg conferred quickly with the navigator and settled on a direction. He motioned to everyone to follow his lead. The dog handler started carefully moving while the radio operator reported their suspicion.

It could be locals walking around in the woods, but he had an eerie feeling this wasn't the case. *Like my brother*, he thought. *He always gets suspicious when his kids are too quiet.* Locals wandering the woods would have no reason to be silent. They would more likely be talking and walking at pace. He motioned to his group to slow down and stay low. Whoever was out there might have heard them coming and taken cover.

Moving at a snail's pace, every man paid attention to where he put his feet to avoid making a sound. The dog handler at the front would focus on what the dog was doing. That meant he, himself, wouldn't be best placed to look around and be ready for contact. Hence, the group's fire support was close to him. That would be the group's strongest man, regularly equipped with the heaviest weapon.

Because they left in a rush and collected live ammunition as they left, they were all equipped with the same weapon on this patrol. The Swedish version of the Heckler & Koch G3, known in Sweden as an AK4. A 7.62mm assault rifle with long-range and high penetration. It only carried a twenty-round clip, but was still a long and heavy weapon to deal with.

The dog was highly excited but did not make a sound, just as it had been trained. The handler pulled the dog in and put an arm around it to keep it calm.

They heard low voices but couldn't see anything. The sun was dropping low, and the shadows thrown through the trees and bushes made it hard to see. He motioned for the dog handler to stay where he was while the remaining men kept creeping forward, one slow step after the other. He heard a car start and could briefly see tail-lights between the trees as the vehicle took off down a narrow forest road. Another car was parked there, with what looked like three men standing around it looking at something—a map perhaps.

The man to his left stepped on a branch. It always surprised him how sound carried in the woods when all was still. He saw the heads of all the three men jerk up and look around. A second later, the three unknown men drew their weapons. Zetterberg instinctively broke silence but only managed a single word.

"Down."

The four of them dropped where they stood just in time for the first shots to ring out. He heard the zing of a bullet as it passed overhead. The same sound they heard at the firing range and while practicing for this very scenario. Who the hell was this, and why were they shooting at them?

The men by the car seemed to be armed with handguns only, so a hit on a prone target at this range was unlikely but not impossible. A bit of luck on their part, and this could be the end of Zetterberg and his group.

Landgren, to his right, was all over the place. He seemed to struggle with their situation and was still casually looking for cover. Like he was walking around looking for something he had dropped. Bengtsson, to his left, was lying perfectly still and had taken aim, but wasn't firing yet. Bengtsson was from the deepest woods of Dalarna and one of the calmest people he had ever met.

Zetterberg tried to think, but his mind worked in slow motion. Seconds passed but felt like minutes. No clear thoughts came into his head; he had no idea who the three other men were or why they were firing at them. There was only one question he couldn't get out of his head. Who would start firing with a handgun at this range? Probably someone who just wanted to suppress them to get away and didn't care much whether they hit anything or not.

The thud of a bullet hitting the tree next to him brought him out of thought. His theory then fell flat when he saw one of the men moving toward them, trying to close the distance. *Fuck, we'll get killed this way.*

For now, they had the advantage in range, but they would lose some of it for every meter the other men advanced.

Landgren had now come to terms with himself and sat crouching behind a tree, weapon at the ready. Zetterberg wrestled with his mind and eventually reached a single conclusion. Landgren and Bengtsson wouldn't die today—not this way. Weapon pressed hard to his shoulder, he lined up his sights. "Fire."

All three soldiers fired at the same time. Firing at semi-automatic setting, squeezing the trigger once for every round. The AK4 was a powerful weapon, and it was hard to fire rapidly while maintaining good aim. However, they all had stable firing positions, the range was short for an assault rifle, and they were all excellent marksmen. On paper targets anyway.

They were supposed to keep track of how many rounds they fired, but Zetterberg immediately lost count and kept going until his weapon stopped. After hesitating for a second, training kicked in, and he put a new magazine into his weapon and took aim again. Landgren and Bengtsson did the same thing.

The sun shined through the smoke while the woods were perfectly still. Still, like a scary old tale of trolls and fairies. Zetterberg looked around. He was shaking like a leaf but wasn't injured. Landgren and Bengtsson didn't seem hurt. Behind him, the dog handler gave him a shaky thumbs-up, holding onto his dog with the other hand. Even the dog seemed fine. He turned his attention back to the car. He looked at it for several seconds but couldn't detect any movement. He motioned for the other three to move forward, and they carefully started moving again, weapons at the ready.

* * *

Stockholm, April 15th, 1800hrs

"What the hell is going on here?", Löfgren hissed at the man he had met yesterday already.

"I'm neck-deep in trouble with this submarine being missing and reappearing. What happened?"

The man took a long pull on his cigarette and looked at Löfgren.

"Your submarine surprised one of ours as we were departing. It was supposed to be in a different place. We don't know who ordered it back to its original area."

"So, our submarine will have your guys on tape, and this will be a big fucking incident before the end of today."

"Well, we wanted it to be a big fucking incident. As far as the tapes are concerned, they've been taken care of."

"Taken care of?"

"Yes, taken care of. You don't need to know more than that."

"Listen, I'm in this as much as you. I need to know what the hell is going on."

The man looked at Löfgren for a few seconds. "We decide what you need to know, but if it helps you sleep at night, we're now in possession of the tapes, and they will never see the light of day."

"You stole them from our submarine?"

"We have the tapes, and that's all you need to know."

Löfgren leaned back in his seat and let out a sigh. How the hell they got ahold of the tapes already was beyond his imagination, but it was helpful to keep this somewhat contained. This could have ended a lot worse.

"Lucky you didn't hit our boat then."

"They never tried to hit it. Your submarine came through a temperature layer right on top of one of ours. They both went to full power, and while yours maneuvered, ours just tried to get as far away as possible to make sure his partner realized who was who."

"You had two of them there?"

"Yes, and underwater combat quickly becomes very confusing, so they had agreed on actions for a scenario like this. The boat closest to the contact runs away at full power to show who he is and create as much distance as possible if the torpedo guiding wire fails. Without a wire, the torpedo doesn't give a shit which language the crew speaks, if you know what I mean."

The man smiled at him. Löfgren shivered. Was this a game to him?

"The second boat fired a torpedo to make sure your guys got something to think about other than chasing us. The torpedo was never intended to hit but to be destroyed."

The man paused to take another pull on his cigarette. As he exhaled the smoke into the air, he made a dismissive gesture with his hand.

"The torpedo missed anyway. If it wasn't for all the secrecy surrounding this, we'd have to pass on our compliments to your crew. They disappeared below the layer before our very eyes, and we never managed to reacquire them on sonar. Some fine submarining, apparently, says the people who know about these things. Textbook."

The man looked down at his hands for a second, spinning a metal cigarette case between his thumb and index finger. "However, your submarine also shot at us."

Löfgren didn't say anything. If their crew had confirmed a kill, he would have heard about it.

Realizing he wasn't going to get a reaction, the man simply continued to answer the question that Löfgren never asked. "It was close, and our boat suffered substantial damage. She didn't sink or surface, but let's just say we are expecting it to take a while for her to get back home."

"And where is home?"

The man looked at Löfgren, pocketed his cigarette case, and stood up to leave.

"Good day, Commander Löfgren."

* * *

Woods north of Oxnö, April 15th, 2000hrs

Zetterberg was sitting against a tree, looking at his hands. They were still shaking after the encounter. They had moved up toward the car and found all three men dead. His team had fired sixty rounds of 7.62mm at them, and it wasn't a pretty sight. Landgren had vomited immediately and was still retching. Bengtsson was shaken up but still in reasonable form considering what just happened to them. The dog handler and dog were okay and in terms of Zetterberg himself, he was better than expected.

They reported the contact, and additional Navy personnel swarmed the location fifteen minutes later. People were digging through the men's car with flashlights, apparently looking for something specific. Helicopters had briefly hovered above them before heading off down the road.

Chapter 13 – Signal

N 58°42'00" E 18°29'11", April 15th, 2030hrs

It had been a long day, and the Captain of the Swedish Minesweeper was preparing for some well-needed sleep when the officer of the watch called him. Something about a signal they couldn't identify. He put his knitted Navy sweater back on, on top of his pajamas, and shuffled his way up to the bridge. He was in a rotten mood, but he forgot all about that when the watch officer pointed to some of the signals they had picked up.

"What? What is that?"

"We don't know. It's actively transmitting. Seems to be at a low effect and at just over 105Khz, very high for an active sonar looking to find anything at even mid-level range."

"And it's stationary?"

"It hasn't moved an inch since we first caught it. Seems completely stationary. I was going to mark the bearing here and start moving us a few hundred meters east to see if we can get a cross-bearing."

The captain thought for a second and then

nodded. "Ok. Move the ship and see if you can pinpoint the position and then call it in. Any chance it comes from any of our units?"

"Theoretically, I guess, but there are no ships on that bearing, and damned if I can mention one of ours transmitting at this frequency. I'll double-check it but would take it as highly unlikely."

The watch officer was probably right. He was young, even for a lieutenant, but was excellent at his job. If he didn't know of any Swedish devices transmitting like this, it probably wasn't Swedish.

"Okay, take her east to evaluate and call it in. I need some coffee but will be back in ten minutes."

* * *

Stockholm, April 15th, 2100hrs

Nylund had been at home for thirty minutes when the phone rang. *Not one minute to rest*, he thought. He could feel this whole situation making him age quickly. Nylund had left for home to get a break and a chance to think things through. Some peace and quiet in his office would do the trick.

Having diverted the Navy to search for the naval craft was very satisfying. He had felt enormous energy as he observed the radar picture change and heard the radio traffic. Like the good old days when the Navy had some power to be reckoned with. No news had come from the search of the craft and he reminded himself to call the watch commander as soon as he finished his sandwich.

Eriksson was running things like a man possessed. Nylund couldn't remember the last time the watch commander slept, and it was now critical that Eriksson got some rest or he would start making mistakes. Nylund admired Eriksson for his work. The man had been on top of this from the start. Eriksson had even dared to disobey orders and do the right thing when his admiral hesitated. *I should write him up for a commendation once this is over,* he thought. He picked up the phone on the fourth signal.

"Yes, Nylund speaking."

"Admiral, Eriksson. We've got a few pieces of news, and there are some decisions to be made as far as I am concerned."

"All right. Give me the news first."

"Okay, first, one of our minesweepers has found an active transmission, 105Khz, nothing we know anything about. They are moving in to investigate and pinpoint the location. They should know more in two or three hours, hopefully. Given recent events, I see this as serious and have put the submarine back on station, to the east of the signal. She submerged twenty minutes ago. Two other submarines have aborted their exercises down south and are working their way up as well. As soon as I know more, you'll know more."

Eriksson continued without missing a beat. "A few hours ago, Yankee 6-7 found a naval craft that fits the description of what pulled alongside the submarine and took the tapes. While they were looking for a vehicle of some sort, one of our base security groups ran into a group of unidentified men. The end result was a firefight."

"A FIREFIGHT?" Nylund exclaimed. "This is Sweden, and this is peacetime. What happened? Is anyone injured?"

"I know, it is hard to believe, but it's all confirmed. The base security team reports no injuries. Three unknown men are dead, and they have proven hard to identify, at least quickly. We have found no ID of any kind."

"So we have no idea who they are?"

"No, we're still trying to identify them. Apparently, they were armed only with handguns while our team had standard-issue AK4. Not a fair fight at mid-range, if you see what I mean. According to the group leader, a sergeant that seems well in control of himself, all things considering, the dog signaled a contact. They saw a car take off, and as they moved in, the three men opened fire on them. As the unknowns moved forward, the team decided to return fire, and the result you can imagine. Sixty rounds of 7.62mm, from which probably a third struck their targets. Not much left to interrogate."

"God, and what about the car that left?"

"We diverted the helicopters to look for it but with only a vague description it's a long shot. That's our decision point, Admiral. We have seven helicopters flying low over civilian housing with a low chance of finding anything. This will create a mess publicly. I would suggest we pull them away. Maybe this is a case for the police?"

Nylund thought about it for a moment. Eriksson was right. With darkness and a vague description, there was zero chance of telling one car from another.

"You're right. Get them back for refit, but keep them ready to go if need be. And keep the police out of this for now."

"Yes, sir . . . and Admiral?"

"Yes."

"What the hell is going on?"

"When I know, you will know." Nylund hung up the phone. A commendation for that man, indeed.

* * *

Berga Naval Base, April 15ᵗʰ, 2105hrs

Eriksson slowly put the phone down on the other end. Explosions, lost submarines, and now Navy ground personnel shooting and killing unknown civilians. This was entirely out of control, and either the admiral doesn't know or won't tell us what's going on. He spent a few seconds contemplating which of those scenarios would be his preference.

Either way, he had started to respect the man. At the start of this, the admiral had seemed hesitant to do anything. He had been passive and wanted to wait and see about most everything. Now Nylund was all over this. He had surprised everyone as he had marched into the command center yesterday evening. The admiral hadn't taken charge of things, as he knew they all could do their jobs without him and were more adept with the latest technology. Nylund had just been around to make decisions when needed, and the rest of the time had stood there looking lean and mean in battledress showing everyone he was there to support them. *Signature of a leader*, Eriksson thought.

* * *

Stockholm, April 15ᵗʰ, 2130hrs

Nylund was in his study preparing for his meeting with the high command. The room would be filled with more politicians this time as well, and it would take most of tomorrow. There was plenty to discuss, as the press had now caught up with recent events. The Muskö Communications officer was hit with a barrage of questions from all over the globe as the news spread.

That the submarines were from the Soviet Union was not an unreasonable assumption. It was the weaker part of the Soviet Navy, but it was still a sizeable fleet. They would be interested in the Swedish Navy's capabilities, as Sweden was a neutral buffer between the closest NATO members and the Warsaw Pact.

Most wargame scenarios were explicit, stating that the central theatre of a war between the two would have its main front around Poland and Germany. Shipping through the Baltic Sea would be critical to the Warsaw Pact and also the ability to get its Baltic Sea fleet access to Skagerrak on the Swedish west coast. First of all, that area was supposably the main launch area of American Polaris missiles aimed at Moscow. Secondly, having the option to send ships from its Baltic Sea fleet into the North Sea and the Atlantic was a welcome addition to come charging across the Barents Sea and NATO's fixed sonar lines. The Öresund Strait between Sweden and Denmark was tight, and they needed to have a good grip on Swedish Navy capabilities.

Nylund sat up straight. What was that? He

was old but not deaf just yet, and it sounded like someone had just stumbled and fallen over in his garden. He decided to ignore it, but a gnawing feeling grew in the back of his head. A lot of unexplained things had happened in the last few days. He walked over to his combat uniform that lay across the couch in his office and dug out his revolver.

He walked downstairs and let his eyes slowly sweep the living room and its windows. After standing still and listening for a few moments, he walked over to the big doors toward the back garden. It was dark, and the back garden was in a long shadow from the streetlights on the front of the house. *Probably nothing*, he thought. He pocketed the revolver and walked toward the kitchen. He had forgotten about the sandwich he was going to make. His stomach now reminded him.

Nylund jumped in surprise, as there was a knock on the back door that he just turned his back on a few seconds ago. Almost losing his balance, he spun around, digging in his pocket for the weapon. As he was struggling to get the weapon free, he looked up and noticed a familiar face. It was Wikström. Nylund stood still for a few seconds, hands-on knees, trying to get his heart rate under control. Then he walked over and let her in.

"What the hell are you doing? You scared the hell out of me." His breath was still strained.

"Seems like I wasn't the first to do that," Wikström responded and nodded toward the handle of his gun sticking out of his pocket.

"Since when do Swedish Admirals walk around armed in their own homes?"

"Since there are too many things happening that can't be made sense of. You have no idea about the tense situation that's ongoing here."

"I have some idea. See, I spoke to the witnesses, and there is only one with any degree of detail about the sighting. I left him at his fishing cabin in Nynäshamn to call you. When I returned, he was missing."

"Segerfors is missing?" Nylund asked, surprise on his face.

Wikström carefully studied Nylund's face as she told him the news. Would he have known this already? Most people recognized a surprised facial expression when they saw one. Raised eyebrows, slightly open mouth, and eyelids that open more than usual. The upper lid raised and the lower lid drawn down, usually exposing white sclera both above and below the iris. What most people didn't realize was that surprise is a split-second expression. It doesn't stick. Anyone that looks surprised for several seconds isn't really surprised. They're faking it.

Wikström looked at Nylund in silence for several seconds. Then she eased the grip of her own weapon, concealed in her jacket pocket. He didn't know anything about this. Probably best to keep an eye on his right hand still, but she would almost bet her life that he didn't have anything to do with this.

She continued, "Yes, missing. There is a sign of struggle in his cabin and some traces of blood on the floor. Not sure what happened, but it would seem to me he didn't exactly leave voluntarily. There' isn't enough blood to think anything serious happened to him. A punch in the face maybe—to make him come along."

"He realizes that the sketch has been changed, updates it, and once you leave he gets taken away by force?"

"That's what it looks like. He could have tripped and fallen, of course, and be somewhere in a bar with a block of ice against his head."

"But you don't believe that, do you?"

"No, I don't."

"Why not?"

"Can't say. Just feels like too much of a coincidence."

Nylund paced the room for a minute. "I can't make sense of all this. A submarine gets ordered to switch its operational area. That has never happened before. As it returns, it runs into a foreign vessel and almost gets sunk. Tapes get taken by people in Swedish Navy uniforms. Base security gets attacked, and now the only person who can clearly identify the other vessel is also missing." He shook his head and then went on to rub both of his eyes. "And you have a feeling something isn't right."

Now it was Wikström's turn to briefly look surprised, "Tapes? Base security attacked?"

Nylund walked over to the kitchen counter and started to mess with an unopened pack of coffee. "Have a seat, Frida. This is going to take a while."

* * *

Muskö Naval Base, April 15th, 2230hrs

Rough evening, Edvinsson thought as he looked at his watch. It was ten-thirty in the evening, and he had been on the phone non-stop since the evening press had dropped the bomb earlier this evening. Administrative staff from the call center had been in his office all evening, concerning both information on the press release and also some noise complaints.

Helicopters were sweeping across civilian housing at low altitudes. An older man had refused to shut up about it until one of the operators simply hung up on him. He had gone on and on about how the Navy would never find any Soviet submarines if they kept flying over land. *Reasonable observation,*

Edvinsson thought, but one might imagine that even the Navy would realize that without help.

A whole neighborhood called in and reported gunfire in the area. He found that hard to believe and instructed the staff to tell them there was no reason for worry. The Swedish military wasn't firing wildly in their area. All was under control.

European and American media were quick to react as they were awake as the big story was published in the Swedish press. He should have suspected this as that reporter called and tried to trick him. In retrospect, he should have reported it upward, but he hadn't thought about it as it was one single call from one individual. Usually, several journalists got the whiff of something simultaneously and hit him within five minutes of each other. That one journalist alone was so well-informed was unusual.

Well-informed may be the wrong word, he thought. *Might as well be ill-informed, but I guess that remains to be seen.* He looked at his watch. The damn Australians had just woken up, and would hit him next.

Chapter 14 – Return to the Scene

N 58°43'10" E 18°25'30", April 15th, 2300hrs

They were all surprised when the order came through. The captain spent some time in the radio room, before immediately giving the order to prepare the boat to dive. The process started with clearing the conning tower of gear. The engineer calculated how much water should be held in the main tank as the dive happened. This would ensure the submarine was close to balanced as it slid down below the surface. A few minutes later, all sections reported in. Ready to dive.

"Clear the bridge," the captain ordered.

The conning officer on the bridge closed the top hatch and climbed down into the pressure hull. He closed the main hatch behind him, and once he was down, the torpedo officer climbed up to the hatch and checked it.

The conning officer reported, "Hatch closed and secured."

A few seconds later, the torpedo officer reported. "Confirmed, hatch closed, hatch secured."

The captain turned to the engineer and helmsman and made the final call. "Dive the boat, balance her at two-five meters."

The engineer turned a few controls on his console, and a valve at the bottom of the five ballast tanks opened to let the water in. At the same time, he opened the air vents at the top to let the air out. Slowly, the tanks filled up with water, and the submarine soon disappeared below the waves.

The diving alarm sounded throughout the ship—one single long tone. The captain then came on the speaker system—"Dive, dive"—before the long tone sounded again.

Lindberg was pissed. They had been attacked, for crying out loud, and now they were being sent back out there. They only had one live torpedo left. They could carry many more, but it was standard to carry only two live ones under peace conditions. The last encounter had involved at least two submarines. Who knew what might await them out there? He figured he wasn't the only one but that the entire crew was in desperate need of some debriefing and some time off after this ordeal. Instead, they were now passing the ten-meter mark. The conning tower would be just about visible but would be gone from the surface in thirty seconds.

Confirming Lindberg's reading of the depth gauge, the engineer came across the speaker system.

"Ten meters, pressure check."

All hatches and all compartments would be closely monitored during the dive to make sure there were no issues with the integrity of the submarine as she disappeared downward, approaching her ordered depth. All compartments reported in one by one. No leaks.

The slightest issue with the watertight integrity of the hull would trigger an immediate order to abort the dive by blowing the ballast tanks. The engineer would close the air vents at the top of the tanks and then push high-pressure air into them to push the water out. As the five tanks started to fill with air, the submarine would quickly rise to the surface again.

The check procedure was repeated a minute later.

"Twenty meters, pressure check."

No leaks.

The helmsman reported reaching the ordered depth a minute later. "Two-five meters, balanced."

The captain looked at the chart and conferred quickly with the executive officer, known as the XO. He then handed over the con of the ship and left the command center. The XO ordered them onto the new course and increased speed to twelve knots.

* * *

Stockholm, April 16th, 0730hrs

The meeting had moved to a bigger room. It was no longer a meeting room but a small lecture hall. Nylund sat on the first row, looking at his notes as the last participants stumbled through the door. It was early morning, and most people congregated at the large table with coffee and sandwiches. Nylund was tired too, but he couldn't handle any more coffee at this time. Wikström had left Nylund's house at 0200. He was then up again at 0400 to prepare for this briefing. For how long he could keep this up was an open question.

He would be in focus and would have to explain recent events the best way he knew how. Yesterday was worth the loss of sleep, though. Wikström and he had systematically worked through a timeline of some of the events. Clearly, something wasn't right here, and he felt better knowing a plan was in place about how to straighten a few things out. He would get to it once this briefing was over and done with.

The minister of defense was accompanied by his usual entourage. There were also some new faces he knew were from the government. He would try to establish facts, and they would have to decide how to deal with the press and with involvement from the police, security services, or anyone else.

"Good morning," Nylund said as he stood up and turned toward the crowd. He started by showing the timeline he worked up with Wikström, excluding a couple of bits that would need further research. . . or maybe just less of an audience.

"1330hrs, yesterday, April 15th, one of our helicopters spotted a flare in the water and shortly thereafter, our surfacing submarine. The good news is that our submarine is no longer missing, but we learned there were worrying circumstances of her delay to report in. The radio transmission included contact with what has been designated a 'certain submarine.' As you understand, this is significant, as all other sightings usually start as possible submarines before, in the rarest of cases, move on to be probable submarines."

"Our submarine tracked the contact and almost ran into it coming through a temperature layer. During the close encounter, the foreign vessel ran away at maximum speed. Our submarine prepared a torpedo while confirming they were in Swedish territorial waters, but before they could finalize, a torpedo was fired at them from a different vessel. Almost certainly a second submarine. Our captain fired a torpedo, broke the guiding wires, and dove for cover. The foreign torpedo missed and likely detonated against a countermeasure, hence failing to damage our submarine. It did scare the hell out of the crew, however. The Swedish torpedo detonated four minutes later. We're unsure of the effects of that."

"Torpedo?" one of the government officials almost screamed.

"Swedish submarines are firing torpedoes and then disappearing. Why didn't they radio in or something? The captain of the boat should be charged with all this mess. We'll all look like idiots to the foreign press."

Nylund clenched his teeth, taking his time before answering. He was already using up a large amount of his self-control, and the meeting had only just begun. "Our regulations give the captain the right to fire a live shot at a foreign vessel in Swedish waters. However, this is irrelevant since technically; he was returning fire."

The politician was about to start talking again when Nylund decided to run him over.

"To radio in, the submarine needs to be close to the surface. They judged the torpedo was fired at them from shallow depth, and they suspected an enemy submarine might be waiting for them to approach the surface to report. Hence, they proceeded south to evaluate their own torpedo detonation and to clear the area. And if I may add, you are doing an excellent job looking like an idiot without any help from the Navy."

The government official almost launched out of his chair and would have continued the argument if not for the supreme commander. Rosenfeldt slammed his hand so hard on one of the fold-out tables that it broke clean off its hinges and fell to the floor.

"Enough of this, both of you. This is highly sensitive, and we have some tough decisions to make today. Focus, gentlemen. Focus." He motioned for Nylund to continue.

"As I just explained, after the explosions, our submarine turned south to evaluate the detonation and to search the area. They didn't find any indication that the Swedish torpedo hit anything and no trace of any other submarines. As this was going on, we initiated submarine missing protocol and were launching a major search.

"As our Navy closed in on them, the captain judged it likely the foreign vessels had moved out and that it would be safest to surface, to not be mistaken for a foreign vessel himself. He launched a flare and surfaced the boat. That's when he got spotted by Yankee 6-4."

The other defense clown opened his mouth in a considerably more respectful and reasonable tone than his colleague. "Any chance to determine the nationality of the submarines? I take it your submarines would have been able to record some of this?"

Nylund wasn't looking forward to this part, but it had to be done. "During the encounter itself, the submarine crew couldn't determine the origin of the foreign vessels. There are tapes of the encounter, but we are uncertain of where they are at the moment."

He could see the audience's surprise. They were all thinking the same thing. The Navy lost all the tapes? The minister of defense quickly recovered. "You don't know where they are?"

"No, we don't. According to submarine logs, a Navy lieutenant boarded the submarine from a small Navy craft and picked up all the tapes. There is no log of orders for this, and we suspect the man was not, in fact, part of the Navy."

"What?"

Now it was the minister's turn to lose his self-control. "What the hell are you telling us, Admiral? A man dressed in uniform picked up the tapes from the submarine, and he wasn't one of ours? How is this even possible? My colleague is right. We will all look like a bunch of idiots, not just to the foreign press but to the whole damn world. You need to get the hold of these tapes, now!"

"Yes, Minister. The Navy is looking into this while we are preparing a briefing for the security services. I'm afraid it gets worse."

The minister sagged in his chair and let out a long sigh. "It gets worse, does it? Well, that's just great."

"We ordered the pickup of the tapes

ourselves and realized within minutes that something was wrong. The helicopters were diverted to search for the craft while we prepared our base security search units for land operations. One of our helicopters found the craft at a similar time as a dog patrol ran into a group of three unknown men in the woods close to Oxnö."

"So, you got them?"

"No, as the search group approached, they came under fire from the three men. Our people took cover, but as the individuals advanced on their position, they had no choice but to return fire. The three unknown men are unfortunately dead and very hard to identify."

"Good God, what's going on here?" the minister said. "Submarines, gunfights. What do we do now? It must have been heard by a hell of a lot of people."

"Navy communications have been answering calls all night and assured everyone that there is nothing out of the ordinary going on and there is no need to worry. However, the question posed in the *Evening Press* about the nationality of the submarines must be answered. Our communications officer is doing a great job holding half the world at bay, but he will need help to come up with a reliable story to tell them."

"Yes, coming up with that is the first priority as soon as we're done here. What else do you have?"

"On the note of nationality, we do have a Navy operation in motion at sea at the moment."

"What kind of operation?"

"One of our vessels picked up a very unusual signal and is moving to investigate. It seems to be intermittent, and they're having difficulties pinpointing the exact location. The signal could be an underwater beacon, transmitting on a frequency not used by us. Not anything that our NATO friends would use either, as far as we know. Meanwhile, our submarine has been ordered back to sea to watch the area."

"Wait, the missing submarine is not in port yet?"

"No, it was the submarine closest to the area. It submerged late last night to take up its station, watching the area around the transmission."

"You haven't lost it yet, have you?" clown number one asked acidly.

He got a very stern look from the supreme commander. Say what you wanted about Fredrik Rosenfeldt and his sometimes-hesitant behavior. The former tank commander looked the part. The staff member from the defense ministry lowered his gaze and leaned back in his seat again.

"I'm lost," the minister said. "Too many things happening at the same time. Let's focus here. We've got a journalist claiming there are Soviet submarines in our waters and that the Navy is being cagy about it. That's our priority before the entire world starts to speculate. If nothing else, I would expect to hear from the Soviets today."

The minister continued, "So, it's simple. Who was it?"

"We don't know," Nylund answered

"Can we exclude that it was a Soviet submarine?"

"No, we cannot. We have some characteristics on the submarine that would exclude certain types, but many nations will have boats with a single, five-bladed propeller. That includes both the Soviet Union and several NATO countries."

"NATO, what the hell would they do here?"

"I don't know, but based on the evidence we have, we can't exclude that either. We're hoping the signal device we're tracking will provide some clarity to the nationality. We can't prove that the signal and the submarine belong together, of course, but it seems likely."

"If 'seems likely' is the best the Navy can do, we'll pick this up now." The minister gestured toward the two members of his staff.

Nylund tried to object but was interrupted.

"You find the source of the signal and confirm that it's a Soviet device. And find the damn tapes. We'll take care of the political implications of this before it gets any worse. Not to mention the entire Swedish population is up in arms about the Soviets being about to attack us. You go do your job, Admiral, and we'll do ours."

Chapter 15 – Analysis

N 58˚45'30" E 18˚37'47", April 16th, 0330hrs

Lindberg sat next to Sandberg in the mess hall, a grand name for the area that fit ten people packed like sardines. Both had difficulties sleeping after the last couple of days and were up earlier than necessary. The torpedo noise stayed with them both, and it wasn't a pleasant noise to have stuck in your head, especially while still aboard a submarine not far from where it happened.

Torpedoes had small propellers, working at a remarkably high RPM to propel them at high speed. The resulting noise was nothing like a ship but an awful screeching sound, suitable for banshees carrying the message of death. It would also have an active sonar to search for the target. Unlike World War II movies, they didn't transmit frequencies the human ear could pick up through the hull. The sonar crew would, however, pick it up through their headphones, and though transmitted digitally, the sound was still equally frightening. An electric-sounding chirp told the crew a torpedo was inbound on their ship.

Lindberg looked at Sandberg. Both men looked worn out after a few days of close to no sleep. There was enough time to get some rest, but the banshees kept them awake. Lindberg figured that sleeplessness would eventually work itself out. How tired did you need to be before you would just fall asleep no matter what? But sleep seemed elusive, and he figured being busy with something valuable would be the next best thing. Still two and a half hours until their shift started.

Lindberg looked around. "Sandberg."

"Yes."

"Want to do something useful for a change and listen to a tape I have?"

"Tape of what?"

"A tape that I didn't give that arrogant prick of a lieutenant when he was here picking them up."

Sandberg looked depressed, "I hear that shit in my head all night anyway."

Lindberg could sense Sandberg's curiosity across the table despite what he had said. "Come on. You want to know as much as I do. I can feel it from here." Lindberg walked over to a small locker with training equipment for the sonar crew, and pulled out a tape recorder with multiple output sockets for headphones. He handed Sandberg a pair of headphones and declared, "I'm listening to it. You do whatever you want."

Sandberg plugged his headphone into the

machine before Lindberg even had the tape out of his pocket. They played the tape back, starting with the section where they came through the layer almost on top of the other submarine. Both men closed their eyes and focused on the noise. After a few minutes, they started rewinding sections of it.

"I'll stand by my first observation," Sandberg said. "I can only hear one screw, and I make the blade count five."

Lindberg nodded. "Me too. That excludes a hell of a lot of boats. Not sure how many Soviet submarines would have one screw."

"We don't know if it's a Soviet boat," said Sandberg.

"Come on. They shot at us. Can you see any of the NATO nations shooting at us?"

"Good point."

"Do you think it could be a double-screw boat that only runs on one of them?"

"Nah, she accelerated like crazy. If you were going to run from someone you knew to be dangerous, would you jump on one leg? And there would have been flow noise around the other propeller if that was the case. I'd say single-screw design for sure."

"Minisub?"

Sandberg shook his head. "I don't think so. Too powerful. Think we would have picked up more noise at the slower speed if it was a minisub. More cavitation at lower speed. I'm thinking attack submarine."

"Okay, so Soviet standard boats then. Whiskey class is a no. Double screws . . ." Lindberg started to make some notes on a piece of paper.

"Echo class, no, twin screws. Kilo-class?"

Sandberg thought about it for a second. "One shaft, but as far as I know, that would be six or seven blades. Would have to look up if we know of any five-bladed versions. Damn, let's listen to it again. What if the sucker has six blades?"

They both spent a few more minutes listening to the contact. None of them could come up with any indication that Sandberg was wrong in his initial estimate. Five-bladed propeller for sure. They would have to revert to checking if there were any Kilos with a five-bladed screw. They kept going through some other options of submarines that could be likely candidates.

Foxtrot class was a common submarine, but like most Soviet submarines, it had multiple propellers and was likely to have six blades on them.

"Tango, no, more than one propeller."

Lindberg checked the time. It was soon time to start the six-hour watch.

"How about a Bravo class?"

Sandberg let out a chuckle. "Bravo class? Are you smoking something?"

"They have a single screw, don't they?"

"They do, but it's a training vessel. Hardly anything you would send to engage another Navy with, and I have never heard of them operating in the Baltics Sea. But fair enough, to be thorough, we should check. I can't remember the number of blades on a Bravo."

"And the Torpedo?"

"Hard to say. It is not Swedish, that is for sure. It blends with our own screw as we turn our tail to it, and as we go through the layer, it is hard to get any clear characteristics on it. Extremely hard to say without being able to listen to comparisons, but the torpedo could be USSR, for sure."

"Oberon," said Lindberg, switching countries as he could not come up with any more submarines belonging to the Soviet Navy.

"You think the submarine was from the UK? I mean, I don't doubt that they have been sniffing around here, but shooting at a Swedish submarine, that is farfetched. You said so yourself a minute ago. Besides, as far as I remember, Oberon has double screws."

"Ah shit, we are not going to solve it here, are we? We'll need access to the libraries and be able to compare things."

"Not to mention a few weeks of peace and quiet," Sandberg added.

"It's 0535. Let's get some breakfast before the watch starts."

* * *

Stockholm, April 16th, 0735hrs

Eivor Falk was cleaning the kitchen table. The kids had just disappeared out the door for school, and her husband, working shift at the hospital, wasn't home yet. On a chair next to the table was the evening press from yesterday. The first page had a huge headline about Soviet submarines operating in Swedish waters and how the Navy did not offer any insight of value about what was going on.

She opened the paper and went through some of the regular garbage until she got to the big piece about the submarines. Jesper Bergman certainly didn't hold back in his article, working with layout and font size to give the impression that Soviet submarines had been here for sure while the Navy was asleep at the wheel. Unable or unwilling to do anything about it. Journalists, they are all the same, she thought. The truth was flexible if it generated good sales and stirred things up.

On the next page was a picture of a sketch that a witness had apparently made of the submarine. Well, "submarine" was a generous description of it. It was a small box on top of a bigger box. Yes, it did look like you would imagine a submarine. That was true. It could also be a barge transporting a sauna. Eivor remembered first seeing drawings of the sighting when preparing the briefing materials for Löfgren.

Bergman probably wouldn't let this go. He would stay with it for weeks if he thought it could get his face in the paper more frequently. Perhaps even interviewed on a TV show. He'd like that.

Done with the paper, she stood up and went into the bedroom to get dressed. Time to get to work. Edvinsson, the call center, and administrative staff were working all around the clock to keep up with the requests coming in from all over the world. It would be good to be there as more information came in. High command must be having a meeting this morning after all this.

* * *

N 58°45'40" E 18°18'10", April 16th, 1000hrs

The watch officer had maneuvered the minesweeper back and forth for more than twelve hours, searching for the intermittent signal. It came and went, but not according to a regular pattern. The first time it had been gone for only a few minutes, and he was sure they could re-acquire it quickly even if that kept happening. The second time they had lost it for almost three hours before picking it up again. This cannot be a coincidence, he thought. This must be deliberate. The third time it had been gone for twenty-two minutes.

It had taken some time, but looking at his plot, he had the area marked clearly and was sure enough for them to get closer to make an observation. Signal frequency did not check out with any known beacons. Not NATO, more likely to be a Warsaw pact device if it is what I think it is. He lifted the telephone next to him.

"Let the captain know we are coming up on the position. And get the divers ready."

He checked his bearings to make sure he was in the correct position. Once pleased with his position, he continued upwind for a minute before dropping the anchor and allowing the vessel to drift backward. Imagine if he dropped the anchor on the signal source. That would be something. He had contemplated it before but figured that the risk was one in a million, and trying to stay on station without an anchor in this wind would be a pain in the neck. Deep down, he still drew a sigh of relief, as the signal continued well after the anchor would have hit bottom. Just imagine the jokes he would have had to put up with.

The divers were briefed about the upcoming operation and were ready to go on short notice. The captain checked their position and then gave the green light to the dive officer. The two divers sat in the little rubber raft and immediately dropped over the side. They came back up shortly to signal they were all ready to go and got a thumbs down from the dive officer. Slowly, they disappeared below the steel gray surface of the Baltic sea, leaving only a trail of bubbles behind.   The captain was tense. Dive operations were a regular duty for them, and he had taken part in work like this more often than he could remember. This time he had a feeling he knew what they would find, and it scared him. It must be an underwater beacon. That would make a lot of sense. What made him nervous was that he had only heard about 105Khz once in his life, which was in discussion with a Polish counterpart. This beacon frequency was commonly used by the Soviet Union. If he was about to dig up materials belonging to the Soviet Navy, it could only mean trouble. Or worse, where was the submarine that was supposed to use the beacon?

* * *

Stockholm, April 16th, 1200hrs

Bergman watched the interview re-run at midday. He looked good and figured he made a good impression as well. Radiating professionalism and gravitas, he said to himself. The morning news had called him the previous day and invited him to take part in an interview, and as a guardian of information being provided to the Swedish public, he had arrived at the SVT, Swedish Television, studio at 0700 that morning.

The interview had started abruptly, without any pleasantries, but that was okay with him. He didn't much like chit-chat anyway.

"You make some bold statements about Soviet submarines operating in Swedish waters. Where does this information come from?"

"Well, the source will remain confidential. We know there have been sightings of a submarine, and my source has provided information that strongly suggests that they belong to the Soviet Baltic Sea Navy."

"Okay, but I assume this isn't confirmed evidence as of yet?"

"That's right. As I said, there is a strong suggestion this is the case. I'm still working to verify some of the information, but we deemed it necessary this information reaches the Swedish public now so that we can make sure our government takes this very seriously."

"So, won't you be running the risk of jumping the gun on this?"

"In real-time journalism, there is always a risk that further facts down the line will put a new light on things, but the indication is strong. I find it imperative that the Swedish public stay informed of this as our government follows up on this potential breach of Swedish territorial borders. If I turn out to be wrong, I can live with it, but the Swedish people need to know what's happening. We need to be comfortable that our government protects our borders and has our safety as their primary concern."

"Yes, indeed," the interviewer continued. "Indications of submarines have been seen before, but I think this is the first time there is a sighting of one running on the surface. It would make me feel safer if we could work out who's behind this. So, can you just help us determine the line between fact and indication?"

"Of course, there isn't really much information to process here, so it should be simple. There's been a sighting of a vessel. That's a fact. The vessel looks like a submarine, and the fact that it suddenly disappeared strengthens that. We know this is within Swedish territory and that it's been witnessed by almost ten different people. We know the submarine isn't Swedish."

"And how do we know it isn't a Swedish submarine?"

"Well, first of all, a witness has made a sketch of the submarine. It doesn't fit the shape or form of a Swedish submarine of either Sjöormen or Näcken class. Second, the positions of the Swedish submarines have been checked. Neither of them is reported in this area at the time."

"So, we can draw the conclusion that

Sweden has had its territory breached by another country? That is a fact as far as you are concerned?"

"Yes, that's a fact. And as I just mentioned, we need to see determined action by the government now to confirm the nationality of this submarine, and we need this information immediately. The safety of the Swedish people is on the line. This is no time for cloak-and-dagger games. We need the government and the Navy to provide complete transparency here on what has been happening and what they plan to do about it."

I look good, he thought. Once this was out and had been translated, he would be contacted by some of the international press. No doubt. This was good for him.

Chapter 16 – Salvage

Divers from the minesweeper swam search patterns for almost an hour before finding something on the bottom. Closing in on it, they saw something that looked like a piece of steel piping attached to a metal board. This item was definitely man-made. It was perfectly horizontal on the bottom, making it clear it had been placed there rather than lost overboard from a vessel. The divers spent half an hour reviewing the device, taking pictures and measurements, and drawing specific details.

On board, the captain radioed headquarters in an attempt to work through what this could be. It seemed he had been right in his assumptions. The item appeared to be an underwater beacon sending out a signal that submarines could use to navigate. The irregular transmission patterns were likely some way of tracking time. Orders could be given to approach the beacon once it had come back after so and so many minutes of pause in transmissions. The minesweeper had plenty of data on the transmission pattern, but it all looked random at this point. They would need an expert to analyze it.

One of the divers who inspected the item guessed that the device could be from the Soviet Navy. Looking at welding and materials, more likely that it is from the East than the West, he had said. That wasn't proof of anything, but the captain still added it to his report. He figured more information was better as long as it was clear it was an assumption and not a fact. One hour later, he got a reply from headquarters regarding the next steps. Salvage the object and proceed at top speed to Muskö Naval Base.

* * *

Muskö Naval Base, April 16th, 1230hrs

Löfgren was in his office, leaning back in his chair. It had been a rough couple of days. He was highly uncomfortable that night when the thought finally struck home he might have contributed to the loss of a Swedish submarine. The plan he had agreed to was simple. If there, hypothetically, would be a sighting of a submarine on the surface in Swedish waters. Someone would need to make sure that such a sighting was taken very seriously by the Swedish Navy and the Swedish government. That was all. Not overly complicated, and nobody gets hurt. Just making sure that the potential submarine threat to Sweden got taken seriously.

Sightings of submarines throughout the past few years had mostly been taken with a pinch of salt. With *U-137*, it was serious, but people had short memories about these things and there was always room for political distortion of facts. In some cases, political opposition even doubted the reported sighting had taken place at all. Political chatter about "Budget submarines" being made up to get funds for the Navy was common throughout the seventies. A fully visible submarine would remind the Swedish public that the Soviet Union was not a friend, and the Navy would finally get the adequate funding to run proper antisubmarine operations.

Not to mention his own branch, Military intelligence. They had been restructured so many times that by the end of the seventies and early eighties, it took real effort to understand who was supposed to do what. A hopeless situation. Löfgren was first supposed to report to the Navy itself, but after further review intelligence was completely separated from the regular military branches. It had taken some work, but thanks to his relationship with Rosenfeldt, it all worked out well in the end. For many others, reporting lines and unclear responsibilities still absorbed most of the effort and effectively prevented any actual intelligence work.

The sooner, the better, he thought. Once the damn socialists were back in power, they would keep running Eastern errands and cut the defense budgets further. That a Swedish submarine would be involved was never in the cards—not to mention the fact it would almost be lost.

Either way you chose to look at this, all he needed to do was get the planted intelligence orders out of the archive, and he should be in the clear. He had done nothing wrong. Perhaps it would be seen as inappropriate to bypass the head of the Navy and inform the Ministry of Defense directly. That was something that would probably go unnoticed, but otherwise would call for a slap on the wrist at most.

Nylund was the one who made up the intelligence mission. He told Löfgren to plant the evidence of the mission, and if push came to shove, he had done what he was ordered to do. It could work against him this time, that Nylund was not technically his commanding officer, but he could probably work around that. Yes, this should come out all right. He was in the clear. Nylund couldn't get him back into trouble without risking his own skin.

* * *

Rosenbad, Stockholm, April 16th, 1230hrs

"We will not get away with this much longer," the minister of Defense said, shifting in his office chair. "The public is fuming about this—about the threat from the East—and we'll need to do something soon. We'll look like sheep to the whole world. We couldn't catch a submarine running on the damn surface. What message would that send?"

The defense minister gestured toward the others to get some response. His two associates, who attended all briefings with him, sat on the couch, and next to them the supreme commander of Sweden's military forces.

One of the minister's advisors spoke first. "Is there any evidence at all that we can use in order to determine the nationality of this submarine?"

Rosenfeldt shook his head. "No. Jesper Bergman's source, which he claims has provided strong indications, is completely unknown. We don't know where he got this information from. Some items suggest the Soviet Union, but they are somewhat vague."

"What items?"

"The sketch we have seen is quite rough, but the general shape of it—with a lower and longer conning tower—is more common in the Soviet Navy. The placement of it is further aft than most NATO boats. As I said, very vague."

"Well, it's something to hold onto," the

advisor said, "and there's nothing else at all?"

"We have salvaged an underwater beacon from our waters. It's being brought into Muskö Base now for inspection. It could be Soviet Navy, but we can't tell yet. The frequency has been used by the Soviet Navy before, but everything needs to be confirmed. Apparently, some diver remarked about it looking Eastern in general craftsmanship. That's all we have. Circumstantial at best. Not enough to make a positive ID on the intruder."

"Oh, come on. Of course it's the Russians. Who else would fire a damn torpedo at one of our submarines?" The advisor was now worked up and out of his chair. "Who else would it be?"

Rosenfeldt nodded. "I agree with you. It seems like a Soviet submarine. I'm simply saying we can't prove it—not for now at least. Nylund and his Navy are working hard on the beacon to see whether it brings any clarity, but for now, it seems the device is Eastern."

The advisor gestured angrily in the air but did not say anything. He turned away and paced the room while looking out the window.

"Damn Navy losing the tapes, our real shot at identifying the damn Russians for sure. If we go out with this uncertain gibberish of indications and possibly this and that, we'll all look like idiots. We need to be decisive here. Swedish public opinion is against the Soviet Union. The enemy is always red and always comes from the East. What else can we say? NATO shot a torpedo at one of our submarines?"

"Nobody knows that a torpedo was fired," his companion advisor interrupted.

"Oh, please. There are thirty men on that submarine. Do you think one of them won't get drunk and spill their guts to their wife or whatever? Besides, we fired a torpedo too, and we don't know the outcome of that yet. As far as we know, we may have killed a whole boatload of foreign sailors."

He was walking back and forth at a ferocious pace now. *If he goes any faster,* the supreme commander thought, *he'll miss his next turn and walk straight into the wall.*

The advisor continued, "The only politically plausible solution is to go with a firm statement that this is a Soviet operation. We condemn it, and we go to Moscow with a formal complaint. It's basically out there already, and if we say anything differently, public opinion will kill us. There's a damn election in five months, and the socialists are looking better than ever."

"The public may accept that it's a Soviet intruder, but what do we actually do about it, except for writing an angry note to Moscow?"

"Show the public that we take their safety concerns very seriously. Increase Navy spending, increase the number of Airforce exercises over densely populated areas. The roar of fighter jets is an effective and relatively cheap way to showcase how serious we are."

"And what about the Soviet Union? They may not like to be called out in public."

"What are they going to do? Invade us? We're not a NATO country, but we may as well be. You know there are agreements in place."

The defense minister nodded.

"I know. Okay, let me brief the prime minister and get his backing on this. Then we go."

He turned to Fredrik Rosenfeld. "We have no single piece of evidence telling us this is anyone else?"

"Circumstantial evidence tells us this is the work of the Soviet Union. There is no evidence suggesting anyone else."

"Okay, that's it then. I'll get back to you once I've spoken to the prime minister."

* * *

Evening press, April 16th, 1300 hrs

Bergman swiveled in his office chair, a big smile on his face. *Explosions. I love it.* A friend of his, working communications for civilian sea traffic, had seen his article and called him up. Apparently, the *M/S Taurus* called in a significant underwater explosion two days after the sighting. They were still working on it, but it looked like there were at least two of them. The Navy called it a planned and controlled mine detonation. There was an explosives-dumping ground in the area, but it was still almost twenty nautical miles away, and it was nearly four-hundred meters deep.

Bullshit, Bergman thought. Submarine sighted, underwater explosions, and then half the Navy casts off for what they call an exercise. Absolute bullshit. The explosions were a fact, and he could still get it into today's paper. This news added on top of yesterday's headlines would put the Navy and the government under such pressure they would have to respond. Come clean? Maybe not, but once they had released their statements, he could probably stay on the first page for weeks if he questioned every detail of it.

* * *

N 58˚45'00" E 18˚44'09", April 16th, 1330hrs
What seemed to just be warm air close to his ear slowly materialized into a whisper. Lindberg had fallen asleep quickly for once and felt groggy as he opened his eyes in the dark compartment. He saw the silhouette of the cook leaning over him.

"What's up?"

"Combat crews to stations. Captain's orders."

Lindberg quickly sat up in his bunk. Without thinking about it, he didn't sit up fully. Even when tired, his subconscious knew he would hit his head on the bunk above him if he did. The cook disappeared while Lindberg swung his feet over the side of his bunk and got his shoes on. He had slept in his uniform since the encounter, too tired to take it off. He climbed the ladder, swung around into the main corridor, and passed the mess hall on his way to the command center.

His mind was already coming up with scenarios to explain what could be going on. This time last week, he would have walked this way muttering about the untimeliness of the exercise. The encounter changed all that. Calling the combat crews to stations was a light version of battle stations. It was used when contacts needed tracking and evaluating but without the immediate expectation of combat. The engineers and other crew members would continue to sleep. At least for now.

As he entered the command center, the atmosphere was tense. Wikingsson and Sandberg were in consoles one and two. They were quietly talking while pointing to the BTR, clearly trying to evaluate a sonar contact.

"Lindberg, good morning," the torpedo officer greeted him. "We need to start a Q-plot and a tactical plot. Get with Sandberg, and get going."

As it turned out, Wikingsson had reported a faint contact ten minutes ago. While he and Sandberg were working to figure out if it was anything, the captain eventually made the call to get additional eyes and ears onto the possible contact. Lindberg prepared his Q-plot and looked at the BTR for initial data points. Bearing 081, then bearing 082 five minutes later.

"That's all I get to work with?" He gestured to Sandberg.

"That's all we have at the moment. It's intermittent and very faint, but I think Wikingsson is right."

Sandberg pointed to his sonar screen. "You see this group of merchants—it's three or four of them. Hard to distinguish. They all seem to be moving south to north. They obscure almost everything, but now and then, we got a faint noise coming through. The contact seems to move south slowly, so once these merchants get out of the way, we should get a better view."

Sandberg was his old self. Seemingly relaxed and just focused on what was in front of him. He didn't have time to feel any fear. Lindberg hadn't had much time for fear either as the torpedo closed in on them, but the last few days had offered ample time to for it.

The mere thought of another submerged contact close to them set his imagination on a one-way road to disaster. The screeching noise of the incoming torpedo would follow them as they tried to get away. The digital chirp from its active transmission would increase in frequency as it closed the distance.

Even if the pressure hull could withstand the force generated by the explosion, it was likely that the weak point, where the propeller axle penetrated the hull, would collapse. Depending on the depth, they wouldn't have much time before the pressure built up and the engine compartment flooded. The crew would blow all ballast in an attempt to get the boat to the surface. They only needed one minute on the surface to get everyone off the boat and launch the rafts.

It would be a race between water leaving the ballast tanks and water coming through the damaged hull. If the damage won, they would never see the surface again. After a few moments of weightlessness, they would slowly start to disappear deeper and deeper into the dark, cold waters of the Baltic Sea.

A shiver ran straight through his body. The depth at their position was over a hundred meters. He could imagine standing in the tight escape chamber, feeling the panic build up as he was pressurized to match the outside depth. If the escape hatch was undamaged, it should open automatically, and he could start his free ascent toward the surface. It would be twenty seconds before he was on the surface. Once he could breath fresh air again, he could only hope to be found before he froze to death.

"Bearing 082 still. Target Bravo, weak signal."

Wikingsson reported a brief contact again. The merchants had moving north, and Sandberg worked to keep a hold of the contact this time. Lindberg could hear him whisper under his breath as he was working.

"Got you, got you. Nowhere to run for you now."

Five minutes passed until Sandberg declared a success. "That's it. Got him. Target Bravo, now bearing 083, is an actual contact—probable submarine. Quiet bastard too."

"How quiet?" The captain was now standing behind Sandberg.

"Very. I need to run it through the library and compare a few things."

"Hurry up then."

Sandberg shot the captain a look that signaled he already knew what to do and he was going as fast as possible. Maybe if the captain got off his back, he could go a bit faster. The captain understood the silent comment and took a few steps back to his regular place next to the periscope.

Sandberg continued to mumble before himself as he was working. "You think you can get away from me, do you? No, no, no. I got you now."

Lindberg marked his Q-plot, but it was impossible to get any insights from the minimal movements in bearing. They would have to start maneuvering to get some angles for him to work with.

He listened to Sandberg in his right ear as he heard the captain discussing actions with the XO on his other side. They were outside Swedish borders, so whatever this was would be in international waters. They could choose to push forward and go for identification, or they could back off back to Swedish waters and hold their country's border.

A surface vessel or a different military unit of some kind would have radioed in to get some advice. That wasn't an option for a submarine at this depth. The captain was in tactical command of the situation and would make the decision by himself. Push and risk confrontation or fall back to never know what was there. Stefan Lindholm quickly made his decision.

"Helm, make your depth one hundred meters. Course 045. We'll do a sprint northeast. Then, we'll creep up again and see if we can't reacquire this one and see what we can find out."

The submarine dove to a greater depth and accelerated. An increase in depth would increase the pressure, which would help to minimize any cavitation as they moved position. Getting a different angle on the target would enable a cross-bearing for them to work out a course and distance of the target.

Twenty minutes later, they returned to a depth near the layer again. Sandberg was glued to his console. You could barely hear him breathe.

"Got him, Target Bravo. Bearing 106. Got her more clearly now. The merchant's interference with sonar is decreasing."

Sandberg was all over things. He read leaflets from a binder, which contained previously recorded submarines, at the same time as the low-frequency sound analysis pin-pointed engine frequencies. His eyes darted between the binder and the sonar screens.

The sonar officer was sitting in SESUB, also working on getting a range to the target. With the bearing not moving much, it was hard to tell how far away it was. Lindberg was looking at his Q-plot, but he had the same problem.

"My best guess is that she's moving more or less straight away from us. Getting a weak movement in bearing, left now." Lindberg looked over Sandberg's shoulder as the sonar picture changed.

"Turn. He's turning. Bearing moving left now. Medium and increasing. She must be changing course."

The captain looked at Sandberg. "Identity, Sandberg. I need to know what it is."

"Target Bravo, now bearing 104, moving left, course 047, calculated range 60 hectometers."

The captain had a serious look on his face while staring at the plot. "Go to battle stations, flood tube six. Everybody, stay calm. We're not in Swedish waters. It's just a precaution."

The captain turned to the navigation officer. "How far are we from Swedish waters?"

"Four nautical miles."

Sandberg interrupted them. "Target Bravo, course change. She's turning to starboard. She's zig-zagging away from us."

"And what is it?"

"Double shafts, three-bladed prop. Looking at the frequencies now. Not sure yet, but I'll keep at it."

The captain and XO exchanged a few words before they nodded in agreement.

"All stop. Commence hovering. We'll stay here for a few hours and see if she turns back. Then, we make our way back to Swedish waters. I'm not provoking a fight out here. We'll stay beneath the layer for now. We can radio this in when we're sure about it."

The crew looked relieved. Lindberg looked at his watch. He hadn't noticed, but the sonar crew had been at their battle stations for almost five hours, and they were all drained. Back to Swedish waters meant one step closer to home. Just maybe they would make it back in one piece.

Chapter 17 – Politics

Muskö Naval Base, April 16ᵗʰ, 1245hrs

Something's not right. Löfgren looked at the report that showed the location of the Swedish submarines at the time of the sighting. Not that Bergman had published them in his article, but he seemed too sure of himself. Did Bergman know the location of Swedish submarines?

If he did, that would mean a severe security breach somewhere in the Navy, and it wouldn't be hard to find the source. Not many people would have access to this information. Himself, Melker Nilsson, Nylund, Rolf Eriksson, one or maybe two radio operators. It wouldn't be hard to plant information for some of these people and see if any of it showed up in the press tomorrow. He made a mental note to think it through later this evening. Right now, he needed to sort out his own situation.

Löfgren got out from behind his desk and looked around the open area outside his office. Most people weren't back from lunch yet, and this was probably as empty as it would get. He put a folder with some random papers under his arm as an alibi and walked around the corner with steps that showed as much determination as he could muster.

At the door, he swiped the card of Eivor Falk that she had left on her desk. The swipe would show in the log, but Eivor used the archive a lot, and nobody would think twice about her entry. Closing the door carefully behind him, he continued straight down the middle corridor, while scanning the codes at the end of the shelves. The box was where Mrs. Falk should have left it, and he quickly opened it up to remove the evidence he handed her a few days earlier.

A few minutes passed while he went through the thick folders with documents. Had someone been going through these? It should be a simple matter to pull out the papers. After a few more minutes, he was sweating and could feel his pulse reverberate through his temples. He couldn't find the papers. The documents that stated the submarine's alleged intelligence mission were nowhere to be found.

After fifteen minutes, he gave up. This just couldn't be. Someone must have been through the files and taken them out. The only person except for himself who knew about this was Nylund. He was the one who made this up in the first place. Had Nylund set a trap? No, Rolf Eriksson confirmed the submarine was missing, and half the fleet had been looking for it.

Back at his desk, Löfgren sat down, trying to clear his head. Nylund told the group that the submarine had intelligence orders when it disappeared. Most of them wouldn't have clearance to request the orders from the archive. Nylund was one of them—maybe Melker Nilsson. If one of them had looked at the orders, there would have been questions to answer already. Who else would have an interest in the order disappearing?

* * *

Stockholm, April 16th, 1600hrs

Jesper Bergman didn't hold back as he published his second first page about the situation with the Swedish submarine and the evasive behavior of the Swedish Navy and politicians. He had a confirmed sighting of a foreign submarine—likely a Soviet one. He had confirmed underwater explosions, and anyone in the Stockholm archipelago would have seen the Navy's presence and activity the last few days. He could add Navy helicopters roaring across rooftops. Whatever they were doing was obviously important enough to get the Navy flooded with complaints from the public.

He leaned on his desk and looked at the article he just finished. *Not bad given the time frame*, he figured. This would break government and Navy silence. No way that they could keep this up without saying anything. *U-137* on the rocks last year outside Karlskrona and now this. With a bit of imagination—or a lot—you might believe we were about to be attacked by the Soviet Union. Some military men would probably find that a good thing. They would finally get to use their invasion defense plans and likely force Sweden to join NATO. Officially this time.

* * *

Stockholm, April 16th, 1630hrs
Nylund looked at the sketch that Wikström had brought him again. He wasn't a submarine expert, but as far as he was concerned, it was more similar to a German submarine than a Soviet one. A German submarine in Swedish waters. He didn't doubt they had been there. They needed the ability to play hide and seek with the Soviets while fulfilling their primary purpose of intercepting Soviet shipping to the main European front. Things like that required practice.

The UK and the US would have been there as well, for that matter. He hadn't been personally involved, but he knew that there had been verbal agreements of joint exercises in conjunction with naval visits. A German submarine had appeared in Swedish waters before, but it voluntarily surfaced, and Sweden received a formal apology from the West German government.

West Germany, the UK, the US. All had one thing in common. They would never fire a torpedo at a Swedish vessel, would they? Covert visits to other countries were one thing. Even Swedish submarines were guilty of that. Firing at foreign vessels and potentially killing their sailors was another. Then the attack on the base security team. It seemed very unlikely to be anyone else than the Soviet Union.

He had decided to submit the original sketch to the Navy analysis group. They oversaw processing of all the tapes, sighting reports, and other materials surrounding contacts with potential foreign vessels in Swedish waters. A driver had picked up the original an hour beforehand. The analysis group would probably share his opinion. The most likely intruder was the Soviet Union. But that sketch looked an awful lot like a West German boat.

* * *

Rosenbad, Stockholm, April 16th, 1700hrs
"Have you read the paper?" The defense minister was worked up, which was unusual for him. "Now we've got the sighting, underwater detonations, helicopters flying low over people's houses. We've

got to say something about this. The socialists have caught on as well. They're telling the paper they're demanding to take part of the evidence in this matter before they are even willing to admit a foreign vessel was ever here."

"I know," Rosenfeldt said.

"They've even dubbed it another "budget submarine," as they think it's fiction. An excuse for us to increase Navy funding."

Rosenfeldt muttered to himself, "Not that we've never played that game, but this one isn't on us."

"The conclusion is that we have to say something. I know it's exactly what this little shit Bergman wants, but we will have to do it. Any news on the nationality?"

"Nothing binding. We have received evidence that the Soviet radio chatter in the Baltic region has intensified last few days, which normally follows on increased activity. Not conclusive, but indicative."

"And Nylund—is he going to keep his shit together and not serve up any more surprises?"

"I wouldn't worry about him. He had a slow start but has done a good job on a tactical level after that. I doubt he will interfere in anything political. After this, we can retire him with honors, remind him about his lifelong commitment to confidentiality, and send him home."

A phone rang, and a staff member picked it

up. A few seconds in, he held out the phone toward the supreme commander. "It's for you."

Rosenfeldt took the phone and listened carefully for half a minute. He hung up and turned toward the Defense minister. "The Navy analysis group says it's undeniably a Soviet submarine."

"That's it then. Call the press conference for tomorrow. Get Nylund there, in his best uniform."

* * *

Rosenbad, Stockholm, April 17th, 0800hrs
The defense minister would have center stage on this press conference, and he would be flanked by the supreme commander and the head of the Navy. The prime minister would be present to show how serious the matter was and to signal his support. The conference was a few days overdue in the eyes of most foreign press members. Some of them had arrived the same evening that Bergman's original article hit.

On the other hand, the group that now had worked their way into the quickly set up conference hall was 750 journalists strong. This was a reflection of the level of interest in this topic, including how it could influence the ongoing posturing between east and west.

Nordin made his way to the platform where the tables and microphones were set up. Rosenfeldt and Nylund were already standing in one corner of it, ramrod straight, looking serious and military. They had their briefing late the previous day, where Nylund got the word that this would be the official statement about what happened. He wasn't happy about claiming the Soviet submarine as a fact.

Despite not being very politically involved, he did understand the need to come across as competent and confident in this matter. Telling the world that Sweden had no idea what had happened wasn't an option, and neither was blaming a NATO nation for trespassing. The prospect of claiming it had been a Swedish submarine was forcefully rejected by everyone in uniform. That would signal severe incompetence to the world.

Before he handed the word to the defense minister, the prime minister took to the microphones and opened the press conference with a few remarks about how serious the Swedish government treated this situation. The defense minister followed up by running through the events of the last couple of days. He described the sighting that took place, which they could confirm was the sighting of a foreign submarine within Swedish territorial waters. The submarine disappeared, and the Navy scrambled from Muskö and Berga to ensure that the intruder left Swedish waters.

On the matter of the underwater detonations, it was confirmed that the Navy did conduct some antisubmarine warfare. The intent was to make it clear for the intruder he would need to leave Swedish waters. This was a warning, and not to be considered an attack on the foreign vessel.

There were rumors about a missing Swedish submarine—something that Nylund had to step in and explain.

"It is true that a Swedish submarine was late in reporting its position due to the sighting and the search that followed."

He explained standard Navy protocol required the Navy to change the status to submarine late and subsequently to submarine missing after a certain amount of time. Hence, it was correct that the naval force also worked to locate the Swedish submarine. However, this was done quickly. The submarine was safe and sound, though still at sea at this point.

Reporters questioned the first official statement about this being an exercise. Nylund explained that too many things had been in motion simultaneously and surrounded by too much uncertainty.

"The Navy is committed to full transparency on these matters, but we cannot make statements ongoing operations. This is both for the safety of the Navy personnel that take part in these operations, and to protect the public from misinformation."

The latter statement was met with evident

skepticism from the crowd, but the issues got dwarfed by the shadow of the bigger question. Who was operating in Swedish waters? The defense minister answered this question, his tone mild but direct.

"We have secured evidence supporting the conclusion that this is a Soviet submarine operating in Swedish territorial waters."

The crowd exploded with questions.

"Why?"

"Is this the only operation you've seen here?"

"For how long will they get away with this?"

Thomas Nordin raised his hand. He didn't manage to stop the barrage of questions but got enough of a decrease in intensity to continue on.

"The Swedish government will submit an official protest to the Soviet Union and demand cessation of this type of behavior. It should be clear to them that we will have our military forces at a higher alert level until they can give us some guarantees in this matter."

There it was. What the Swedish public had been waiting for. Public confirmation of what everyone already thought they knew—that Soviet submarines consistently breached Sweden's sovereignty. They were precisely the big bad Eastern bear they were made out to be. The Navy, as well as the military in general, would be looking at increased funds. NATO would be looking at increasing its presence in the Baltic region. A more formidable challenge for Soviet submarines entering the Skagerrak to interfere with the Polaris missile boats seemed likely. One statement set back Swedish-Soviet relations by decades.

* * *

Stockholm, April 17th, 1030hrs

When the message arrived, Rosenfeldt, Nordin, and Nylund were all sitting in a room adjacent to the press conference hall. Their Swedish submarine had radioed in this morning and reported contact with a certain submarine. It had been in international waters and on a course away from them. They stayed there for a few hours before looping back to Swedish waters in a wide arch to make sure the area was clear. No further contact. The other submarine had most likely left the area.

"Do they know the nationality?" Nordin asked.

The messenger looked at the form and read out loud as he scanned it. "Certain submarine, zig-zagging away from Swedish territory. The best guess of the sonar chief at this time is an Oberon, whatever that is."

Nylund and Rosenfeldt sat up straight when they heard the verdict. Nordin gave them a puzzled look.

"What's an Oberon?"

"An Oberon is a diesel-electric submarine. It's a British Royal Navy boat, minister."

The three men looked at each other. They had just proclaimed that the intrusion into Swedish waters was by a Soviet submarine.

"But this one was never on Swedish territory?" Nordin continued.

"It seems it was never seen or heard on Swedish territory. No. That doesn't mean it was never there." Nylund started to think aloud about what this could mean when Nordin held up a hand and stopped him.

"I'll speak to the Americans. If that was a British boat, the Americans will know about it."

He looked up at the messenger. "None of this leaves the room."

Chapter 18 – Doubts

Alexander Markovski served as the Ambassador in Stockholm since only two years, taking on his post while Sweden was under center, or even right-wing governance, depending on one's point of view. It wasn't an easy task, and it October 27th last year did not make it any easier. Early in the morning, he had received the news a Soviet submarine had run aground in Swedish territorial waters. The story of *U-137*, or *S-363* as was the Soviet designation of the vessel, reached news outlets worldwide. "Whiskey on the rocks" was an expression well known to the world now and would probably stay that way in naval circuits for decades.

He knew about it before the Swedes did, but there was nothing he could do to get a ship off a rock or control what the Swedish government did once they found it. The Soviet Navy lined up at the Swedish border, trying to scare Sweden into handing the submarine back. Apparently, the Swedish prime minister didn't let himself get

215

deterred but ordered his coastal defense forces to defend Swedish waters at all cost. He certainly wouldn't have made this decision if he believed Sweden stood alone against the tremendous Soviet war machine. Sweden wasn't a member of NATO, but he was sure agreements were in place. They weren't able to work out precisely what they were, but their existence was a certainty.

What was entertaining in the aftermath was the circus that erupted in the Swedish military. Not only was there a foreign submarine in their waters, but it also stood on a rock all night, diesels engaged, trying to get off it. And this while the Swedish Navy was sleeping. The Navy was embarrassed and received tremendous criticism, even from the Swedish Army and Airforce. The Navy blamed budget cuts, and the politicians questioned the competence of the Navy. The military and political landscape was one big, confusing mess.

It was a beautiful thing to watch for an outsider and the supposed enemy. The fact was that he never saw a real plan for the Soviet Union to attack Sweden during his entire career. That was especially true now. The might of the Red Army was faltering under financial pressure, and striking a country like Sweden wasn't discussed. The sole focus was on keeping defenses at an acceptable level and preventing the West from spotting the cracks in their armor. Deception became more important that force.

Markovski stood by the window of the Stockholm embassy, watching the views across to Långholmen, one of the many islands that constituted Stockholm. As his expected call came through, he walked over to his desk and picked up the phone.

He expected no pleasantries or small talk.

"You reported that the Swedish government made the official statement and named us as the intruder. Is that correct?"

"That is correct. They held a press conference where the defense minister stated this in no uncertain terms. The room was full of journalists, so you will see this in every paper and on every radio and TV station over the next hours and probably for days or weeks to come."

"And they didn't provide any evidence for it?"

"Nothing. They stated there was evidence strongly suggesting a Soviet vessel, but they didn't presented anything. The cat's out of the bag, as they say in the West. What do you need me to do now?"

"It's time to take to the offensive now. We will prepare an official press release, and I need you to set up a press conference of your own as soon as the first statement is out."

"And you want me to deny our involvement, I take it?"

"Of course. The Soviet Navy had nothing to do with this. We'll deny our involvement and find it outrageous to have the finger pointed at us this way. They're just using the unfortunate mistake of the *S-363* to further hammer a wedge in between Sweden and the Soviet Union. It's their damn right-wingers that are behind this. Then, we give them a couple of days to doubt us before suggesting an international investigation into this. We welcome international transparency, but it would mean Sweden will have to release all the evidence."

The voice on the other side laughed. "Come on, Sasha. If they still don't believe you, just tell them to sink the damn thing next time. That should throw them off the scent."

Markovski smiled to himself, picturing the regular meeting room in the office of the Swedish government, telling them to do a better job next time and simply "sink the damn thing." Even for a diplomat, it was sometimes hard to deny the elegance of straightforward delivery like this when talking to international colleagues. Some Swedish defense associates would need a non-diplomatic dictionary if he ever got to use this statement.

* * *

Stockholm, April 18ᵗʰ, 2100hrs

Nordin sat completely still, arms folded on the table in front of him, simply looking at his phone. It should ring at any moment now, as their scheduled call with the NATO representative had been set to begin a few minutes ago. He wasn't sure who he'd be speaking to but hopefully someone who knew something about NATO military movements in Europe. Someone from SACEUR's staff, not a politician.

His secretary walked by the open door and gave him a thumbs up. The call was on its way. Since she knew the importance of the call, she closed the door to his office without him asking.

Nordin's phone rang. If the NATO representative was already on the line, he didn't want to seem too eager, so he let it ring four times before he picked it up. "Yes. This is Thomas Nordin."

"Mr. Nordin. Tim Morris. I'm an aide to General Rogers. You probably know him as Supreme Allied Commander Europe. I was told you had some points of discussion on NATO operations?"

"Mr. Morris. My pleasure. Yes, I do have a few things I need to discuss. This specifically concerns NATO naval operations. I take it you are in a position to discuss or relay question on this matter?"

"Rest assured, Mr. Nordin. I have a direct connection to Northwood and CINCEASTLANT. Whether I can answer your questions now or will have to take them away depends on the nature of your discussion points. We have read your newspapers the last few days and seen your press conference. Your call is not a complete surprise."

"I imagine you are well-informed, Mr. Morris. The matter is both delicate and complicated. The nature of underwater operations, I take it."

"Yes, there is always complexity surrounding locations and actions of underwater vessels. That is the general idea of them, I believe."

"Yes, it is. And sometimes, it would be useful to have some clarity. If simply as a matter of ruling out certain options. Avoiding misunderstandings, if you see what I mean?"

"I completely agree with you, Mr. Nordin. It would be a shame if mere misunderstandings were to destroy ongoing and future relationships. I can reassure you that General Rogers feels the same way."

"Thank you, Mr. Morris. That is good to hear. So, you see, I'm trying to rule out any ongoing NATO activity that the Swedish Navy may be aware of but that the country's elected leaders are not."

"Well, we don't have full transparency to the information flow between Sweden's military and its government, but let me assure you that there are no secret schemes in place to create any inconsistency on information there."

The diplomatic language of this was a necessity, but after years of playing by these rules, Nordin was tired of it. The good thing about people who were used to operating this way was their susceptibility to being shocked into making a mistake.

"Well, Mr. Morris. That is reassuring, but I really just need to know whether you shot a torpedo at one of our submarines."

The line went silent. Mr. Morris apparently just got something to think about. He was a smart man, and he would understand what Nordin was trying to accomplish. The line was not silent for long.

"Mr. Nordin. Let me assure you that no NATO vessel has fired any torpedoes at Swedish vessels."

"That's good to know. But you have been snooping around in our waters lately, haven't you?"

"Mr. Nordin. I'm not sure what you want, but again, let me assure you that no NATO vessel would fire a torpedo at a Swedish vessel. Nor would we enter Swedish waters without authorization, for that matter."

"No, that would be breaching the sovereignty of Sweden, and of course, you would never do that."

"That is correct. That being said, it is in both NATO's and Sweden's interest to have a solid and alert Navy presence along the Swedish coastline. I am sure you would understand the need to regularly test such a capability."

"Of course. Practice makes perfect."

"Yes, it does."

"It would just be a shame that while practicing, something like an Oberon-class submarine would be detected in Swedish waters. That would really create a big problem in terms of the public view of all this. As you pointed out, we made some announcements concerning this matter already."

"I hear you perfectly, Mr. Nordin. No such event will take place. You can trust me on that. We have nothing to gain from you having to change your already public statements."

"Thank you, Mr. Morris. That's a relief. That was all I needed to confirm. No misunderstanding. One could even say, common goals."

"Absolutely. Thank you for your call, Mr. Nordin."

* * *

Stockholm, April 19th, 0800hrs

Nylund poured himself a cup of coffee and looked at the water through his kitchen window. It was the first day in a week he had been able to get some proper sleep. The press conference hadn't solved anything, but it had relieved some of the pressure accumulated during the last few days. The Swedish public finally got their theories of evil Russians confirmed. Nylund shrugged for himself. Ten minutes after the press conference, most of the Swedish people would have gone back to normal. A normal that didn't include thinking about their ability to defend the territorial waters of their country.

The international press was telling their stories, but once they realized this was now a diplomatic operation, not a military one, the news were slow and less groundbreaking. For the Navy, this didn't mean less work, but it meant somewhat less urgency. Sitting at his kitchen table, Nylund walked through a list of priorities he had to work on. Some of them were official, some of a more personal nature.

The defense minister expected all the evidence to be collected and appropriately documented. This was important but not a big task. There was no objective evidence at all that this was a Soviet submarine. With the background of *U-137* the previous year and the general perception that

223

the enemy always was red, it had been the only option. There was no lack of indications that this was a Soviet submarine. There was just nothing solid.

The Oberon trail was worrying. If the sonar chief on the Swedish submarine was right, and this was indeed a UK submarine. What would that mean? They never caught it in Swedish waters, and it never acted aggressively. On the contrary, it maneuvered further away from the Swedish coast. Maybe because it heard the Swedish submarine approaching, or perhaps because it was done with whatever it was there to do. Regardless of how you twisted the information, there was no evidence of any NATO wrongdoing. There was, on the other hand, no evidence of any Soviet wrongdoing either.

The Swedish head of the Army didn't take the news well. He was now convinced that this had been a Navy stunt to increase their share of the military budget. He was worried it would leave less for the Army to maintain its capacity to repel a significant land-based attack.

* * *

Stockholm, April 19th, 0900hrs
Nordin was sitting with his face in his hands. He let out a long sigh, then leaned back, leaving his palms on the table.

"Did they say that?"

One of his helpers looked about as tired as Nordin himself. "Yes, the official response is that no Soviet submarine has been operating in Swedish waters. They're making a big deal about the misfortune of *U-137* and us just taking the easy way out, turning them into a villain in the international press. They're not very pleased. On the other hand, if it was them, they would still react like this. So, no surprise there."

"Yes, of course. They wouldn't just agree to it and apologize. So, what did Mr. Markovski say when you spoke to him?"

"Off the record, he was quite aggressive about it. After telling us that the Soviet Union would welcome an international investigation on the matter, where we all put our cards on the table for a commission, he told us our Navy should have done a better job and sunk the thing."

"There's a thought." Nordin nodded in agreement. If the Navy had caught the intruder, this would all have been cleared up by now.

"On the matter of the international investigation, I think he's bluffing. There's no way they would actually go through with that and let international inspectors check all their communications and visit their naval bases. What do you think?" Nordin nodded toward his aide.

"I think that they will put that in more official

terms before it becomes a real threat. What about our records?"

"What about them?"

"Can we prove it was a Soviet submarine?"

"Well, maybe not completely at the moment, but soon enough, we will have an archive that removes any doubt. It's being worked on."

* * *

Muskö Naval Base, April 19th, 1000hrs

Löfgren was in an excellent mood. He received a call from the Supreme Commander himself this morning. New orders directly from the man. Sensitive enough Rosenfeldt told him no written order would follow. Löfgren would need to make sure this happened, and if he ran into any roadblocks, the Supreme Commander would make himself available to remove them. *In one way, you could see it as him working for me*, Löfgren thought. Nylund wouldn't be allowed to interfere, and Löfgren would have the authority to ignore any wishes from the head of the Navy. He would just have to keep the Supreme Commander in the loop so they could keep that man under control.

Perfect timing, Löfgren thought. Special assignment. This gave him the excuse he needed to run free in the archives. He needed to find the orders he planted.

Closing his eyes, Löfgren went through what he needed to do. He didn't want to write it down but still required a checklist to make sure all the evidence in the archives lined up with what was communicated by the defense minister. The man said it was a Soviet submarine, so a Soviet submarine it would be.

The reports on the transponder and the shooting with the three unknowns would have to be located and redacted—or removed. That could be done in the next day or so, though. The main issue now was to organize what to do with the crew of the Swedish submarine. He would have to find their scheduled return time. They must be due back soon.

Their reports couldn't identify the intruder, but they would have to be thoroughly debriefed. Then what do we do with them? We just let them out into the world where they can tell whatever drunken stories they want? There is no other option, but maybe we could keep them for a little while until we get the situation under control. For sure, they could keep them locked away somewhere in the name of confidentiality, psych evaluation, and debriefing . . . or whatever other reason they could come up with.

* * *

Stockholm, April 19th, 1000hrs

This was the second time Wikström unexpectedly showed up at Nylund's house. She apparently didn't trust telephones anymore and felt most comfortable being unpredictable in her movements. This time, she knocked at the front door, however, like a normal person.

"Any coffee around? We need to talk about a few things."

"Indeed, we do, Frida. One of them might be you showing up here unannounced again."

"Ah, get over it, will you."

Nylund smiled at her directness. She never changed in the slightest. She had been this way since the day he met her, and it was part of the reason why he liked her. Straightforward, no-nonsense, and with a single focus on getting the job done, whatever the job might be. *No wonder she was a good police investigator*, he thought. They must have been sad when she left.

The truth was very different. Wikström's superiors had all sighed in relief as she left. Brilliant and goal-oriented, she also had a knack for breaking the rules and a reputation for being brash with colleagues who were less engaged or skilled at their job. A lot of problems in the department were solved the day she resigned.

"I can't make this work," she said.

"Make what work?"

"The timeline and the things that have happened lately. The switch in the operational area . . . Bergman's reports. They were too timely and convenient for my liking. Who got him onto the story in the first place? How could he be so sure it was a foreign submarine? Was he that sure because he knew the positions of the Swedish Navy submarines?"

She shook her head angrily and then buried her face in her hands as Nylund put a cup of coffee in front of her. She sat up and continued, paying no attention to her coffee cup.

"Segerfors, the tapes, the shooting. However I twist and turn all this, it all comes down to one thing. There must be a leak somewhere in the Navy."

"I know."

"And you know the darndest thing? For a while, I thought it was you."

Nylund looked at her with surprise on his face. Unlike last time, this was fake surprise. Of course, he understood how she would think that. He was the only person with access to anything in the Navy and who also knew about her investigation and her trip to Segerfors.

"So, how did you exclude me from your little conspiracy theory then?"

"You had true surprise on your face last time when I told you about Segerfors. And it wasn't as if

229

you needed me to find him for you. You already had his name and address. If you wanted him out of the way, it would just be annoying to have me around."

"Unless I used it as an alibi," Nylund said with a smug voice

"Then you would have used a more official resource. They would make for a much more reliable alibi than some tired ex-cop."

"Right you are. So who is it?"

"Well, given the fact that no one besides you would be aware of it all, it seems that there's more than one, doesn't it? Navy information must come out of the Navy. Harder to tell where this info about Segerfors came from. Maybe someone who followed you?"

"Me, being followed? I'm not so sure about that."

"I'm not sure of anything. That's why we need to take this investigation to the next level."

"Look, I paid you to look through all this with the witnesses and see if it was trustworthy information. I won't, and can't, pay you to take on the Navy at this level."

"Are you mad? This isn't investigating whether the neighbor is having an affair or not. You're the one who told me about the shooting, the missing tapes, and the fact that one of your submarines was actually fired at. That is an act of war, Klasse. Come on!"

"You're right, I know, but I can't."

"Don't patronize me like that. I know what I'm getting myself into here, and I know there may not be money on the table, but we need to look into this."

Nylund sipped his coffee and looked out through the window. "I know you're right. You always are. So, how do we set this up?"

Wikström was worked up now and had already found a pen and paper. Nylund noticed she had forgotten all about her coffee, but he figured she didn't need it. More likely, she would need something to slow her down throughout this process. Wikström started to draw a long horizontal line on the paper, and she talked as she marked it up to turn it into a timeline.

"We'll need a place to keep our own archive. Can you get copies of the reports as they come in? The tapes are already gone, and I just have a hunch more things might go missing. There's a self-storage facility not too far from here. I have some space there from before we can use."

"I can probably get hold of copies of certain things," he said. "We're not supposed to do that obviously, but let's say there are certain ways around it. Mrs. Falk, one of the secretaries there, knows me well and she's quite flexible."

"Hmm, we could use her help then, but she needs to be covered in all this as well."

"Covered?"

"We need to figure out who's telling what to whom. The easiest way is to plant a few different pieces of information with different people and then see what information turns up where. We need copies, but then we can gamble with some of the reports to see if they move or disappear."

Nylund's heartbeat increased as the grave nature of what they were discussing started to sink in.

Chapter 19 – Budget Submarines

Stockholm, April 19th, 1100hrs

Though Nylund was tired, he felt a rush of almost childish excitement after they conceived their plan. *Like when I was ten, and we played detectives in the backyard,* he thought. He had to remind himself the stakes were higher this time. Life and death even.

He picked up the phone to dial Löfgren. Old differences apart, military intelligence must have thought the same thing about Bergman claiming to know the positions of the Swedish submarines. Löfgren picked up on the second signal and sounded like he had seen better days. "Ola, this is Klas."

"Klas, yes, what can I do for you?" Löfgren's response was automatic and without engagement, which Nylund noticed on the other side of the line.

"I know, I know. We have our differences. Whatever you think of me, we are tied together around this sighting and the other events, and we need to sort this out."

"Yes, your idea of planting evidence hasn't

panned out so well."

"What evidence?"

"When our submarine went missing, you told them all we could hold off reporting it since the submarine was on an intelligence operation—something about maneuvering in mined waters."

Nylund had to stop and think for a second. That had completely slipped his mind. They were a few minutes from declaring submarine missing, and he needed more time to figure things out. Löfgren was right. He did tell Eriksson and the salvage crews about this.

"Yes, you're right. That was hasty, but what evidence are you talking about?"

"I told you there was no intelligence mission, hence no orders. You told me to fabricate some. And I did."

"You filed evidence of this in the order archive?"

"Yes."

"Well, get it out of there then."

"Trust me, I have tried. It's missing."

"The evidence you put in there is missing? Who would have known about those orders?"

"Nobody, as far as I'm concerned. I've been looking around for it, but I can't find it anywhere."

"Okay, but we have more important things to do."

"More important than being caught

fabricating evidence? If this somehow comes out, we're both finished. I'll make sure of that. I'm just the poor commander who was coerced to do it by the Navy Chief."

Now he recognized Löfgren. Worried about his own skin above all else. Nylund would take the blame for the intelligence foul-up. That wasn't a problem. They had been under enormous pressure and made a bad call. Getting threatened by some political game-playing bastard was something different, though there was no time for this argument now.

"I'm sure you will get your star eventually, but we have other things to worry about."

"You mean Bergman's interview and claim that he knew the locations of the Swedish submarines?"

"Yes, exactly. Who knows whether he's lying or not, but if we assume he's not, we have a big problem. Someone in the Navy is leaking information."

"And you have an idea of who this is and how to find out?"

"I have someone who can potentially help us find out what Bergman knows and how he got to that information. That may be everything we do for now. In the meantime, you do your best to find that evidence."

Nylund hung up the phone. If there was

something in it for Löfgren, he would probably play ball. A star on his commander's uniform might be enough for him to stay in check and cooperate.

On the other side of the line, Löfgren was having similar thoughts about Nylund. Could he trust the old man?

* * *

Stockholm, April 19th, 1100hrs
Nordin was tired. He just hung up the phone with the head of the Swedish Army, who had urgently needed to speak to him. It had all started this morning when he had no choice but to speak to reporters about the submarine issue. His political adversaries suddenly turned aggressive and claimed there was no foreign submarine at all. This was all a hoax where the evil right-wingers of the government had run a Swedish submarine through Danziger Gatt to create this commotion. All to distract the Swedish public from the failed election promises, raise more money for the Navy, and put a wedge between Sweden and the Soviet Union. They had primarily driven hard on the budget question and repeatedly referred to it as a sighting of a 'budget submarine.'

He had to smile at his first reaction. *Why didn't I think of that?* He had to give the damn socialists a point on the scoreboard for this one. Not bad. Not bad at all. They obviously saw the uniting effect an external enemy had on the country and were worried this could influence the election negatively for them.

They were right. There had been an uptick in the polls for Nordin and his party following all of this, and there was no reason to believe it would stop as Sweden armed itself for this future conflict. More money for the Navy was already in the works and would be expanded further in the future if they could stay in power.

He wished was true that this was his idea. Then, he could have been softer in pointing out the nationality of the submarine, and these political points would be the result of his strategic genius. Unfortunately, this was now a real foreign submarine, and the uptick in political points, though encouraging, was offset by the fact they didn't know who this was and what to do about it. *Just roll with the punches, I guess. Make it stay a Soviet submarine, play the game, and roll with the punches.*

He spent an hour answering questions about this, ensuring everyone there was no right-wing plot in place, misusing the Swedish armed forces to create some sort of fake war. He felt comfortable with the press, but as soon as he was done and retreated into his office again, the head of the Army caught him on this urgent matter. Thinking it was related to the high command briefings, he took the call, only to get an earful of complaints.

Now the Navy would get too large of a share of the defense budget. Nylund would get more ships, submarines, and helicopters to hunt foreign submarines with. In the meantime, his Army, the branch of the military that would really repel the Soviet invasion, was going to suffer.

Nordin ran the same speech for the head of the Army as for the press. This wasn't a government scheme but an actual sighting of a foreign submarine. The head of the Army was in the room when they talked about it. A Swedish submarine got shot at, for Christ's sake. The Army chief believed him, as far as he could tell, but it didn't stop him from immediately continuing with new theories.

Probably Nylund and the Navy made this up to steal funds from the Army without the government's knowledge. Yes, it must be the Navy that was behind all this. That would explain it all. And what about this missing submarine that suddenly turned up unharmed? Was it ever really missing?

At this point, Nordin hung up on him. For crying out loud, he would have to give Rosenfeldt a call and tell him to get his underlings under control. These people were supposed to signify the discipline of society. *Feels more like a chicken farm.*

Stockholm, April 19th, 1300hrs

Nylund was back in his office, and Eivor Falk passed by with a folder in her hand.

"A report from the Navy surgeon," she said, "from the incident the other night."

Nylund took the folder and started to look through it. It was a surprisingly concise document, given that three people were killed. *On the other hand, I take it the cause of death should be clear enough*, Nylund thought.

He started reading the conclusion. All three men had been hit by several bullets, and their state was as one could expect after that. Only one of them had enough pieces of his jaw left to make a dental print and analysis possible. Teeth were surprisingly valuable in determining where people were from and how they lived.

He skimmed over the pictures but quickly looked away. *Dear God. That's what 7.62mm of lead flying at 800 meters per second will do to people.* Turning the page, he got to the comments. The men didn't look to be Eastern, but looks could be deceiving.

The dental work on the body with an intact jaw had several fillings in his teeth. The conclusion said they would not commonly be seen in the East. The materials used for the dental work were more likely to originate in Western Europe or the United States. With some further investigation, the coroner figured he would be able to narrow it down to country.

He threw the folder on his desk. That didn't help much, did it? Some man related to the tapes' disappearance had dental work that wasn't likely to be Eastern. The dental imprints, alongside other information, had been sent off to Swedish authorities and some international ones. Perhaps there was a match in some register somewhere that could help them find something out about the nationality and identity of these men.

On second thought, he would need a copy of this to hand to Wikström.

* * *

Muskö Naval Base, April 19th, 1305hrs
Eivor Falk returned from lunch and sat down, ready to continue the day. One would think the military had a very disciplined process around documents and administration, but that was never the case. Naval officers considered themselves to be above administrative tasks. They had wars to run or something. Hence, they would routinely drop the ball on documentation, probably equally split between "by accident" and "on purpose."

Falk was used to it and now didn't think too

hard about the chaos, simply doing the best she could during her workday. Several piles of paperwork were on her desk, primarily active investigations or operations, with some added backlog on top.

It was probably about time to deal with the big pile on her right, she figured, looking at the calendar on her desk. It was the 19th of April now. Eight days had passed since the sighting—four since the Swedish submarine surfaced and the tapes were stolen.

She pulled at a paper that was sticking out of the pile and looked at it. Requisition form for equipment. She had kept the document handy in case she needed it. With the pressure building around this, it might be time to launch a bit of a diversion. In front of her, she had a submitted order fulfilled from the primary storage and marina. One small watercraft and four sets of Swedish Navy uniforms. Flipping through some of the other paperwork, she read the report that was submitted by the submarine again.

Four men in a small Navy craft had come up alongside the submarine and boarded it, acquired the tapes from its sonar system, and disappeared as fast as they turned up. This was the prelude to the shooting that had then taken place in the woods around Oxnö.

She looked back at the requisition form

again. Small craft, four sets of uniforms. The order had been fulfilled by one of the regular staff from the storage and maintenance crew. She recognized his signature. The signature of the person who had picked it all up was just a scribble. Good. That would do.

Looking further down the form, she confirmed it was both submitted and approved by the same person. That was against protocol, but the storage crew often didn't read the forms that thoroughly. Unlike the unreadable signature of the person who picked it up, she had made sure the approval signature was clear.

* * *

Muskö Naval Base, April 19ᵗʰ, 1400hrs
Nylund found a note on his desk when he came back. It was from Mrs. Falk, and it asked for him to get ahold of her urgently. Maybe it had to do with the missing evidence Löfgren planted. Mrs. Falk was one of the more common visitors to the archives, and if anyone was going to stumble across this, it would be her.

He looked outside for her, but she wasn't at her desk. He was tempted to ignore it and wait for her to come back, but in the last decade she had never left an urgent message like this. He decided to find her and picked up the phone to call the archive. Given what he had just been thinking about, it was a likely possibility. He was right.

"Archives, Falk."

"Eivor, it's Klas. I just saw your note. What's happening that's so urgent?"

Falk explained the matter of the requisition form to Nylund. The materials requested and the timing coincided well with the tapes being taken from the submarine. She wasn't sure it was anything, but it seemed a bit too close to be a coincidence. She continued to explain how she didn't recognize the name of the person who picked up the materials and how the submitter and approver were the same person. Before she finished, Nylund interrupted her.

"Who? Who submitted and approved the form?" he shouted.

"It's signed by Commander Löfgren."

Chapter 20 – Jenny

Muskö Naval Base, April 19th, 1500hrs

Nylund sat at his desk, trying to make sense of what he just learned. Löfgren signed the requisition for the craft and the uniforms used when the tapes were stolen. If he had something to do with this, for sure, he wouldn't have used his real name. Löfgren might be many things, but stupid wasn't one of them.

He was the one who had briefed them on the sighting in the first place, so he wanted it to be known. Something might have gone wrong, of course. The Swedish submarine received orders to move to a different area and then back again. Maybe it was a failed attempt to move the Swedish submarine out of the way. A failed attempt by whom? Once there was an exchange of torpedoes and close contact, we got the bastard on tape. Because of that, he needed the tapes to go away to deny us the chance to identify the intruder.

Nylund leaned back in his chair. That was speculation only of course. He'd known Löfgren for many years. If it clearly had been a Soviet boat,

Löfgren would have paraded that tape around the entire high command and probably the press as well. He would have made sure he got the credit for a second confirmed Soviet boat in Swedish waters. On the other hand, if it was someone else, would Löfgren have any reasons to avoid this being clarified?

Either way, unfortunately, Nylund already spoke to Löfgren about a possible leak—and about finding it. It would be ironic if Löfgren turned out to be the leak. He would have to speak to Wikström and make sure this was included in their investigation. True or not, given the materials they had, it looked like Löfgren was up to something. They would need to understand what.

* * *

Baltic sea, April 19ᵗʰ, 2300hrs
Nothing had happened since the contact three days earlier. Lindberg was tracking merchant traffic and not much else. They followed their regular routes without the slightest deviation. During the few days, the most excitement they had was to raise the periscope no more than fifty meters in front of a sailing boat they couldn't heard on sonar.

The captain was fast to lower it again, and they got away with the periscope in one piece. The family in the sailing boat narrowly escaped what

245

would have been the scare of a lifetime.

Together with Sandberg, he continued to listen to the recording of the encounter with the foreign submarines when they had free time. Sandberg guessed the most recent contact was an Oberon. That never became official, but they suspected it was noted in the report to the Navy headquarters. They still had no idea about the type from the first encounter and determining the nationality of the torpedo would be damn near impossible without a direct comparison from the sound library in the training studio.

The regular ship library didn't contain torpedoes. Generally, it was supposed to be clear who you were at war with, and all they needed to know about torpedoes was that they were dangerous. Stay away. That's what the high-pitch noise told them.

The tension was taking a toll on the entire crew. The relief of surviving the encounter was replaced with silent despair as they were ordered to take up their current patrol area instead of running straight for home. Most of the crew was sleeping poorly, eating badly with a non-surprising state of exhaustion and irritability accompanying it.

Several heated discussions broke out over minor things that would normally go unnoticed, and it didn't get any better when the cook announced they were out of coffee. They weren't scheduled for a tour this long, and in contrast to food, where he could stretch the supply, coffee was in high demand and painfully finite. One of the engineers had woken up one morning and exploded as the news was delivered to him along with a cup of herbal tea.

The signal officer entered the mess hall. It was packed with crew members who would typically be asleep but could find no peace of mind. Instead, they were watching a movie and kept dreaming of drinking a cup of coffee along with it. Something stronger wouldn't have hurt either. There was unfortunately a no-alcohol policy on Swedish naval vessels.

"Orders came through," the signal officer proclaimed shortly. "We're slowly going to make our way back to Berga."

The entire mess hall drew a sigh of relief in unison. Finally, they would be going back to land, where they would be safe from whoever was shooting at them and hopefully be able to get a good night's rest. Lindberg wasn't sure it would be enough for him. He and Sandberg had been listening to the tape so intensely that he couldn't hear anything but the sound of the high-pitched torpedo both while awake and asleep now. He didn't have any visual nightmares about it, but he could hear the propeller's pitch, screeching as it closed in on them.

Once he got ashore, at least he could call Jenny. He met her at a party in Wikingsson's apartment in Stockholm. Lindberg had noticed her immediately when he entered the apartment as she passed right in front of him on her way upstairs. They spoke later in the evening, but it wasn't exactly love at first sight for any of them. Instead, they kept meeting now and then through Wikingsson and other common friends. For months this was ongoing without anything romantic happening. Then, one day when they were all at a small local lake for an early spring barbecue, it was like they both suddenly snapped out of it, and it all happened at once. Maybe it was the cold evening and the warm fire that set the scene for it. He made a clumsy move to make it look like he ended up next to her by accident. She smiled and simply took his hand. No words needed.

He reported back to Berga and first submarine division the following Monday morning and embarked on the "regular" patrol that would now forever be etched in his mind. The screeching noise of the torpedo. Lindberg wasn't sure he would ever sleep well again.

Chapter 21 – Pincer

Stockholm, April 20th, 0900hrs

A message was on his desk again. Nylund preferred to get his briefings verbally if possible, so he directly called the head of engineering. The head of engineering was usually in charge of planning significant overhauls on the ships, but he was called in to deal specifically with the beacon that the minesweeper had retrieved. Nylund exchanged the usual pleasantries with the man but was quick to get to the point.

"I saw the message. You were done with the beacon, or whatever it is. What do you have for me?"

"It's been an interesting task for sure," the engineer replied. "As was noted in the report from the minesweeper, the device does look like some sort of transponder or beacon. From the looks of it, the diver's comment that it looks Eastern is correct. Welding and outer materials would definitely suggest that this is right. The frequency that it transmits is at a frequency we have seen in use before by the Soviets. So far, it looks like a Warsaw pact device."

"So far? Then what?"

"Then, we took it apart. The inside is considerably different from the outside. Sleek, well made, and most of the electrical components are not Russian. They are more likely to be Western."

"Yes, but for sure they could find and use Western components to build it, as a diversion, I mean."

"Yes, they could. Not all of these things are that easy to come by, though. Some of them might even be a struggle for us to get hold of. In my opinion, it would be considerably easier for us to fake the Eastern-looking outside than for them to find and build the Western-looking inside. That is just speculation, of course."

"You think it's a Western device?"

"I can't tell. I am just saying that it would be easier than the other way around. Anything is possible."

"Where is the device now?"

"Well, we have filed the full report with the main archive, and the device was picked up by a storage crew an hour ago."

"Find it."

"Find what?"

"Find the device again. Find the device and sit your ass down on the box. Don't you dare leave that thing out of sight until I say so. And send me a copy of the report."

"But . . ."

Nylund had already hung up the phone. The device could be Western. It could have been put there by a Western submarine. Either way, since it was clear the sketch was modified before reaching them, the archive or storage facility didn't seem the best place for it. He can sit on the box until we get a hold of the report and can save a copy. Nylund needed to talk to Wikström. She would need to help with this.

* * *

Stockholm, April 20th, 1100hrs

Nylund picked up the phone. The caller on the other end was the Navy coroner.

"There was a hit on the man's dental records. We got a name."

"Tell me."

"Michael Wozniak, born 1955."

"So Polish, not Russian," Nylund confirmed.

"Of Polish descent, yes, but there's more information to this story. According to the record, Mr. Wozniak has two Polish parents, but he was born and raised in the UK. We got the record from the British Army. Enlisted straight out of school in 1972, Airborne infantry, 3rd Battalion of the 16 Air Assault Brigade. Based out of a place called

Colchester. I have no idea where the hell that is. My colleague here thinks it's up the East Coast somewhere."

"Yes, yes, Colchester. What else do we have on him?"

"An excellent soldier apparently. Solid service record; promoted to sergeant in a hurry, it looks like. Surprisingly left the service in 1979. Seems he disappeared off the radar at that point."

A shiver went down Nylund's spine. "Deniable operator? It's not a UK operator who assaulted our men, is it?"

"Well, it certainly fits the profile, but I doubt the Brits would have handed us his file if he was operating on their behalf. Then, he wouldn't be deniable anymore, would he?" The man on the other end chuckled at his own joke, but he continued in a more serious tone as he got no response from Nylund. "I would think soldier of fortune if anything. He has an old wound on his left calf that looks like it could be from a bullet. His service record mentions no deployment to a war zone where that could have happened. No mention of training accidents either."

The man definitely wasn't Soviet regular then. The British Army history would be a bit of a problem. He had to agree with the coroner they wouldn't have received the file if Mr. Wozniak was acting on behalf of the UK. More likely, he was working for the highest bidder. That could be anyone.

"It does seem farfetched that someone with that much military training would engage armed soldiers with a handgun. He must have known the chance of coming out on top in that firefight would be slim to none," Nylund speculated.

"If up against equal opposition, yes, but they would also know our active soldiers mostly consist of nineteen-year-old enlisted men with no combat experience. If you take a shot at them, they may freeze and fail to engage at all. One hell of a gamble, however. And it clearly didn't work this time around." The coroner refrained from laughing at his own observation this time.

"You're right. Anyway, I need to go. Do you have anything else for me?"

"No, that is about it. There are some details in the file, but I doubt they matter. I'll send it over. Just one thing."

"Yes."

"The British Army has been most accommodating, but they do want to know why we requested the file of one of theirs."

"I don't know. You'll have to make something up. Under no circumstances will they be informed of what he was actually doing here or the nature of how he expired."

"Okay, leave that with me. Was there

anything else you needed?"

"Yes, there is. I need you to send me a copy of this report by courier immediately. Then I need you to file the main one in the archive under section HC58d."

The man on the other side hesitated, "That is not the designated section for this."

"I know, but you're to file this thing at HC58d, and you're not to tell anyone about it. I want to test the alertness of some of the staff in the archive. We'll move it later. Is that clear?"

"HC58d, consider it done."

* * *

Rosenbad, April 20th, 1130hrs

"I don't want to hear it. We have communicated that this is a Soviet submarine, and it will stay a damned Soviet submarine." Nordin was clearly unhappy about the latest pieces of information coming in.

"What do you want us to do, tell the world we made a mistake and that our sovereignty was breached by our NATO allies?"

"I understand. I'm just saying that more and more material is piling up in the archive suggesting this may not be a Soviet operation. At least one of the men shot while searching for the tapes is a UK citizen, and the components of the transponder that we fished out of the water seem to be of Western origin. This doesn't prove it's not a Soviet boat, but it will raise doubt about our quick and concrete conclusion that it is. That's all." The supreme commander shrugged his shoulders to stress that he was simply presenting facts to the defense minister.

Nordin stopped to think for a second. "What we need is an archive that doesn't suggest this is something else than a Soviet submarine."

"Clean it up?" Rosenfeldt's eyebrows went up.

"Oh, come on. It wouldn't be the first time you people lost or accidentally misplaced things to promote the outcome you want. Nylund needs to sort his Navy out and make sure that whatever we have in the archive makes a strong case to suggest this is a Soviet submarine. End of story."

Rosenfeldt stood up and straightened his uniform, then quickly nodded before turning to exit the room, pleased that he had already spoken to Löfgren and initiated this very clean-up.

* * *

Berga Naval Base, April 20th, 1400hrs

Finally, it was time. The submarine was still submerged but ran at periscope depth with the radar mast up above the surface. Lindberg could clearly see the outline of Utö and Ornö, the two large islands that lay as the outer rim of Hårsfjärden outside Berga Naval Base. The captain raised the periscope and had a look at the entry to Hårsfjärden. The weather was beautiful, though a sense of freezing April temperatures was visible even through the periscope lens.

The captain ordered a report of all sonar contact from Wikingsson. As Wikingsson called out the bearings, the captain visually confirmed them through the periscope. There was nothing close by they needed to worry about.

Lindberg left the command center and started to prepare the survival suits. The order hadn't been given yet but would be soon enough. All deck crew would wear the survival suits this time of year as they prepped for tying the vessel down at the pier. In April, water temperatures in Stockholm would typically be around four to five degrees Celsius, and submarines were very clumsy to operate on the surface and in narrow waters. If one of them would fall into the sea, it could take ten minutes for the submarine to turn around and be in a position to pick them up again. Ten minutes in four-degree water was enough to be a severe problem.

Eager to get ashore, Lindberg and the rest of the deck crew were almost dressed up and ready as they heard the captain give the order to blow the ballast tanks. A valve at the bottom of the tank would open, and the high-pressure air was flowing in to push the water out. As the tank filled with air instead of water, the submarine slowly floated toward the surface.

To confirm what they already knew, the orders came over the speaker system.

"Surface, Surface, deck crews stand by at main hatch."

They could all feel the slight movement from the waves affecting the submarine as it rose to the surface. With a round hull and no keel, the submarine would roll violently on the surface in rough seas. Today was a good day and it was barely noticeable.

The engineer confirmed. "Ballast is blown. Valves are closed. We are surfaced, Captain."

"Understood. Open the hatch. Man the bridge. Deck crews, prepare for docking, port side."

They had been through it many times but never had the sound of the hatch opening been sweeter. A small click and a short lived rush of air as the pressure between inside and outside equalized. Like opening a can of soda. A few seconds later, they could feel the first gust of cold April air hit them in the face. Every man closed his eyes to take in a deep breath through the nose. Fresh air was normal to most people. For the crew of a submarine, it was a sign of home.

The navigations officer, set to man the bridge, locked the hatch in place and started his climb up the conning tower. Lindberg and the deck crews climbed into the tower and used a door on the side to exit onto the submarine's deck. The weather was surprisingly cold for the time of year but not cold enough for ice to form on the hull.

The crew opened the deck hatches holding the lines and laid them out in wide S-shapes across the deck. That way, they wouldn't get tangled as the land crews started to pull them ashore. The deck crews then took station on the front of the submarine from where they would throw the docking lines.

Lindberg was busy working the rear lines, feeding line or holding it in place as the submarine slowly moved into the correct position at the pier. Once he had tied his line down and confirmed the order that docking was complete, he looked around the dock for the first time. The regular four-man land crew that would run land operations for the submarines was there. Further up the pier, there were dozens of people waiting, next to an entire fleet of minivans.

"Everybody off the boat," someone on the pier shouted.

"Get off and gather in a line right here," he pointed at the pier next to a man with a clipboard. Slowly, the crew started to leave the ship and line up where directed. The man with the clipboard checked them off a list and directed them to one of the vehicles at the base of the pier. "Rank, name, and ID number."

"Sonar Petty Officer Lindberg, Carl, 630327-2953."

"Good, take your seat in vehicle two."

"And the sub?"

"Another crew will take care of the boat and your gear. Just move to the second vehicle, please. Nothing to worry about. We just need to get the debriefing sessions started as soon as possible."

Debriefing made sense, Lindberg figured. As far as he was aware, they were the first Swedish submarine crew to ever fire a live torpedo at an actual contact. Not to mention being shot at. No wonder the top brass of the Navy was interested in knowing what had happened and how both men and materials were holding up.

Lindberg walked up to the second vehicle in the column. As soon as it was full, the driver entered and quickly drove through the gates of the first submarine division at Berga Naval Base. He made a left and passed Amiralsholmen, hosting a whole fleet of small sailing boats. The driver made a right turn up the main road, passed the big exercise field in front of the swimming hall, and continued through the main gate, driving off in the direction of Västerhaninge.

Though vague, Lindberg's feeling of uneasiness was building with every turn.

Chapter 22 – Cleanup

Rosenfeldt sat at his desk looking through the latest financial reports. He sometimes missed the simplicity of platoon and company command from his earlier days. He had spent a lot of his time at P10 Armored Regiment, where the focus was on operational and logistical matters. How to maneuver, how to train your troops. Now he spent most of his time reading reports and meddling in political matters that he neither understood nor found interesting.

He had risen fast through the ranks. A natural talent for soldiering and a will to do whatever it took to get ahead was accompanied by a well-developed sense of how hard he could push it before his colleagues would dislike him. He had good friends among his soldiers, but the ones that knew him well tended to distance themselves, as they recognized his prowess to throw them under the bus if it would benefit his career. At the same time, they wanted to stay close because they knew he would succeed, and success rubbed off on the people surrounding him.

A knock on his doorframe brought him out of thought. Nylund stood there in his battle dress. He had been wearing that thing ever since this all started, apart from at the press conference. The admiral looked like an old war dog, but Rosenfeldt figured that this was the purpose.

"Come in, Klasse. Have a seat."

Nylund entered the room with more than a little apprehension. Being called like this to the supreme commander's office outside of the regular briefings wasn't very common, and it rarely meant good news. This had been a few rough days, and Nylund understood he hadn't acted perfectly, especially not at the start of this. He'd been numbed by sighting after sighting that turned out to be nothing. He couldn't remember the lady's name on Utö, but she must have seen four periscopes last year alone. A submarine, fully visible on the surface was different. He should have been faster to act and not written it off. Nylund took a breath to start talking, but Rosenfeldt beat him to it.

"How are you, Klasse?"

Nylund was surprised about the mild and almost friendly tone in his voice, but he knew Rosenfeldt well and sensed this was not as good a start as the supreme commander wanted him to believe.

"I'm okay, all things considered, but I doubt you brought me here to check up on me?"

Rosenfeldt smiled. "You're right, Klasse. I'm glad you're all right, but we have more important things to do than to talk about our feelings. I'll skip right to the point. This submarine story is over. The sighted vessel belongs to the Soviet Union, and this is the end of it. You know as well as I that this must stay this way. No loose ends floating around."

Nylund was surprised for the second time in one minute. He understood that politics had its place and was a form of necessary evil in all this, but it sounded like he was just ordered to stop all investigations on what had happened.

"I'm not completely sure I follow."

"We need to make sure that this stays a sighting of a Soviet submarine. To clearly state it for you, I need an archive full of information that this is a Soviet submarine and that lacks indication that this was someone else. Is that about clear enough for you?"

Surprise quickly turned to anger. Nylund threw his hands into the air as he started to speak.

"General, that is outrageous. This is not a sighting. Someone shot a torpedo at my Navy. If it wasn't for the skill of Captain Lindholm, we would have thirty dead sailors on our hands. This isn't something we can sweep under the carpet based on indications. I agree it did seem like it was a Soviet boat, but more and more evidence is looking questionable or even pointing in the other direction. This needs to be properly investigated. The beacon is made of Western components, and the bloody thug we shot seems to be a British citizen."

"There will be an investigation of this, Klasse. We'll have a real look through a proper commission."

"No, it gets investigated now. Not by a commission next year that will find nothing but selective evidence. We need to know who shot a torpedo at our ship. Fredrik, come on. This isn't a game. This is an act of war."

"So who was it, Admiral?" Rosenfeldt threw his hands to the side in a questioning gesture.

"I don't know yet, I don't know, but we need to find out."

"So, what do you actually know? As far as I'm concerned, you're fighting shadows, looking for something that simply isn't there. You have to let it go. You know that the only political solution to this is a Soviet submarine, and that is what will happen. Nothing else. Do I make myself clear, Admiral?"

"I hear you, but we can't do that."

Rosenfeldt sighed. "Klasse, the only other option is that it was a NATO submarine, and you know about our relationship with them."

"Yes, I know, and I know they are occasionally snooping around in our archipelago, but this time it includes a war shot."

"Even worse then, you want to accuse NATO of firing a torpedo at our submarine?"

"No, but—"

"No buts, Admiral. we need to close this out."

Nylund said nothing. He looked down at the floor, shaking his head in disbelief.

"What has this come to, Fredrik?"

Without waiting for a response, Nylund stood up and turned on his heel. Rosenfeldt saw him leave the room and turn right down the corridor toward the exit.

Nylund was an uncertain card at this time. He understood what was going on, but it went so against his grain that the supreme commander wasn't sure he could completely trust Nylund to take care of this the way it needed taking care of. He reached over and picked up his phone.

"It's me. I think Nylund might be a problem."

* * *

Berga Naval Base, April 20th, 1800hrs

"Nylund, it's Eriksson."

"Hi, Roffe."

"I was just at the pier, and the submarine is back. I heard it would come in, so I wanted to check in on the crew, but they're nowhere to be seen. Do you know where they are?"

"I don't know exactly but assume they're being debriefed. Anything wrong?"

"Well, the boat looks like it's almost been abandoned. Like they have left in a rush. There are still food scraps in the sink, like the cook just dropped what he had in his hands and walked away. Fair enough they get debriefed, but the land crew said they were pulled off the submarine within a minute of docking. You know as well as I that there is plenty of preparations due before you power down completely. Besides that, the hatch is wide open. It's supposed to be closed and padlocked once docking is complete."

"Well, the circumstances are quite unusual, so it's no wonder things weren't done completely as usual. Can you get another crew to sort the boat out? I'll have a look at where the crew is."

"The other crew won't be happy to clean up someone else's boat, but sure, I can get it done."

* * *

Stockholm, April 20th, 1800hrs

"He won't let go of it. I have a sense he will dig into this until he finds out who shot a torpedo at his Navy," Rosenfeldt stated.

Thomas Nordin shook his head. "It's not his damn Navy. We just allowed him to manage it for a while. He must understand there is no other option in this case. No discussion."

"He could be a risk to all this. He is a good man but highly emotional right now."

"Look, it's simple. If he can't make this happen, you need to find someone who will."

"Replace him, you mean?"

"Not officially, no, that would create too much attention and cause a whole plethora of other problems. Leave him where he is, but limit his effectiveness in official naval channels and find someone who can circumvent him."

"Well, that's already underway. I had a feeling this would happen. I got someone working on it. Someone loyal and likely to do whatever needs doing to get ahead. Commander Löfgren will do it. Military intelligence. He sits next to the archive, has full access, and will do what we tell him to if there is something in it for him. Like an additional star on his uniform."

"I don't care about the shoulder boards of you people. If he wants some stars or gold or whatever, feel free to give it to him."

The defense minister leaned back and stretched in his chair. Managing the information in this matter required some time and effort, but it could potentially have exponential returns. If he successfully contained the situation and hammered home the message of a Soviet submarine in Swedish waters, this could really become a problem for the damn socialists. They were gunning for his government and, unfortunately, it looked as if they would be successful. It depended a bit on which poll you chose to believe, but there was a chance he could put a spanner in the works of the Soviet-friendly behavior of these people.

And if it didn't work? If it didn't work, he would sacrifice the man in front of him. Him and the head of the Navy. If the archive were only partially cleaned up, he could blame the military for incompetence, and the military could blame the budget cuts made by the socialists all through the seventies. *Not bad*, he thought. *Not bad at all.*

"Tell this Löfgren that he will have authority to do whatever it takes to sort this out. We need it done as soon as possible."

"He is working on it. I'll confirm this with him."

* * *

Muskö Naval Base, April 20th, 1930hrs
Nylund slammed down the phone. Attempt after attempt to find the crew of the submarine had been met by shaking heads and shrugs. *What is wrong with the damn Navy when the admiral cannot find his own crew? First, the boat goes missing, and once we find it again, the crew goes missing.*

Undoubtedly, this was the work of the supreme commander. As Nylund resisted the idea of cleaning up the archives, they must have taken precautions to limit his reach within the Navy. It was now clearer than ever that he and Wikström would have to continue their own investigation of how all this fit together. And if he needed copies of more things from the archives, he was now in a race with time before his access was blocked altogether. They might be looking at replacing him, but he figured it would draw too much attention at the moment. It would rather be a silent blocking of him doing his job, and they would let him retire at a later date.

He picked up the phone to the head of engineering at Muskö Naval Base. Maybe he could still get a hold of the transponder device. There was an answer on the first signal despite the hour of the day.

"Yes."

"It's Nylund. I hope you're still sitting on the box with the transponder."

"No, the box is no longer here."

"What are you saying, man? Didn't I make it clear to you that you would guard that box until I said so?"

"Yes, you did, but Commander Löfgren turned up with some paperwork about it being moved. I had to move. What was I supposed to do?"

Löfgren again. It was starting to make sense now. The tapes that would potentially identify the submarine went missing. The transponder with Western components that could cast some doubt about the Soviet angle suffered the same fate. The transponder could be the work of Rosenfeldt, asking Löfgren to clear it up. But would Rosenfeldt have anything to do with the tapes? People had been shot over those. Moving some items from the archives was one thing. Taking part in shooting people was another. This was peacetime after all, was it not?

Chapter 23 – Suspicions

This isn't good, Löfgren thought. Within fifteen minutes, he was hit with two different pieces of information from two different places, both suggesting he would have further issues. This wasn't good news—not for the Navy and not for him.

The naval analysis group had received a sketch directly from Nylund. Apparently, he had collected it from one of the main witnesses, one Alvar Segerfors, who had also submitted a sketch when this all started. Now looking at the sketch in front of him, he had a problem. They didn't even look similar. The first one in his briefing file was vague and would need some imagination to be sure it was a submarine.

The second one that Nylund had sent through from the same witness was very different. There was no mistaking this was a submarine. The bow was higher than the aft, and it had a conning tower toward the back. The conning tower had an unbroken front and a clearly shown rounding on the back. There was an object on the front deck about the height of a man—potentially a sensor of some sort.

He had to smile about the naval analysis group. How convenient that they were all so biased that they couldn't possibly come to any other conclusion than this being a Soviet submarine in question. You could report Jesus walking on water, and this group would somehow turn that into a Whiskey-class submarine.

Nylund's handwritten notes sent along with the sketch suggested it could be a West German submarine type 206. It had a characteristic rounding on its tower that made it look different from many other submarines. The report from the analysis group had gone to great lengths to reject this idea. They had suggested the angle of the drawing was wrong based on the position of the sighting and somehow got to the conclusion that this might as well be a Soviet Whiskey-class submarine. Did they not have a different character in terms of its snorkel mast sticking out on the back? Whatever. He wasn't a submarine expert. This report would stay in the archive, though. That was for sure. This was formal confirmation that the Navy's own experts considered this a Soviet vessel.

For Löfgren, getting a better sketch wasn't a problem. His problem with this sketch, in conjunction with what he had overheard this morning, was twofold. How the hell did Nylund get ahold of the sketch? Was he running his own investigation on the side, interviewing witnesses? Then, if this Alvar Segerfors had submitted a sketch at the very beginning, why did it look different in his briefing papers? Assuming Segerfors hadn't suddenly woken up and vividly remembered additional details, someone had been tampering with the sketch.

Once the materials came through, only one person would be part of both archiving it and helping him prepare briefing materials: Mrs. Falk. She would almost certainly have been the only person with an opportunity to do this. Remove the detailed sketch and replace it with a vaguer version that would make it impossible to determine what type of submarine it was.

To add to this suspicion, he had overheard Mrs. Falk talking to another employee who had lost their access card. She had talked about how that would never happen to her, as from the time she left her house until she got back home, her access card never left its place. She carried it in a sling around her neck. If it never left its place, how would he have found it on her desk the other day when he was using it to access the archives? Had she left it there on purpose? Leaning back in his chair, he felt more and more uneasy as the minutes passed. Mrs. Falk would have had access to everything and everyone for years without anyone taking notice.

* * *

Berga Naval Base, April 21st, 1030hrs

Eriksson had been right. The other submarine crew that was available hadn't been happy to get called out to clean up their neighboring submarine. *They have some incident, and suddenly they're too important to take out their own trash?* Grudgingly, they had wandered across the pier and embarked on their cleaning mission.

As they had been through the most obvious items, trash, and food, they started to clear out the personal gear of the crew and put it in piles on the pier to label it. They had asked Eriksson about what to do with it, and he had simply told them to lock it up in the barracks behind the main building at the division.

"And this?" One of the enlisted men waved a tape in front of Eriksson. "Does this go with the personal gear or stay on board?"

Eriksson looked at it. The tape was the same make and model they used in all the Navy's recording devices. They were all numbered so that the Navy could tell if any tapes were missing. Generally, on their submarines, the sonar crews would make sure there were always recordings running and that the tapes were in good order and all accounted for.

"Where did you find it?"

"I found it in a personal locker, along with this gear," the sailor nodded toward a pile of clothes on the ground.

"Whose gear is that?"

The sailor bent over to look at the tag on the bag that the clothes were about to be packed into, "Sonar Petty Officer Lindberg, sir."

Sonar Petty Officer Lindberg had Navy tapes in his locker even though all the tapes had been stolen. It was also strictly forbidden to remove these tapes from their designated place.

"I'll take it," Eriksson said. The sailor shrugged and handed it over to him, happy to have one less thing to pack up and carry over to the barracks.

* * *

Unknown Location, April 21ˢᵗ, 1400hrs

The entire crew had been taken by motorcade out through Västerhaninge. They had continued through Tungelsta and made a right turn. That was as far as Lindberg could follow them.

After that, they were passing areas unknown to him. All forests and lakes. They followed Road 257 toward Botkyrka but turned left instead of right when they got to the final turn. Somewhere between that turn and Västerby, they turned right off the main road and onto tiny gravel roads. As it cleared, they were dropped off at a big house in the middle of nowhere, looking like a big barn that had been turned into a regular house.

The crew was checked off the clipboard again, standing in two lines in the garden. The main house was in front of them, and a second house, almost as big as the first one, was on their left. There was a high fence around the property, not military grade with barbed wire on top but high enough that it would be a challenge to climb. It had started to rain, and as the count was finished, they were invited into the big house.

On the inside, it looked like a simple hotel. Each man was handed a set of new clothes, towels, and toiletries and assigned to a shared room with one or two other crew members. As Sandberg was up, Lindberg was surprised to see he was sent off to a room alone. Wikingsson was sent to a room alone as well, and Lindberg too once it was his turn. It seemed like the sonar crew was all in their own rooms. What happened to the rest? He didn't have time to tell before he got escorted into his room.

His mind twitched as he heard them lock the door behind him. As a general rule, you couldn't simply lock people up in a country like Sweden unless they had done something wrong. Maybe the military had some special privileges in this area. He hadn't done anything wrong, had he?

Through the trip, the man with the clipboard that had been riding in Lindberg's vehicle told them that though the whole thing seemed a bit odd, it was standard practice in terms of debriefing crews. As Sweden hadn't been at war for two hundred years, it just was not very common.

* * *

Berga Naval Base, April 21ˢᵗ, 1400hrs

Rolf Eriksson walked across the smaller exercise field next to the main assembly hall at Berga. Across the field was the training facility for both submarine and anti-submarine sonar crews, where they were trained in the use of sonars and sound analysis. He hadn't set his foot there for ten years, and the receptionist looked at him with some question.

Eriksson signed in and proceeded over to one of the sound training rooms, checked that nobody was using it, and then entered and closed the door carefully behind him. It was a small room that would fit eight people training at the same time. Eight seats with tape recorders and headphones and piles of paper where the trainees could check boxes and write comments around what they were listening to.

The trainee would mark which tape they

were listening to and then mark the sheet according to what they could identify. Cavitation, engine noise, exhaust or rudder sounds, blade count. The list had grown since he did his own training, but the principle remained the same.

He sat down at one station and put the headphones on. Carefully, he put the tape in the recorder, and once he had double-checked that it was in there right, he pressed play. There were only a few minutes of sound on it. He listened intently to the recorded sound and rewound it several times, using one of the training sheets to make notes of what he heard.

It was a while since he served in active duty on board a submarine and his knowledge of sound analysis was slightly dated. He still knew the basics, though, and could quickly make out roughly what he was listening to. Rudder sounds perhaps at the start; then, the contact accelerated, and you couldn't hear the sounds of rudder hydraulics anymore. He lost count as he tried to find the rhythm. It was a long time ago he practiced this. Still, confident he would have recognized the very distinct and familiar rhythm of a three or four-bladed propeller, he determined that this must have at least five.

The contact started to cavitate as it accelerated. It had to be a submarine, and he could only make out one propeller shaft. Multiple shafts would almost certainly have propellers where the rhythm wasn't completely synchronized. He struggled with the blade count for a bit longer and couldn't find any indication of the submarine having more than one propeller. He'd have to leave that to an expert to confirm. Sandberg, who was the sonar Chief on board should have a listen. He would be able to tell.

Single shaft Soviet submarine. That would exclude an awful lot of them. Whiskey, Foxtrot, Echo, Tango. All of them had multiple propellers. It could be a Kilo. They had one shaft. They had six or seven blades, if memory served, but okay, it could've been a Kilo. Eriksson had heard enough and focused on the sound of the torpedo that was also on the recording.

The incoming torpedo's pitch would help identify what type it was, but it was almost impossible without access to a library that could be used for reference. That would have to wait for an expert as well. This would have to go to Nylund. As far as Eriksson was concerned, this didn't prove that it was a Soviet boat. It could have been any number of things with one shaft and five or more blades.

Eriksson pocketed the tape and walked across the exercise yard again toward his car. Eriksson wondered why Lindberg had kept a copy of this among his personal gear in the first place.

Had anything happened on board that made Lindberg suspicious?

* * *

Berga Naval Base, April 21st, 1700hrs
Eriksson picked up the phone and dialed Nylund's number. He was unsure whether this tape would make any difference, but the man should be aware it existed.

"Admiral, it's Eriksson. I got some interesting news."

"Yes, go ahead."

"It seems that one of the sonar crew on board made a copy of the tape from the encounter."

Nylund exploded with questions from the other side of the line. "What? Where did you find it? Do you have it? Have you listened to it?"

"It was found by the second crew that was cleaning the boat. We sorted and tagged the crew's personal gear and found a tape. I took it off them, and I have it here on my desk, along with two copies that I've made."

"And what is on it? Have you listened?"

"I have listened to it. Look, I'm not an expert, and I can't tell you exactly what it is. There are rudder sounds. Strong acceleration. Screw with at least five blades. One shaft as far as I can tell. As I said, I'm not an expert at this. Someone with better knowledge would need to go through this and compare to all available libraries to make a more certain identification."

"So, the tape proves nothing?"

"Not yet, but that's just because we haven't had it looked at by an expert. With some time, maybe it's possible to make out exactly what this is. So far, it doesn't prove it's a Soviet submarine like the press said, but it also doesn't prove it's not."

"Okay, okay, Eriksson. Listen. We need to make sure these tapes are safe until we can get them analyzed. With the missing tapes and the shooting, things are a bit tense now. I'll put you in contact with a person I trust that can make sure the tapes are kept safe. She'll call you later and set a time and place."

"A person, as in a naval officer?"

"A person, as in someone I can trust. Too many things have gone wrong in the Navy lately. Don't worry, we're just diversifying a bit to make sure things don't disappear again. Just wait for her call."

Eriksson confirmed and hung up the phone. He couldn't blame Nylund for being cautious around this stuff. He was right. There were too many things that had gone wrong in the Navy lately. The whole incompetence spiel had been started by the press the year before. *U-137* ran its diesels all night to get off the rock she had run onto, while the Navy didn't notice. The press had a field day with that for weeks.

The Swedish Navy can barely catch a submarine when it's stuck on land. It had been a tough time to be in the Navy ever since. Now, this incident wasn't only about almost having a submarine sunk. They had also lost reports and evidence along the way. In the back of his head, Eriksson had his doubts they would ever be able to find out who it was. The tapes could help, but he wasn't sure they could determine with any certainty who the intruder was. It might be better just to voluntarily retire from active duty before they were all fired. The "old men's shelf" at the Swedish defense materials administration seemed to have an endless supply of open positions for former officers.

* * *

Unknown location, April 21st, 2100hrs
Lindberg wouldn't be able to sleep tonight. He already knew it. The screeching noise of the torpedo that had followed them came back as soon as he closed his eyes. His breathing and heartbeat would increase, and after a few minutes, it became unbearable to the point that he had to open his eyes. As the sight of the ceiling and the lamp attached to it came back into view, his body realized

that he was safe and started to lower its guard again.

The troubles to sleep had become worse and worse over time. The first few days hadn't been all that bad. Occasionally, he had caught himself waking up due to a screeching noise, and he had needed a few seconds to determine whether it was a dream or reality. As the days passed, the torpedo noise came back more often, ten or twelve times a night. He did not know the psychology of this, but the noise's recurrence and the difficulty to find sleep had led to a much worse problem. Fear of sleeping.

He already knew it would be unpleasant to try to sleep, and his body knew it as well. It was easier to act against your will when it required force and action. Anyone could walk into the dentist's office, even if the mind resisted. Sleep wasn't an action that could be forced, however. It was the lack of action. The lack of thinking. As he lay down to try to sleep again, his body already knew it was time for another visit to Hell, and he could feel the fear coming back.

It was like slowly being lowered into icy water. Discomfort as it passed his knees, the intensity increasing as it crept up past his waist. As it hit his chest, breathing normally was already impossible and the thought of being submerged in black, icy water, never to surface again, caused his brain to panic. By then, he had to open his eyes to escape.

Chapter 24 – Interrogation

Military Headquarters, April 22nd, 0900hrs

Löfgren had been waiting patiently outside the office of the supreme commander. It wasn't easy to stay calm through all this, but he felt like he was getting a better grip on the situation for every hour that passed. He would be able to clean up the archives. People in high places would be forever grateful if he could pull this off.

On top of that, if he could get enough suspicion pointed toward Mrs. Falk and make a case for her leaking Navy materials, he would be able to pin each and every foul up on her and Nylund. Nylund acted late and ordered Löfgren to plant evidence. Mrs. Falk then tampered with materials and the archive. How was he supposed to do an excellent job under these conditions, surrounded by incompetence and treason?

Rosenfeldt's secretary waved at him to come through, and he quickly stood up and marched into the office of the supreme commander. Rosenfeldt was standing behind his desk with his back toward the door. *Admiring the view maybe*, Löfgren thought, but this was unlikely, as the view was across one of the main freeways under construction in this part of town. Not a pretty sight.

Rosenfeldt turned around and motioned for him to take a seat, before sitting down across from him.

"So, Commander, how are we moving ahead in our little operation?"

"Main parts of the cleanup are on track," Löfgren responded confidently.

He picked up a thin file from his Navy bag and opened it in his lap so he could follow his own checklist.

"The transponder itself and the report on it have been relocated. We had to argue with an engineer who apparently was ordered by Nylund to guard the transponder. That's been solved through some very official-looking paperwork. No issue there."

"But there are several people who have seen this thing. How do we convince them that it doesn't exist anymore?"

"We can't, but we can build a compelling story through evidence that this was indeed a Soviet submarine. Once we accomplish that, what these people think they remember will be irrelevant. The human memory isn't flawless. It will misremember and change facts all the time. That is one of our main advantages. What's in print is true.

The rest is just conspiracy theory."

Löfgren looked down at his list and continued. "The autopsy report from the shooting and the documents received from the British Army have been removed as well. It doesn't prove the UK was involved, of course, but the document raises doubts about the official story. From now on, the nationality of the three men is unconfirmed. You could support a thesis from their behavior that they were Russian operatives, and nobody can prove the opposite. The bodies have been released from the naval base and will be cremated . . . right about now." He looked down at his watch. "Yes, right about now."

"And this new sketch you got—the one with the rounding on the conning tower. Has that been relocated too?" Rosenfeldt was running through his own mental checklist.

"No, we've left that one in the archives."

"Why? Didn't Nylund suggest it could be a West German boat?"

"Yes, he did, but that suggestion got torn to pieces by his own naval analysis group. Handy bunch those people. Patriotic and heavily biased toward the enemy always being red, if you know what I mean. Besides, it would be good if we did have something left in the archive."

Löfgren looked at his file. "The crew is being debriefed."

"By the Navy?"

"No, by independent contractors."

"You're not planning to hurt the crew, are you? They're Swedish officers and enlisted men."

"The defense minister confirmed to do *whatever it takes*, but no. We don't plan to hurt the crew. Most of them will provide a short statement and then be released back into service. Machinists, engineers—they have no real way of knowing any of the details of the incident. They'll know they were shot at but could never tell by whom. There will only be a handful of the sonar crew who would have heard anything and would also have the expertise to understand what was happening. It may take a bit longer to debrief them to make sure we know what they know. If they have any indication that this was not a Soviet boat, we may have to suggest that they recalibrate their memories."

"Recalibrate their memories?"

"Drugs, interviews, psychology. Most of them are very young men who just want to go home to their girlfriends. Easy to influence."

Impressive, Rosenfeldt thought. The man is all over this and will stop at nothing to get it done. He liked what he was hearing at first, but as they diverged into drug use and something that sounded like brainwashing of the poor men, he started to wonder if Löfgren wasn't enjoying this *whatever-it-takes* order a bit too much.

"Okay, but nobody gets hurt."

"There will be no visible harm to anyone."

This made Rosenfeldt cringe in his seat. What the hell did that mean? He quickly got a grip on himself again and nodded toward the folder in Löfgren's lap.

Löfgren looked down at it again. "Yes. Sonar crew. That brings me to the tapes. They were taken, and I don't know where they are or who has them. That's a major problem. It's a loose end we can't tie up."

He knew very well who had the tapes, and he assumed they would never see the light of day. He still wanted to make sure this wasn't his problem. He watched Rosenfeldt lean back and interlock his fingers behind his head, looking at the ceiling.

"Are there any other recordings?" Rosenfeldt asked after a few moments of silence.

"We're looking through the crew's personal gear and searching the whole submarine to make sure no other tapes are around. So far, we haven't found anything."

Löfgren closed the folder as he had now worked through it all the way to the end.

"Speaking of problems. We got a few different ones as well."

The supreme commander didn't flinch—just raised his eyebrows to encourage Löfgren to continue.

"I'm unsure how Nylund got ahold of the updated sketch he submitted to the analysis group. I think he might be running his own investigation on the side after being denied full access and authority to run it officially. I'll investigate that. If he is running something, he might have been able to get copies. I don't know."

"Yes, you investigate that, and you make sure he doesn't have anything in terms of personal archives on this. We can't afford any contradicting evidence floating around."

"I'll see to that, but there is another problem as well. The sketch I originally used in the briefing looked different from the new one, though it came from the same witness. Either the witness suddenly remembered new things, or someone swapped the original sketch. I have reason to believe that it was Mrs. Eivor Falk, one of the secretaries at the Muskö Naval Base."

"And what would those reasons be, Commander?"

"Well, she's the only one with access. I'm not sure of any concrete motive, but it's highly worrying, and I would take care of it now if it was up to me."

"If someone alters things in the archive without orders from the top, they need to be removed immediately. The military and especially the Navy, are being ridiculed for incompetence. If you need to clean out your crew there to make sure you've got a well-working machine, do so."

* * *

Unknown Location, April 22nd, 1000hrs

Perfect, the young man in front of her looked utterly destroyed. Arousal from combat experience followed by prolonged exposure to perceived or real danger. Add some sleep deprivation to that, and you would have a potent amalgam for exhausting a human being within a very short timeframe. The couple of Benzodiazepines he was issued last night probably didn't help either. He might have slept some, but he would be drowsy. Either way, there wouldn't be much resistance or resolve coming from this young man today.

She wouldn't be called upon unless there was an emergency. There were many psychologists, but she had done extensive work with combatants following Swedish forces deployed in the Congo. She had quickly recognized this as a niche and set up her own company. Her services didn't come cheap, and they were usually deployed under, let's say, questionable legal conditions. Discreet solving of complex tasks of a psychological nature. That made for a premium markup.

She had her crew with her and most of them were not psychologists. It wasn't all talking and evaluating. She also needed things done. Things of a more operational nature. Ex-military, both Swedish and foreign, usually disgruntled with their previous governmental employer. They would make it to her payroll. It was an excellent payroll to be on, and as long as missions were accomplished, there was limited scrutiny on the legal aspects of things.

So far, this hadn't been difficult at all. Her job was simple. Identify anyone in the crew who could suggest this wasn't a Soviet submarine. If she found one, do anything needed to suggest they should reevaluate their opinion on the matter. Place enough doubt in them until they were unsure. You didn't have to work with soldiers to understand the scope of things. The tobacco industry had caught on to the same measures as soon as the first suggestions surfaced about smoking and cancer. They didn't need to convince the public that cigarettes were good for them, they just needed to doubt that they were bad.

Her situation was the same, and she knew the look very well. The look on someone's face when a certain memory started to become fuzzy around the edges. Then the slow exhale that followed as the obscure memory ceased to mean anything.

The start of the list was child's play. Engineers and personnel from the torpedo room. They knew about a torpedo. They knew about the two explosions, but that was about the end of it.

They couldn't tell what actually happened outside the submarine. They didn't know more than the average Swede reading the evening press. She talked to them for fifteen minutes and checked them off her list to send them home.

The man in front of her now was from the sonar crew. According to reports, he was the one to report the initial contact, manning the sonar for the entirety of the engagement. Fresh out of submarine school at Berga in December 1981, he'd started his twelve-month stint on board in January 1982. Three months on a vessel would have brought him to a reasonable level of proficiency, though she would probably get more out of the next man on the list, Sonar Chief Edward Sandberg. *Well, let's see what we have here then*, she thought while opening the man's file.

Applying her most understanding and caring voice, she started, "Can you give me your name and rank, sailor?"

"Sonar Petty Officer Lindberg, Carl."

"Good, you'll have been told before, but I'll tell you again. This is standard procedure for debriefing. I know it's painful to stay here and answer questions. I know you'd rather go home. Don't worry. You'll be home in no time."

She eyed him in silence for a while. "You look tired. The medicine they gave you didn't help?"

"I'm not sure; I think I slept for a few hours,

but it's all a bit blurry."

"I understand. Don't worry about it. We'll get you home shortly so you can get some rest. After what happened to you, sleep issues and some level of anxiety are normal. They'll pass but it may take a bit of time."

"Maybe we could get started slowly. Just start with your description of what happened out there on April 13th."

Lindberg explained the contact. How unclear and difficult it was to pinpoint. It turned out to be a submarine, so his estimate was that it let the current push it the right way while maintaining propulsion for two or three knots. Just enough to enable the use of its rudders. He described his thoughts about whether to report it or not and how he eventually found the contact to be real enough to raise to the captain and the torpedo officer.

They doubted him at first but still knew that it had to be investigated. They ruled out the possibility of a surface vessel. Mistakes like that happened. It wasn't as easy as people thought to identify something from simply listening to it. When they found nothing on the surface, they dove under the layer and came down right in front of the contact.

"Right in front of the damn thing," Lindberg gestured with his hands in front of his face. "Right in front of it."

"And then what happened?" She was still at her very best behavior to make the man feel comfortable and safe.

Lindberg continued to describe how they didn't hear it at first. It was in their wake, and the sonar was blocked by their own hull and propeller noise. As they turned, Sandberg caught it immediately. He had found the intruder's behavior odd, as it ran away in a straight line at full speed.

"I'm sorry. I'm not well versed in submarine warfare. Why is that odd?"

"Because we came around its back and easily lined it up for a shot. Turning your back and running at that range is suicide."

He explained there was a second submarine that fired at them. It must have been because the torpedo appeared from an entirely different bearing. Yes, it was possible to steer a torpedo around in an arch to confuse the enemy, but Lindberg would have heard the launch at that range. The surface was clear, so there was no other option than this torpedo coming from a second submarine.

"Did you ever hear this second submarine?"

"No, all we heard was the torpedo."

If the submarine was at a similar bearing, the torpedo would have masked it and been invisible to them. The captain reacted immediately. They fired a torpedo, which obscured the sonar picture even further, and then they'd dove for cover.

They never reacquired any of the submarines, but they did have the first one on tape.

As he was telling the last bit of the story, he looked up at her. "Have you not analyzed the tapes yet?"

"They're working on that, but for now, we need to focus on what you know."

The young sonar operator didn't know the tapes went missing along the way, nor did he need to know.

"We listened to the tapes and tried to determine what it was. It's hard, but we can make out it has one shaft and a five-bladed propeller for sure. That would exclude a lot of submarines, as many are double-shafted."

"You're unsure what class of Soviet submarine this is?"

"Yes, as I said, it excludes a lot of them. It's not a Tango. Not a Whiskey. Call it a Kilo if we got the blade count wrong, but I doubt it. Sandberg and I spent quite some time on it. Quite frankly, we can't tell for sure that it's a Soviet submarine."

She ignored his last remark and continued. "So, how much time did you spend analyzing this tape? It seems to me you would all have been busy in battle stations from the engagement until you handed them over. Not a lot of time to play with."

Lindberg sensed something was wrong, but in his foggy mind, he couldn't make out what it was.

The lady was suggesting it was a Soviet submarine, but neither he nor Sandberg could know that. And they had listened to it for hours.

"We listened until they told us to return to Berga."

There it was, the man was hiding something. She decided to drop the understanding act and go on the offensive. Maybe she could scare him into questioning himself and think about the implications for himself rather than about what had happened at sea.

"You listened until you were called back to Berga? I find that odd, given that you handed all the tapes over well before that. Do you have any further copies of the tape?" Her tone was stern and pointy now. She stood up and leaned forward over the desk, staring at him. "Do you have another tape?"

It took Lindberg a few seconds to work out what he had said that triggered this reaction. He slowly realized what had happened and began to work through what the correct answer would be. He tried to deny the additional tape with confidence but could hear his own voice swaying like a straw in the wind. She wouldn't be convinced.

"Petty Officer Lindberg, this is very simple. We are debriefing you, and we are also investigating a Soviet submarine in Swedish waters. This is about the integrity of Swedish territory and is of national importance. If you have any further evidence to share, you will tell me. Holding this back is a severe crime, with very severe consequences."

That should put him in the right mindset, she figured. "Lindberg, do you have a copy, yes or no?"

"Yes, I do. We listened to it in our spare time while on station the last few days."

"Where is the tape?"

"I had it in my locker along with my personal gear before we docked. We got pulled off the boat immediately on arrival, so I would think it's still there."

"You better hope it is. You made a copy of the tape, did you? And you have kept it from the people requesting it from you. This could land you in very serious trouble, sailor. Very serious trouble. A Soviet submarine entering Swedish waters, and you take it upon yourself to play around with evidence. We'll see what happens to you once this is done."

She slammed his file shut, picked it up, and walked past Lindberg to leave the room. *Poor boy*, she thought. I'll leave him alone with his feelings for twenty minutes and then have them take him back to his room. He would likely feel devastated. One small price to pay in the big scheme of things. She rounded the corner and walked up to one of her colleagues.

"Lindberg, Carl. Search his gear. He should have a sonar tape among his personal items. I need to get to Muskö to talk to someone. Just keep the men separated."

The man just nodded and reached for his phone.

"Oh, and when you bring him back to his room, handcuff him and push him around a bit. I want him to feel like he has done something terribly wrong. That will make it easier to get him to cooperate later."

* * *

Rosenbad, April 22nd, 1400hrs

"I've told Löfgren to follow up and check what's happening, but it seems Nylund is conducting some personal investigation on the side." Rosenfeldt put one leg on top of the other and looked at the defense minister.

"What's wrong with that man? First, he's a tired old admiral, and now he takes more and more initiative by the hour. Frankly, I'd prefer if he had done it the other way around." Nordin shook his head and let out a sigh.

"Well, this has to stay what it is now. If he's conducting his own research on the side, we need to know what he's up to and then firmly put an end to it."

"And by firmly, you mean?"

"I mean to find out if he's working with someone, get back whatever they have, and then send Nylund into retirement. He needs to shut up, and whoever is helping him too."

"We can formally put Nylund aside—that's not a problem—and we can probably look through his office and home as well under the banner of debriefing and following an exit process. If he has any helpers, I'm not sure what we can do."

"Shut them up."

"We can't shut people up if they don't want to. I know we have weapons and all, but that's not what the military does in a country like ours."

"Yes, yes, I know. Just get someone else to shut them up then. Leave it with Commander Löfgren. He seems to be enjoying himself."

"Yes, he's enjoying it a bit too much. I'd be careful about firing him up even more about this."

"You can be as careful as you want, but he needs to deal with it. There will be one version of the truth, and that will be the Navy archives. They look to be well in order, at least soon. If any official-looking documents are floating around out there, Löfgren needs to find them and get rid of them. End of story."

Chapter 25 – Unraveling

Muskö Naval base, April 22nd, 1600hrs

"This way," said the Navy corporal, gesturing ahead.

Eivor Falk entered the room with a fair degree of apprehension, as most people would if they had been summoned to an extraordinary meeting with someone they never heard of. She relaxed somewhat when she saw only one person in there. A woman slightly her senior and with a generally welcoming demeanor. The woman motioned toward a chair opposite her own and asked if she wanted something.

"No, I don't need anything. I'm just curious about what's going on here."

"Yes, of course. Not to worry. We're just looking into a couple of items that have moved or been misplaced in the main archives, and need to make sure our routines are adequate. You visit the archives often, don't you?"

"Yes, of course, I do. Filing in the archive and pulling materials for briefings is part of my job. I'm in there all the time."

Falk was now getting nervous. Looking into routines would have been done by some old Navy lieutenant who was too tired or too useless to serve on active duty. This woman was clearly not Navy. She was slouching in her chair to seem relaxed and casual, but from the shape of her shoulders, you could tell this wouldn't be her natural posture. She spoke in a mild and friendly manner but couldn't hide a sharp look in her blue eyes. This woman was a professional. In fact, such a professional that she couldn't hide it, despite her best efforts.

No, this wasn't about routines. This was about something different, and Mrs. Falk had a perfectly good idea of what that might be. The time had come.

"So, do you normally work alone in the archive?"

"I have top-secret clearance and can work alone in the archive, yes. Am I in trouble for something that has happened?"

"No, not at all. You can relax. I'm more interested in seeing if you've seen anything in the archive lately that seemed off—something out of place. Things like that."

"Well, it was the requisition for the craft and uniforms." She explained how she had found a requisition form that, in terms of time and materials, coincided with an incident where these had potentially been used. She also explained that she couldn't recognize the signatures. Then, there was the breach in routine. The submitter and approver had been the same person. She naturally left out the part about her forging this form.

"And who was this person?"

"It was signed by Commander Löfgren."

"Where is it now?"

"I handed a copy to Admiral Nylund, and the original is still in the archive unless someone else has removed it, of course."

"Has Commander Löfgren been made aware of this?"

"I don't think so, but I don't know. I just pass on information. I'm not privy to all the decisions that get made around here, you see."

"I'll need a copy of the requisition too. Is there anything else that has seemed out of place?"

Falk moved in her seat. *Was this the time to strike, perhaps?* It seemed like the requisition would be enough to lead them on a path toward Löfgren. No need for further upsets. She would still have the access card as a backup plan if more firepower was needed. On the other hand, it couldn't hurt to give this another nudge in the right direction. Yes, it was time.

"I did just find some information earlier today as I was sifting through materials. It was an order document for the submarine that went missing. Something about their mission being at least partially intelligence based. I didn't quite understand what it meant, but that's normal. We usually read enough to understand where it needs to go—but rarely the entire document."

"And why would that strike you as odd?"

"The submarine's orders were already filed before it left the pier. This addition suddenly appeared, and I'm not sure where it came from."

"And a submarine order needs to be signed by someone, and that someone is . . .?"

"Well, normally, the orders are signed by the division commander, Melker Nilsson, for the first submarine division. Intelligence orders can come through in a different way."

"Yes, yes, and who signed this new order?"

"Commander Löfgren did."

"I'll need a copy of that too."

The woman opposite Falk took some notes down in her notebook and closed the file in front of her. She looked around the room and then waved for the corporal who was waiting outside the door.

"I think we're done here. As I said, there's nothing to worry about. We just need to look into the flow here to confirm that submarine orders don't appear out of nowhere. I think this whole event will cause a bit of an overhaul around here—in terms of process. That's all."

The woman shook her hand quickly and was about to leave the room as she turned around and continued. "Just one more thing. I take it your pass is always with you, and nobody else would ever have an opportunity to use it?"

Falk held up her pass that was in a sling around her neck.

"I always keep it on me. Well, I did leave it at my desk a few days back. The only time in a decade, I would think. It got tangled in my jacket as I was going for lunch, and I left it on my desk, but it was still there when I got back. My colleague let me back in. People leave their passes on the desk all the time, you know."

* * *

Stockholm, April 22nd, 2000hrs

She saw a silver Volvo turn up on the parking lot outside the store where she had told Eriksson to meet her. It was a convenient location since the store also had a small parking garage underneath it. It was hard to see into and easy to track who came in and out. She saw him look for the entrance briefly before he turned to enter the garage. This obviously wasn't his regular neighborhood.

She stepped away from her car as he turned into the garage. Eriksson stopped in front of her and looked her up and down, obviously comparing her looks with what Nylund would have described to him. Convinced she was the right person, he nodded and lowered his window.

"Captain Eriksson, I assume."

He nodded again. "Yes." Without much doubt, he held out a small package through the window.

"That's the tape we found and two copies that I made. Nylund said that you would make sure they get spread out in safe places."

She took the package from him. "Yes, I will. We need to de-risk the information we have." She got a third nod from Eriksson before he simply closed his window again and started to move off. He was clearly uncomfortable with playing cloak and dagger games. Most military men were. They were trained to follow orders on the battlefield. Acting like spies, mistrusting everyone, and working in the shadows didn't come easy to them. They would all prefer a naval battle to this.

She walked over to her car and sat down in the driver's seat. Curiosity got the better of her, and she opened one of the tapes and put it in the tape recorder. Pressing play, the speakers started to give off a deep rumbling sound. She listened to it for thirty seconds and then turned it off and rewound the tape. How on earth could anyone make sense of that? It sounded like someone rattling a chain under water.

She pulled out from the parking garage and back onto the road. She knew it was probably paranoia, but the feeling of being followed was still with her. Last time turned out to be nothing, but she would still take some precautions before driving over to the storage where she intended to keep the tapes. She would need to inform Nylund she had the tapes and then spread them to different locations for safekeeping.

* * *

Unknown Location, April 23rd, 1050hrs

That little bastard, she thought. Her people had been digging through the crew's personal items for a whole day without finding a tape. Not among Lindberg's items and not among any other items either, for that matter. He had seemed broken enough not to lie about it, but apparently, he fooled her.

There was another option, of course—that he did have the tape there but someone had found and taken it. Seemed more likely to her that the little rat of a Navy conscript lied. And she had believed him. This annoyed her immensely as she walked down the corridor toward her team's office. No more being nice to this guy.

She burst into the room, interrupting a discussion about whether the sonar chief, Sandberg, was too tall for submarine service and whether his back would suffer in the long run.

"Is he ready?"

A team-member looked at his watch, "Maybe. He was a bit of a wreck before, and since you called, we've nudged him and made him stand up every five minutes. He will be completely broken soon enough."

"Good, I have some other work to attend to. Keep waking him up every five minutes, and I'll get to him within an hour or two."

Her experience said that of all the possible ways of torturing someone, a lack of sleep and a feeling of futility were the most efficient. The sonar man had been treated like a criminal and threatened with the implications for him. She now had the ammunition to threaten him further.

If she could build the feeling about how this could end badly for him, his imagination would then do the bulk of the work for her. He would imagine life behind bars, perhaps strapped to a bed somewhere where nobody would ever find him. With severe sleep deprivation, making sure his sense of reason was compromised, the level of despair he'd experience would be beyond what most people could imagine. She had seen it work before.

She walked into her office. It seemed like the Supreme Commander had been trying to reach her. It was best to speak to him directly to make sure this all went down in the best interest of her business. Unlike common assumptions that private corporations were the bad and ruthless ones, most of her work came from governments. Once done with the day's business development activities, she would deal with that little worm lying to her.

* * *

Unknown Location, April 23rd, 1100hrs

She picked up the phone on the first signal.

"The log you asked about. It's come back."

"And?"

"You were right. Eivor Falk's pass was used on April 16th, 1251hrs, while she was having lunch. There are at least three people who can confirm seeing her at lunch during that time. There's no way it was her. Someone entered using her pass."

"And Löfgren?"

"We're not sure yet but working on it still. We know he was on base that day, and we don't know where he was during the lunch hour. It could be him, but we can't confirm it yet. We've pulled all the prints off her card. Unlikely it will yield anything but might be worth a try."

"Good work. Evidence or not, there are surely a few things that look out of place for Commander Löfgren. A bit of a hassle, as he's the one who hired us, but let me make some notes of this on the side and talk to some people. I can probably find a discreet way of getting this in front of Rosenfeldt."

"Okay, you need anything else?"

"Keep trying to pinpoint Löfgren's location that day. And maybe look into his movements in general while you're at it."

Chapter 26 – Safe Location

Nylund sat at his desk, looking out the window across the lake. His house did seem awfully large without Christina and his daughter in it. If he was sitting still, there wasn't one single movement at all in his house. Not one. Nothing but complete silence.

He looked down at the pad in front of him. He still didn't know what place Wikström found for the evidence they gathered, but she said she would come by at some point in the next day or two and explain. She had become increasingly paranoid lately and didn't want to tell him over the phone.

None of the boxes he had drawn up on his pad were solid evidence. It wouldn't tell them with any certainty who fired a torpedo at his Navy. Added together, however, he felt like they might be coming to a critical mass, suggesting this wasn't a Soviet submarine after all. It was someone else.

There was a tape. Eriksson hadn't been able to tell what it was, but an expert with access to other recordings may be able to make sense of it.

For sure, they would have West German boats in their library from some previous exercise. He wasn't sure it was a West German boat, but the new sketch certainly looked like one.

The Navy analysis group had vetoed his guess, of course. Hard to tell with those people. After last year's debacle with *U-137*, all they could think of was the great red threat from the East. That this could be more complicated didn't seem to faze them. They had pointed out the angle of the sketch was wrong, but how that would constitute evidence of a Soviet boat was beyond him.

Nylund could feel Wikström's pain and understood why she left the police force. She had told him more than one story about trying to solve a case, while behind her, someone trailed her every step looking for a technicality to prevent progress. Depressing.

He had a UK-born soldier who could have worked for anyone and a missing transponder. They did have a copy of the report, but the device itself was gone. He added one more box. The fact that the damn thing disappeared was almost evidence in itself. It didn't change the fact that a heap of indications told him this was something else, not a Soviet vessel. He looked at the ceiling, indications was one thing, but he didn't have one shred of solid evidence. It would have to come down to the tape. They needed that tape in the hands of an expert, and just maybe, they would be able to get a definite outcome. He looked at his watch. He hoped Wikström had the tapes by now and could make sure they were stored safely.

* * *

Unknown Location, April 23rd, 1330hrs

She stood outside the door, thinking through how she wanted to do this. The man on the other side would be a complete wreck from sleep deprivation, and if she could instill enough fear in him, he should be unable to lie again.

Her conversation with the supreme commander went very well. He was grateful for having received the information, even if it was bad news. They agreed she would continue as planned to solve the problem with the archive and information. He would handle some of the politics before they would speak again and agree on how to proceed with Löfgren.

She stretched her neck and rolled her head from side to side. She found it harder to sustain herself through these short and high-intensity operations as she got older. A deep breath, she lowered her brow and tilted her head forward to get a more aggressive look. Then, she opened the door and stormed inside.

"You're lying, right? You think you can lie to

me and get away with it. If you weren't in trouble before, you're in major trouble now, young man."

Lindberg looked up at her with dull eyes. Her colleague had been standing next to him, slapping him lightly across the face every few seconds to make sure he stayed awake. The other man quickly left the room, and she was left alone with Lindberg.

"You lied. You lied to me, didn't you?"

The young man in front of her just looked confused about the sudden barrage of questions directed at him. Good, he was responding as expected. She should be able to solve this now without giving him another six or twelve hours of this treatment.

"Do you have any idea what will happen to you if you don't cooperate with me? A Soviet submarine was in Swedish waters. This is a major international incident, and you're wasting my time looking around your gear. Do you have any tapes? And if so, where are they? I need to know, right now."

"I did have a tape in my locker. Only one. I promise."

"Well, we didn't find it, so it seems you're lying, doesn't it?"

Lindberg's head hung down on his chest, and he shook his head slightly while repeating to her. "I'm not lying. I'm not."

"Did you identify the submarine on the

tape?"

"No, we don't know what it is."

"And once you were unclear what it was, what did you do with the tape?"

"It's among my gear in the locker. It must be."

"There you go, lying to me again. It isn't there, so where is it?"

"I don't know then," Lindberg screamed in her face. "I had it with my gear when we docked the fucking ship. What do you want from me?"

Surprised, she stepped back to get a better look at him. He wasn't lying. He really thought the tape was among his gear. Damn, that meant nobody knew where the tape was. She would bet her company on the fact he wasn't lying, but she had to give it one more go before she could let this be.

"Well, all we need from you is for you to tell us where the tape is. If you don't, the consequences for you will be grave, son. Worse than you can imagine."

And he can probably imagine quite a bit by now, she thought.

"Have you ever seen what happens to traitors? They end up disappearing, don't they? Where do you think they go?"

"I don't know, I don't know," he sobbed, head hanging low still. "I don't know where the tape is. I had it with my gear in the locker. It was in my locker the last time I saw it. I swear."

She looked at him in silence for a whole minute. He was telling the truth. That's a problem.

She adopted her most caring voice. "Relax, son. I believe you. Everything will be fine. You understand that we're desperate to identify what type of Soviet submarine was in our waters. When national security is at play, things can get a bit intense. Don't worry. You'll be back home in no time."

Lindberg didn't respond, but she could hear his breathing lighten as she told him this was all over. She could, of course, turn on him now and go back to hitting him with more angry questions, but she judged there was no need. Confident he didn't know where the tape was, she instead tapped Lindberg on the shoulder.

"Well done, soldier. You're a hard man to crack."

She left the room and walked over to her team room, her colleagues looking at her as she entered. She shook her head. "He doesn't know. I'm certain he doesn't know. If the tape was there, it's been lost somewhere between docking and now. Who's been on board?"

"It was cleaned by a second crew, led by a Captain Rolf Eriksson."

"See if we can get something out of any of

them, but be careful, okay?"

"Okay, we'll have a look. So, what do we do with the man in the room next door?"

"Give him something to sleep on—something heavy that does the job. Take good care of him and ensure him that he'll be home soon. He'll barely remember this and will likely be happy just to get out and able to go home."

Her colleague nodded. "No problem."

"And flag him for follow-up. We may need to tie up this loose end at some point."

* * *

Stockholm, April 23rd, 1400hrs

Wikström walked up Slottsbacken, the Swedish Royal castle on her right. Royalty. What a joke. Somehow by birth, one family was destined to rule over everyone else and live off their tax money. It might have worked in the Middle Ages, but it should have been left back there.

Her brother had called her and given the rarity of that, she agreed to meet him in the city. He was a city boy, through and through, her brother. A lawyer at one of the famous firms, working all hours of the day. If he had the time to eat, his dear little failed police officer sister would, of course, be expected to show up. It was always like that. He did what he wanted, and the world would adjust

317

accordingly. She didn't know how he did it, but it seemed to work for him.

She made a left turn on Bollhusgränd. Five Small Houses—one hell of a restaurant to have lunch. She decided not to walk back to her car in a straight line but instead to get some air after the meal. She had turned down toward the water with him for a walk on Skeppsbron. He would have to get back to his office, somewhere across the bridge and close to Norrmalmtorg. At least that's where she thought he worked. After a quick goodbye, she turned left before the castle after spending a few moments watching her brother walking away along the waterfront.

He was only two years older than her, but his working hours and lifestyle were starting to take their toll. He was overweight, and he'd been drinking like a dog at a water fountain in July throughout lunch. She was driving and had stuck to water. Retired or not, drinking and driving was out of the question for a police officer. Besides, she had work to do this afternoon.

She closed in on the street, and without knowing why, she turned left again, basically completing a circle and ending up close to the restaurant they left just twenty minutes ago. As her conscious mind caught up with what she had done, her senses sharpened. These things never happened to her for no reason.

Now fully alert, she tried not to speed up—something most people would do in this situation. She carried on past the restaurant again. Either she was getting old and out of practice, or someone was following her.

She walked down the alley again toward the water. As she reached the corner, she casually turned left, and a second later, she broke into a full sprint until she reached the next alley where she turned left again. She stopped behind the corner to catch her breath. An amateur or someone tracking her alone might fall for the temptation to run along the water to reacquire her. She could spot that in her sleep. Someone who was organized would stay calm, think through the surroundings, and trust that a colleague or team member would catch a glimpse of her. A professional would also realize they might have been made. No way she would have made it out of sight in that time if she had kept her pace. A minute passed. She started to move again.

Whoever was following her had picked one hell of a spot to try. The Old Town of Stockholm was a maze of streets and alleys. It would be tough to keep track of someone here while remaining invisible. Too many corners to turn.

Her pulse was beating steadier now, and she felt more confident she could navigate her way south through the alleyways unless they had a damn regiment of people following her.

Unknowingly to Wikström, she was doing the same thing that Löfgren did in this area just a few days earlier.

As she walked past Järntorget, she felt the first drops of rain. There was more to come for sure, and it offered an excellent opportunity for her to adopt a different strategy. She turned on her heel and entered one of the coffee shops on the corner. She found a spot close to the window where she could see both the door and the square outside. Judging by the clouds, it would soon be pouring. Nobody without serious purpose would stick around outside in those conditions. *This will probably take a few hours*, she thought, and waved for the waitress to come by and take her order.

* * *

Stockholm, April 23rd, 1500hrs

Rosenfeldt's day hadn't started well, but as he was moving through the corridors of Sweden's military headquarters, he was feeling better. This place gave him a feeling of normality. He was a lifelong Army officer and hadn't climbed to the position of Supreme Commander for nothing.

All problems can be solved was a motto he had been working by for thirty years. He always instilled it in his troops as well, if they showed signs of giving up hope on things. Don't fixate on the problem. Just keep working the solution. All problems can be solved, whatever they are. He turned left into his own office and met his secretary in the doorway.

"General, the document you were talking about just arrived by courier. It's on your desk."

He nodded thanks to her and sat down at his desk. The supreme commander looked at the envelope before him, reminded himself that all problems could be solved, and opened it. He found a few copies of documents inside along with a handwritten note explaining why it was in his best interest to read it. No signature, but it undoubtably came from the work of the external contractors. They had interviewed the crew and spoke to a few other people who seemed to be involved in this in one way or another.

The note laid it out in simple bullet-point form. There was a suspicion that Mrs. Eivor Falk had tampered with the archives, and for this reason, the team conducted an interview with her. The result stated it was unlikely had done anything wrong—at least not intentionally—but they had uncovered some other interesting and alarming facts.

Commander Löfgren had submitted and signed a requisition form for a small craft and four Swedish Navy uniforms. This was precisely the gear used in the boarding of the Swedish submarine when the tapes disappeared. The requisition had been floating around the naval base sea of paperwork for a while before being found. Who collected the requested gear remained unknown.

There was an addition to the orders of the Swedish submarine. This wasn't part of the original orders but were added at a later stage. It was unclear when and how they had appeared in the archives, but they were signed off by Commander Löfgren as well. The odd thing was, none of the crew seemed to be aware of the order. The investigators were also looking into another lead. Falk's access card had been used at a time where she was confirmed to be elsewhere. There was no further information regarding who this was, though a few things looked unclear around one Commander Ola Löfgren.

This was terrible news. Rosenfeldt appointed Löfgren and personally vouched for him, telling the defense minister what a good job he'd be doing. If he was somehow involved in this, it would reflect very poorly on Rosenfeldt himself. He would need to set another meeting with the leaders of this investigation. They were externals appointed by Löfgren himself and had no reason to throw this type of information around.

If they were professionals and interested in further work from the military and government, they would most certainly keep this under wraps.

Chapter 27 – Loss of life

Wikström turned left onto the parking lot of the construction site. It was a bit of a walk from there to the storage center, but it was easier to check your surroundings on foot. She had to park halfway up the curb to fit her car in, but it wasn't likely to be a problem tonight. She walked fast down the pathway, carefully looking around. The package she received from Eriksson was tucked under her arm. She would deposit it all there tonight and then figure out how to split the three tapes up.

She planned to take one to another location as soon as she figured out where that would be. Then, a classic trick seen in the movies might be employed. She would package one tape up and hand it to one of her trusted friends, with the instructions to mail it to another location one month later. In the package would be further instructions for the recipient to repackage and forward it again, two months later. That would give her three months to work through this, knowing where the tapes were and that it would be hard to find for anyone looking. The feeling of being followed the other day had, again, turned out to be nothing—but still spooked her into being more cautious.

She would have more work to do tomorrow. Before leaving, she received a phone call from one of Alvar Segerfors' neighbors she spoke to on her last visit to Nynäshamn. The neighbour had seen Alvar come up the stairs to the apartment, but he never stopped to say hello. He just hurried to pull his keys out and get into his apartment. It was odd because he always used to have time to stop and exchange a few words. She promised the neighbor to investigate it. And investigate it she would. She needed to know what happened to him and where he had been.

She made a right onto the small parking lot of the storage facility, walking across it toward the front door. It was closed, but with a main key to the front door and the key for the rented locker, she could come and go as she wished. She quickly unlocked the front door, locked it behind her, and then proceeded into the maze of storage lockers and larger spaces inside. It was an old warehouse building with high ceilings, and her footsteps gave off a ghostly echo as she walked. She ignored the switch for the main lights as there were enough exit lights in there to see anyway. Straight ahead and down aisle A to the right. Locker nineteen.

The locker gave off a light squeak when she opened it. She wasted no time. She checked all the previous materials were in order, put the package on top, and then closed the locker again. After a second of hesitation, she re-opened the locker. All copies in the same place made her paranoid brain uncomfortable. She quickly reached back and took one tape out to put in her pocket. *This one stays with me.*

She walked up aisle A again, but as she turned the last corner, she could hear someone sticking a key in the main door. Instinctively, she doubled back around the corner and stood still to listen. There was a rattling of the lock, but it didn't turn yet. She shivered as she realized what was happening. Whoever was coming through that door didn't have a key. They were picking the lock.

This couldn't be a coincidence. There was no way someone random would rob this place as she was here dropping off the tapes. She pulled her weapon and started to back down through the corridor, looking for another way out.

The lock turned, and she heard the door open. This was definitely no coincidence. She heard at least two people come through the door. Nobody said anything but the noise of fabric rubbing against fabric as they moved was clear.

They also ignored the main switch and kept

moving straight into the warehouse, spreading out through different aisles as they moved. She quickly contemplated going back for the materials but decided against it. It would take too long. There were more than two of them, and from the sound of their movements, they knew what they were doing. They were moving fast, like people do when they know what they are looking for.

Her heart rate spiked, and she felt it pass the point where it would start to be detrimental. Her hands were shaking, and her brain struggled to stay focused and compute the information from her senses.

She had to get her pulse out of the red zone and back to a level where she could still function. Forcing herself to shut her mouth, she inhaled through her nose, held her breath for a few seconds, and then slowly let the air out through her mouth. After another breath, she could feel her heart rate decrease some, and her senses left the brink of panic and returned to her.

Hunched over, she moved as fast as she could across the aisle toward a cross-section. She could hear someone moving parallel to her in another aisle and suspected they could hear her too.

Rather than slowing down at the corner to peek around it, she straightened up and accelerated as much as she could through the last few meters of the aisle. Worst case, they would be armed, but it would be hard for anyone to manage to see her and take aim in the short time she would be visible.

She was right. A shot rang out only a few meters away from her as someone came out the parallel aisle. She didn't feel anything and assumed they missed. There was no time to stop and check.

She kept running for a few meters and then turned a left corner. She was tempted to fire a round blindly behind her to make them slow down, but she chose to keep her weapon as a surprise for them. She stopped briefly and tried to force her heart rate down again to stop shaking.

While she was standing there, a shadow appeared at the corner she had just turned. The figure was tall and no doubt a man. Unfortunately for him, he first checked his right side, which gave her a second to aim before he looked her way.

He spun around with the weapon in front of him. She squeezed the trigger as gently as she could and fired three rounds in quick succession. She had never fired her weapon at a real person before. The sound was muffled and she first doubted whether the weapon actually fired. It became clear to her as the man let out a loud noise and toppled backward out of sight.

She contemplated moving toward him to finish the job but decided not to. There must be three or four of them, and she wouldn't get out of this alive if she tried to stand her ground.

She had to run.

She heard pounding footsteps closing in, drawn by the shots, and she started a flat-out sprint down the side of the building.

A sign came into view, signaling a fire exit. She pushed the handle down and lunged herself at the door, pushing as hard as she could. It opened into the now dark evening sky. The cold April air hit her face as she got out, which helped her to catch a second wind.

If she ran in a straight line, she'd get shot in the back, so she started down the gridiron stairs and decided to drop out of view in the shadows underneath the steps.

Her followers reached the door, and one of them went through it, entirely focused on distances further away. They expected her to run. As he came down the stairs, he came level with her, standing only two or three meters away. She aimed her weapon and fired again. There was no doubt of the effect this time. She hit the man in the back of the head, and he collapsed straight ahead without making a sound. Guessing that there was at least one more by the door, she started running through the shadows alongside the wall.

She saw a head popping out from the doorway behind her, and she fired a shot blindly behind her. The head disappeared again. A second later, the man slung a weapon around the corner and fired a long burst her way. None of the rounds came particularly close, and she turned the corner of the big building and continued into the woods.

She threw all her keys away as she started to run toward the trees. Even if they managed to catch her, they would not have any help to find her locker.

She made it thirty meters into the woods before she had to stop. Her lungs felt ready to explode, and she could feel the content of her stomach rising. Her old ankle injury made itself known, but it wasn't too bad. She could ignore it for a while.

With barely enough time to lean over, she vomited behind a tree. She'd been in a lot of violent situations, but she never killed anyone before.

Struggling for air, she walked a few steps before managing to run again. Her sense of direction was compromised. She was unsure where to go, but there was no choice but to continue running away from what just happened.

She would have to get to Nylund and warn him. Or maybe he was too high profile of a target. Whoever sent the submarine into Swedish waters probably didn't want the mess of a missing admiral right now. She, on the other hand, was a nobody. Someone easy to get rid of with very few questions asked.

She heard another shot ring out. It was a rifle this time. Significantly more powerful than the handguns she saw them carry inside.

She didn't feel anything, but as she put her left leg in front to take the next step, it buckled under her weight. She tried to reach out for something to hold onto, but her hands found nothing, and she landed flat on her chest and face.

Turning over and looking down at herself, she could see she had been hit. The inside of her left thigh was in pieces and bleeding profusely, pumping out more blood with every beat of her heart. She knew this would be it. If she didn't get help immediately, she would bleed out.

With no pain reaching her brain yet, she propped herself up on one elbow and tried to see if anyone was coming her way. Her other hand was looking on the ground for her weapon. It was all dark now, and she could barely make out the trees closest to her.

A second shot rang out, and she felt a thud as the round hit her in the chest. As she lay flat on her back, for a second, she could sense the treetops swaying above, and she could hear the followers closing in. Frida Wikström could then no longer resist the urge to close her eyes.

Chapter 28 – Aftermath

Unknown Location, April 24th, 0700hrs

There's news," the man on the other side told her without any introductions. After a second, she recognized his voice as the second team leader looking for the tape.

"I'm listening."

"I was going to call you to tell you that a conscript found the tape among the personal gear and handed it to a captain named Rolf Eriksson. He apparently visited the sound analysis center at Berga. The person working there remembered him, as captain Eriksson hasn't been there in years. They didn't see what he was doing, but they definitely have the equipment to make copies in there."

She hit her fist on the desk in front of her. Damn, several copies of the tape would make this much harder to contain. But this would mean the poor enlisted man they tortured probably was telling the truth the first time around. He did have the tape among his personal gear. *Poor guy*, she thought, without a hint of any actual remorse.

"You said you were going to tell me that, so what are you really telling me now?"

"We just got word from our team following up on Nylund's associate. Apparently, she spoke to witnesses of the submarine sightings. She identified herself as a police officer under the name of Maria Wennergren. They found a self-storage facility under this name and intercepted her there at eight-thirty last night. The team has searched the whole place, and it looks like they have found most of the materials. We only have two problems."

"And what would those be?"

"She was armed. We got one man dead and a second one injured. He will be okay, but major cleanup operations were undertaken through the night to remove all traces of the gunfight. It should look like a break-in now."

"And what about her? They didn't let her get away, did they?"

"No, they shot her. She's dead. They've moved her to a different location where she won't be found anytime soon."

"Okay, I trust they can handle that. What is the second problem?"

"They have found three plastic casings but only two tapes. One in the locker, one in her pocket. One case is empty. We don't know whether it ever had a tape in it, of course, but we assume it did. Also, the tapes have notes attached about what it is, so someone has been listening to them."

"And her car?"

"She arrived on foot."

"On foot, no way. She must have had a vehicle to take her there."

"Yes, maybe, but the search and the cleanup have taken all night. She didn't have any car keys, and we didn't have the manpower to search any larger areas."

She took a deep breath while thinking through what they just told her, "Well, there is a third problem then. If you've shot a police officer, there will be hell to pay. Any police force in the world will pull all stops in an investigation to find a cop killer."

"Well, there's nobody named Maria Wennergren on the force, at least not that we can find. She could be an ex-police officer. We'll find out, but I doubt she was active."

"And the cleanup is good?"

"They're ensuring me it is as good as it can get, and it will likely be seen as a simple break-in."

* * *

Stockholm, April 24th, 0830hrs

Jesper Bergman hung up the phone. He wasn't keen on traveling to the office on a Saturday, but his day just got more interesting. He was unsure what was going on and why someone would have picked him, but his curiosity wouldn't let him ignore it.

The voice on the other side, a man speaking British English, had told him there was an ongoing debate within the Navy on the submarine's nationality. Maybe it wasn't a Soviet submarine after all. Bergman was intrigued, but as with all information that landed on his desk, he would need some proof this was at least sound speculation and not someone playing him for a fool.

He had demanded proof this was ongoing, and the voice calmly explained to him there would be a courier at the front desk in about one to two hours. He would get his evidence this wasn't as clean-cut of a case as per the first glance.

Bergman thanked himself for being cautious from the start, calling it a possible Soviet submarine. Now he could bring new information on this without sounding like he was misinformed the first time. *This is potentially good stuff*, he thought. If this person calling him could deliver on the promise, he was set up for another few days on the first page. He had tried to place the accent of the man who called. It was clearly British but with an undertone of something. South African, perhaps?

* * *

Stockholm, April 4th, 1300hrs

Having passed the front desk on the way back from lunch, Bergman was handed a package that just arrived. He used all his willpower not to sprint back to his office. While running and pushing people aside in his mind, in real life he walked at a regular pace, acting as if there was nothing particular going on in his life.

Getting into his office, however, he did get a bit too excited and slammed the door with a loud bang. He offered a gesture of excuse to his colleagues through the internal window before sitting down.

The package contained a report from the Royal Swedish Navy. High level of confidentiality. That meant seventy years of confidentiality before it could be released. *This must be good*, he thought. Looking through the pages, he could first see a page with a sketch of a submarine on it. This wasn't the same sketch he had seen before but a much more detailed one.

There was no misunderstanding that this was a submarine, and a trained eye might even be able to determine what type. There were a few handwritten notes under the sketch. They pointed out the shape of the hull and the rounding of the conning tower. In the end, there was a comment that said: Type 206? Then a simple signature. *I'll be damned*, Bergman thought. That is signed by Klas

Nylund, the Navy chief. But what the hell is a Type 206?

He skimmed the report to see if he could find any info on the 206. A few pages later, he found it. The text stated how this couldn't be seen as a West German Type 206 submarine but almost certainly was a Soviet Whiskey-class boat.

West Germany. Bergman dropped the report on his desk. West Germany. That was NATO, which would mean that . . . He paused his thought. What would that mean? Would the Navy not be notified if a NATO submarine was operating in Swedish waters? Sweden was no member of NATO, but it was basically common knowledge that the Swedish military was NATO-friendly. The Socialists might throw a spanner in the works on if they were re-elected, but that was a problem for later this year.

Nylund supposedly was no expert on submarines, and his point of view had been well and truly shredded by the analysis group. It would be enough to write a piece about different points of view within the Navy. To throw some light on the apparent disagreement would be enough to start asking some very senior people some very uncomfortable questions.

* * *

Rosenbad, April 24th, 1700hrs

"Damn that guy. Who provided him this information?"

Nordin was furious after seeing what was printed in the evening press. There was official doubt about this being a Soviet submarine. "What's the status on cleaning up the damn archives and making sure this stays what we said it is?"

Rosenfeldt brought his face out of his hands and sat up straight. "It has progressed well, as far as I know. I'll get Löfgren to report in tomorrow and verify this. You know he has taken your whatever-it-takes orders a bit too literally for my liking, but I think he has done a good job."

"A good job? You call this a good job? If he'd done a good job, there wouldn't be doubt on the first page of the damn paper. This is a disaster. The Navy is leaking like a rusty sieve, and these are theories from the head of the damn thing."

"Well, the Navy analysis group pushed back on it with all its might."

"Yes, that's great, but it also makes the Navy look like a fucking circus. The head of it thinks one thing, and his staff thinks another. Then, this information somehow finds its way to a reporter. We look as incompetent as ever, which makes us all look bad, including the supreme commander. Just to be clear, that's you."

"What are you saying?"

"I'm saying that we'll call a press conference and deny this. You will get Nylund up there, and he'll tell the world that this was an off-the-cuff and ill-thought-through comment when he was tired. It was never meant to be seen as a formal opinion. He will confirm the submarine is Soviet or that will be the end of him."

"And if it doesn't work?"

"Your Löfgren will have to make sure there is not a shred of evidence anywhere to prove us wrong. If you can't do that, the military has failed to do its damn job, and this will be your fault. And I don't mean your fault as in the military. I mean, your fault, personally. Make this go away."

* * *

Military Headquarters, April 25th, 0930hrs

Löfgren sat in the office of the supreme commander again. He had just been listening to Rosenfeldt having a long monolog about how they had agreed there was one source of truth and how this needed to stay a Soviet submarine at all costs. There was doubt being printed in the paper, and people's opinions could follow soon.

"You see what I mean, Löfgren. This has to be tidied up right now."

Löfgren shifted in his seat but kept relaxed. He was starting to warm up to the presence of the supreme commander and felt comfortable being chewed out. The man wasn't that bad; he was just under a lot of pressure and found it hard to cope. He should have stayed a tank commander. Apparently, he was good at that.

"General, trust me when I say that all is under control."

"You call this under control?" Rosenfeldt pointed to the issue of the evening press that was in front of him on the table.

"General, first of all, let me point out that there is no evidence at all that this isn't a Soviet submarine. They are indications at best, and why would the Navy not be able to have an internal discussion about the nationality? Nylund had a theory, and it got put down. That's the end of that."

"So, where are the items now?"

"No disrespect, General, but it's probably better if you don't know. In addition to our own archive, Nylund was indeed conducting his own investigation on the side and had some copies of materials in his possession. These have been removed."

"Didn't you say he probably had an associate as well?"

"Well, yes, but she has been removed as well."

"Removed?" The skepticism on Rosenfeldt's face was unmistakable.

Löfgren was unsure how straightforward he could be with Rosenfeldt. For looking like a brutal platoon commander, he didn't have the stomach for this type of intelligence work that, let's say, bent the law a bit to get results.

"I think it would be better if you didn't know that either, General."

Rosenfeldt gave Löfgren a stern look and for a moment looked like he would launch himself across the desk before he settled for shouting.

"Why don't you let me be the judge of that. You will tell me what the hell is going on, Commander, and you will tell me now. I said nobody gets hurt. So, why do I get the feeling that this is what has just happened?"

"She got shot in an altercation," Löfgren said curtly.

The supreme commander fell back in his chair with his mouth open in surprise.

"What? Was she Swedish? You're not telling me you've fucking shot a Swedish civilian, are you?"

"She was armed, which wasn't expected, and there was an exchange of gunfire. She was killed. It's unfortunate, but we can't undo it."

"Are these the contractors you were talking about? They're not simply interrogators who were supposed to debrief the crew and talk to some people. What are they? Mercenaries? Have you gone completely insane?"

This was about all that Löfgren was willing to tolerate. He stood up and put both of his fists down on the General's desk. "I didn't create this mess. You did. I'm just the poor bastard who has to clean up your shit for you. The defense minister told us to do whatever it takes, and we've done just that. Unfortunately, it ended this way for Nylund's associate, but we secured the information we needed. If you get Nylund on the record denying his comments about West Germany, your hands are clean, General. So are Nordin's. Isn't that what you wanted?"

* * *

Military Headquarters, April 25th, 1200hrs

Rosenfeldt had now spoken several times to the female interrogator. That was still what he called her, though he was now aware she had a far more significant role. She was more of a relationship manager for whatever outfit she was running. They weren't exactly listed on the yellow pages.

He was meant to get an update from her in a few minutes to see where this was going. He would have to decide what to do with Nylund, Löfgren, and this whole damn situation. His phone rang, and he picked it up.

"General, it's me."

"Yes, so what do you have for me?" *Whoever you are*, he thought. He wasn't quite as old as Nylund, but he was also brought up in an era where you saw the enemy and fought them with conventional weapons. Dealing with unknown external contractors who had the reach to investigate things in all corners of the military made him very uncomfortable.

"I got two different things, General. First, we have sent all of the submarine crew home. There are two of them that took a bit of work. The sonar chief and one of the enlisted petty officers."

"And by work, you mean what?"

"By work, I mean we had to talk to them for a bit longer." She clearly wasn't happy being interrupted with questions he should know better than to ask.

"They're okay and on their way home. They've been decorated, paid off, and have signed non-disclosure agreements that could have them for treason if they ever breathe a word of this to anyone. Needless to say, this is no guarantee. These agreements have failed before."

"When would they have failed before?"

"Well, let's say that people with combat stress who are unable to talk about things sometimes end of on the wrong side of drugs and alcohol. Then depression, then despair, and then whatever agreement they have signed means nothing to them. The usual."

The usual? Who was this woman? She was talking about this like an accountant talking about money. Rosenfeldt did sense her professionalism, which convinced him the best way out of this mess would be to follow her recommendations.

"What are you suggesting?"

"Depending on how important this secret is to you. I don't think they bought the Soviet thing completely, so personally, I would suggest we tag them for follow-up."

"Meaning?"

"Meaning the most important people, like the sonar crew, would have unfortunate accidents in say a year from now when this has blown over, and there is less risk of connection between events."

Rosenfeldt looked at the phone in his hand with surprise on his face. Did this woman seriously suggest they would simply murder Swedish sailors to keep this quiet? This was getting further and further away from engaging enemy tanks on the battlefield. He had slowly gotten used to the everyday politics that surrounded his job. He still didn't like it and sometimes struggled with it, but he could usually justify to himself what he was doing at the end of the day.

What they were now talking about would mean crossing a different line, one where there was no way back. First, these people had shot what he figured was a Swedish investigator, and now they were willing to follow up with the organized murder of more people who were simply drafted in service of their country. This was all insane. He clenched his jaw in an attempt to not say anything while forcing his brain to slow down.

"Let me think about that. What was the second thing you wanted me to know?"

"Yes, we need to talk about my employer, Commander Löfgren. Mrs. Falk's access card was on her desk while she was observed having lunch in the canteen. There is a partial print on it that doesn't belong to her. It belongs to commander Löfgren. I think it's safe to say that he had something to do with this all, even without being sure exactly how or why yet. I would distance myself from him if I were you. Personally, I would attach as many of the problems as possible to him and then sacrifice him. But that's just me."

Yes, that is you, Rosenfeldt thought. However, this time, he could see her point clearly. He was not concerned about Löfgren. He was highly effective but a snake who cared more about his career than the people serving around him. If he had to go down, Rosenfeldt could live with it. "What are you people doing now?"

"We're backtracking Löfgren's movements over the last couple of weeks. We know he has met someone that's still unidentified. It could be nothing at all but we don't know yet. Other than that, we're cleaning up and getting ready to close up shop."

"And the shooting?"

"What shooting?" Her neutral voice signaled she knew precisely what he was talking about.

"Löfgren said you had shot someone who was working with Nylund."

"Yes, that was unfortunate. She was armed and took us by surprise. That's all cleared up already."

Cleared up. He guessed that was code for; this would never be a problem again.

Of course, it wasn't completely accurate that Wikström had taken them by surprise. They would have preferred to take her alive. Unfortunately, one of the men had seen her dash through the building and instinctively squeezed off a round. Once she had fired back and managed to leave the building, the senior operative on-site simply decided to shoot her. It was the next best outcome.

Chapter 29 – Escape

Military Headquarters, April 25th, 1500hrs

So, how to play this now? After the phone call with that dreadful woman, Rosenfeldt was in his office alone, trying to think through how to solve the Soviet submarine crisis. At the same time, he needed to avoid taking the blame for appointing Löfgren. *We get Nylund to deny the whole 206 debacle to the press; then, we push him aside and retire him in due course.*

The man will look good as a four-star admiral. Weathered face, grey eminence. We can parade him around a bit. Then he can sail away over the horizon, read bedtime stories to his grandchildren or something if he had any. Nordin wouldn't have anything against that.

Löfgren had done a phenomenal job in cleaning up the archives and found every piece of evidence. Hence, Rosenfeldt's recommendation had worked out well. The fact that some disturbing other things had come up was only convenient at this time as they would be able to really push Löfgren if needed.

If he had something to do with the tapes and falsifying submarine orders, they would be able to hold a treason charge over his head if there was trouble. Even cleaning up the archives could be held over him, as there was no written record of that order from either him or Nordin. They could make it look like Löfgren did it on his own accord, and that would make a case for treason even more likely. Maybe he should just make it happen. Like a pre-emptive strike.

He picked up the phone and dialed Nordin directly.

"Yes."

"It's me. Just wanted to confirm something with you before I act on it."

"Shoot."

"We'll get Nylund on the podium and take back his whole 206 thing. Then, he can praise his analysis group and the great work they are doing. After that, I'll gag him before I promote him for his great service to our country, finding the Soviet submarine, and chasing it off. In a few months when things have settled, we retire him and sort a replacement."

"I like it."

"Then we have to do something about Löfgren. I know I brought him forward, but there are some disturbing indications he might have had something to do with this whole thing."

"What? Löfgren has?"

"Some indications in him signing off the equipment for the crew that stole the tapes, and he has put forged order data in the archive for the submarine. It's not completely solid yet, but it's being worked on."

"Worked on by whom?"

"Best not to know the details, but let's say Löfgren brought some contractors on board. Highly effective people that found this on their own employer. I have been speaking with them directly."

"What do you suggest?"

"Give me some time to verify a few things, but I would think we arrest him on espionage. Then, we lock him up and use him as an excuse for why certain things have not worked as well as they should have. They're backtracking his steps, and it seems he has been meeting with a man yet to be identified. We can float some ideas about this to the press to get some strength to the story."

"Yes, yes, I like it." Nordin picked up Rosenfeldt's thoughts and continued. "I can follow up and blame the Socialists for cutting funds to the military, leaving us all in this unfortunate mess. With a well-functioning and funded Navy, this would never have happened. All that. This should improve our chances in the election, and if it fails anyway, a wedge between Sweden and the Soviet Union would be a great welcome gift to the new government."

"Yes, and there's another thing. Löfgren's contractor crew shot and killed a Swedish citizen working with Nylund on an investigation."

The line went silent. Rosenfeldt held his breath for a moment, awaiting the defense minister's reaction.

"Does Nylund know?"

"Well, he'll suspect that something has happened, but there is no evidence."

"Well, shit. Make sure you gag him good. And keep the telephone number for the outfit taking care of this. If all else fails, maybe we can get them to shoot the new prime minister as well." Nordin laughed heartily over the secure phone line.

* * *

Military Headquarters, April 25th, 1630hrs

"It's pretty simple, Klasse. You get on the podium, you tell the world your comment on this being a West German submarine was a premature thought that should have been erased. Then, you take your next star as proof of your service to your country before you shut up about all of this until you end your days."

"So promoted into retirement and gagged then?"

"Yes, something like that. I'm not concerned

with the semantics of it. The comment about the 206 must be a write-off in the view of the public. Then, we'll organize one hell of a promotion party for you. The admiral that found and chased away the Soviets from our Swedish waters. Again. First *U-137*, and now this. The admiral that got a rarely seen budget increase for the Navy. Your Navy, Klasse. Your Navy will be stronger when you leave it than when you arrived, and it will keep getting stronger for years. Besides, a fourth star will look good on you."

"So, that's it then. An official story to please the politicians. Damn Fredrik, you can tell as well as I it looks like a 206."

"I can read a report of your beloved analysis group claiming this is a Soviet submarine and that you're on a wild goose chase. These are your experts, Klasse, telling us this is a Soviet submarine."

Nylund sat quietly for a while. His Navy. His Navy would be stronger than ever if the budget increases came through. Was that not his job? To build and maintain a strong and effective Navy, even if he wasn't the one at the helm anymore? He'd have to sign some paperwork. That was for sure. They wouldn't let him off with swearing on his mother's grave.

"So, when do I retire, and who will take my place?"

"That will be decided at a later stage—a few months maybe. Whenever it can be done without too much of a fuss. But don't misunderstand me. You are the figurehead of the Navy. I will appoint a successor soon who will trail your every step. I don't want one decision out of you without them knowing. You got me?"

"What if I say no? You can't make me shut up, Fredrik."

The supreme commander sighed. "Well, yes, we can."

Nylund looked up and was met with nothing but a blank stare from General Fredrik Rosenfeldt.

* * *

Nylund's House, April 25th, 1830hrs

There was someone at the door. Not many people visited him these days. The social events had been Christina's area, and he had ignored all of that since she left. Through the frosted glass in the front door, he could see two dark shapes. One of the shapes pressed the doorbell again. Nylund walked over and opened the door to find himself face to face with two uniformed police officers.

"Admiral Klas Nylund?"

"Yes."

"We're investigating a break-in and would just like to ask you a few questions. May we come in for a minute?"

Nylund held the door open for the men, who entered, carefully cleaned their shoes on the mat, and then walked straight toward the kitchen table. They politely waited until Nylund motioned for them to sit down.

One of the officers pulled out a few pieces of paper from his pocket and put them on the table in front of him.

The police officer gave him a brief rundown of why they were there. A break-in at a self-storage facility. Someone had searched through a large share of the lockers and storage units. It was hard to tell how much was missing, as only the customers themselves would know what was there to begin with. The police officer deemed it unlikely they would ever be able to assess the losses in full. People often didn't want to tell the police what they kept locked up far away from their homes.

Through the morning, they had received another call from a construction site down the road from the storage facility. Someone had parked a car that partially blocked the entrance to the site, and the construction crew called it in to get it removed.

"This is the thing," the officer started. "Most of the day yesterday was spent sifting through the owners of the storage units. One of them looks like this."

He put a piece of paper in front of Nylund.

"Police ID under the name of Maria Wennergren. She's rented storage locker A-19 since quite a while back. That's a copy of her ID. Do you recognize this woman?"

Alarm bells had been ringing in Nylund's head since he heard the word storage facility. She had talked about this for whatever copies they could get their hands on. Was this where she took the tapes from Eriksson as well?

There wouldn't be much merit in lying. If they hadn't figured it out by now, they probably would over the next few days. Nylund had started the investigation under the radar for the Navy, but hiring a private investigator wasn't illegal as such. Using a fake police ID probably was, but that was her doing, not his.

"I recognize the photograph but not the name."

"Funny that you should mention that. The car that was parked about a kilometer down the road. We checked the ownership and this is the owner of that car." He put the second piece of paper on the table. It was a dark copy of a driver's license.

"Frida Maria Wikström. As you can see, the pictures are almost identical."

"She hasn't called many people from her home phone, it seems, but your number was one of them. Hence, we wanted to check what your relationship with Frida Wikström is. We assume that's her real name since there is no Maria Wennergren on the police force."

Nylund moved in his seat. He was tempted to say he barely knew her and how he knew nothing about this. Whatever would make them leave. Again, he got to the conclusion they would probably figure things out soon enough, and if it was evident he had been lying, they would be back.

"Well, you may have seen the news on the sighting of a foreign submarine in Danziger Gatt?"

Both officers nodded.

"I hired Frida Wikström to talk to the witnesses—the people that claimed to have seen the submarine. We get a lot of sightings every year turning out to be floating logs and other garbage. This one seemed legit, but I wanted a second opinion about whether the witnesses were reliable and how sure they were on what they saw that day."

"And she did this for you?"

"Yes, she talked to all the witnesses and provided me an assessment of their reliability. Needless to say, she figured they were trustworthy. At least most of them."

"Can we see her assessment?"

"That's part of a naval investigation and confidential. I'm sorry."

It wasn't part of a naval investigation at all. He didn't actually know where the materials were, but he thought he sounded official enough for the police officers to believe him.

"Okay, when did you last see Frida Wikström?"

"I don't know, a week ago maybe. She did the thing, and then I'm not sure where she went. I'm afraid I don't know much that I think could be of any help."

"And you wouldn't know where she is now, would you? As you can imagine, we would really want to speak to her about what her car was doing close to the scene of the break-in."

"Yes, I understand. Unfortunately, I don't know where she is. I'm sorry."

That was the truth, at least. Nylund had no idea where Wikström was, and the lump of ice in his stomach grew minute by minute because of it. Hopefully, the officers would leave soon, before he could no longer suppress the panic he was feeling.

"Okay, if you hear anything from her or you come to think of anything else. Please call the police at this number." The officer left a small card on the table.

"No problem. I will."

Leave now, damn it. Just leave now.

The officers left, and Nylund closed the door behind them. He was left leaning on the door frame with a growing sense of panic. That must be the place where she was storing the evidence. This had to be connected. No way that place would have been robbed while her car was parked nearby. Where was she?

He ran up the stairs and dug around for her number. He picked up the phone and dialed, his brain in a haze. She was gone, and it was at least partially his fault. What if the worst had happened?

No, no. That would be too much. There was some pressure from the Navy and politicians to keep this a Soviet submarine and bury the other evidence. But the Swedish government would never murder anyone, would they? That wasn't how a country like Sweden operated. On the other hand, he had seen the stare of the supreme commander. He knew something. He must know something.

* * *

Nylund's House, April 25th, 2100hrs

He had wanted to call Wikström, but he realized they would still check her phone records. He didn't dare to take the risk. The feeling of not knowing was unbearable. Not being able to even attempt to find an answer was worse. All he could do was pace back and forth and do nothing.

The police called it a break-in but mentioned nothing about a fight or any other trouble. What if she was there while these people showed up? She wouldn't just roll over for them. That wasn't her style. Nylund knew about the injuries she had sustained in the line of duty. She had been beaten up by a drug addict at one point, broken bones in her face. It probably would have been worse if it wasn't for her colleague, who caught up with them and, let's say, dealt with the threat.

The colleague got suspended while she got a fractured face. Only shortly after this, she was pushed down the stairs in an apartment block while trying to talk to a witness. She never complained, but he knew her ankle still gave her trouble sometimes. No, she wouldn't have gone down without a fight.

If this was all connected to their investigation and the submarine sighting, maybe he should just get on the podium tomorrow and speak his mind. The damn thing looked like a 206. A West German boat in the Swedish archipelago. He had no illusions about NATO or the Soviet Union. They had undoubtedly both been sniffing around in Swedish waters. But this time was different. This time, they had shot at the Swedish Navy and, even if they missed, it was unacceptable to sweep something like this away.

Retirement and a fourth star meant nothing to him. A stronger Navy, better equipped to fulfill its mission. That was something.

* * *

Rosenbad, April 26th, 1000hrs

Nine days after the first press conference, it was time for the next one. This was a larger arena and held hundreds of journalists from all over the world. Thomas Nordin was cementing the view with the foreign press and Swedish public that this was the intrusion of a Soviet submarine.

Referring to open communications within NATO and an archive with clear evidence the Soviet Union was behind this, Nordin hammered home his message of socialist budget cuts leading to a weak defense capability and how this would need to change. The eastern threat was real.

Nylund looked at the crowd. The flashes from their cameras blinded him, and while he maintained a straight face to the outside world, his feelings were eating him up inside. A lot of the evidence they had collected was gone, and so was Wikström. His genuine opinion of the sketch he had seen was that it was a West German submarine. However, it was also true that the man on the podium would stand up for a stronger Navy and a more robust military, while the opposing socialists would prefer to dismantle them even further.

The questions he had been waiting for eventually hit Nordin. Was it not true what Bergman at the *Evening Press* had reported about? There were doubts within the Navy. Was it not true that the man next to him on stage, the Navy chief himself, pointed to this as a NATO vessel? Nordin assured them that this was not the case, then took one step aside and gestured for Nylund to take the podium.

Camera flashes intensified as he walked from his place on the stage and over to the podium. It didn't show to the crowd, but they were among the heaviest steps Admiral Klas Nylund had walked in his life.

"Admiral Nylund, Admiral Nylund. Isn't it true that you considered the intruder to be a NATO vessel?"

With a grim face, he looked at them across the set of microphones. "The Navy has gone through great lengths to analyze this intrusion. There was indeed a sketch which showed some similarities with a non-Soviet vessel at first glance. I did make a few notes around this, but they were never meant to be seen as a formal opinion. They were simply ideas that the Navy analysis group would have to look into. The Navy analysis group contains the best minds in the sound analysis and naval warfare industry. After reviewing the sketch and the other materials, their conclusion is that the intrusion into Swedish waters was conducted by a Soviet vessel."

Nylund turned on his heel and walked back to his place. At the same time, Nordin was quick to take up the position in the limelight and continue his barrage of the Socialists, the party that had undoubtedly weakened the Swedish military's ability to defend them against the Eastern threat.

* * *

Muskö Naval Base, April 26th, 1200hrs

What a damn mess this had become. It was supposed to be a simple sighting of a suspected Soviet submarine, and because her teenage kids never shut up, it had almost cost the lives of an entire Swedish submarine crew. Eivor Falk was walking back to her seat after passing the operations office again.

It was full of people, and she had no chance of walking in there and digging through the logbooks without being noticed. She would give it another half-hour and then try again.

After the interrogation by this overly friendly woman, she had been left to go back to work as usual. But that might not last for long. She planted enough information with them to chase Löfgren for a while, but with some careful analysis, they might see through it. Löfgren was a useful idiot whose only job had been to make sure the Swedish Navy and government were painfully aware of the sighting. That was all.

Her job had been to get the Swedish submarine out of the way. It was assigned to patrol just across the planned exit route after the operation was already underway. *Amateurs*, she thought. It would, of course, have been much easier to give the intruding submarine a new exit route, but they wanted no transmissions in the air that could be used as proof later. It was supposed to be a suspected Soviet submarine, not a proven one.

On the other hand, who am I to accuse them of being amateurs? she thought. She had made some notes as she received the orders, but her kids were fighting like there was no tomorrow while she was working. She had thought they would stop that once they reached mid-teens, but the arguments only seemed to intensify. What they argued about when they were toddlers now seemed insignificant.

Either way, they distracted her, and she had messed up which patrolling area the submarine was in with the one it was supposed to be in. Once she managed to forge orders to get it moved, she second-guessed herself and recalled it to the original square. Whenever they started to investigate the logs of the naval base, this would stick out like a sore thumb. She did not have much respect for military intelligence, but if they got enough time to dig through this, they might find that the orders hadn't been through the normal process and how Löfgren had nothing to do with it.

Could they work out it was her? With a bit of time and investigating, yes, they probably could.

The pages in the base logbook would have to go. The less they had to work with and the more confusion, the better.

It helped to be a woman in her line of work. Surrounded by seemingly powerful men, too busy playing war to look twice at the woman sorting the paperwork. Such idiots. It would take them another decade to realize that wars were no longer fought with guns and powder. They were fought with information. Whoever could get the best information, or get the enemy to believe the worst information, would win. Women, possibly less able to carry heavy weapons, were just as well-equipped to fight this new type of war. Not to mention probably born with better skills in deception. She laughed internally at her own thought.

She had to disappear after this. She had gotten away with a lot, but as she looked at the men working around her as idiots, an uneasy feeling started to spread through her body. *You are being arrogant now*, she thought. *And when you become an arrogant spy, you become a captured spy.*

Sweden wouldn't likely hurt her if she was caught. Stig Bergling, who was caught just a few years earlier, was sentenced to life in prison but was allowed conjugal visits for crying out loud. He had been a long-time spy for the Soviet Union and would probably still be out of prison in ten to fifteen years. She wondered what her husband would make of conjugal visits for a decade. They could probably both live with that, but she wouldn't manage to be away from her children for that time.

It seemed a long time ago now, but as a younger woman with younger children and a husband still finalizing his studies, she saw it as more of a game to pass on the occasional note with information to her case officer. The Navy didn't pay her well, and she figured it was harmless to write up a few minor pieces of information to hand to her contact.

She was just being tested, of course. She realized that later. The requests became just slightly more prominent every time, and as she had wanted to stop, they just tightened their grip on her. She was caught up in it and there was no way out. She had panicked but somehow refrained from doing anything stupid. After a few more years, she was used to it but also wise enough to work on her own exit plan, should this day ever come.

For now, there was no other option. She had been paid very well for her services during the last couple of years. The pages in the logbook would have to go to leave no written mark of this, and then it was time to pull the plug and execute her exit plan. Telling her husband would be risky, but she could make it work.

* * *

Muskö Naval Base, April 26th, 1400hrs

It was time. They were changing watch in the operations office, and quite a few people were moving in and out while talking about work and random private matters. For all the rigor that went into relieving the watch on board the Navy ships, it was amazing that the main operations office was this relaxed.

They were mainly concerned with strategy and placing the right naval unit in the right patrolling area, and had very little to do with split-second decisions. However, every order usually came through here, and every communication with the Navy ships was logged. The logbook from the 11th to 16th of April was recent enough to still be in here next to the ones that were currently in use.

She brought some papers with her as a made-up reason to be there and flipped through them while quickly walking through the door.

"Falk."

She froze in her tracks, slowly looking up at one of the commanders with her best look of innocence.

"Yes, Commander."

"The new watch is coming on—change of watch, you know. Would you mind grabbing a new coffee pot from the canteen and bringing it over?"

Another self-important idiot thinking his job is more important than it is, she thought. I've been working here for a decade. *I know what a watch change is. I also understand that a real operations officer wouldn't allow me to be in here at all, Commander.* "Yes, of course. Right away," she answered him with a smile. "Just give me five minutes to sort this out," she waved her papers in the air.

The commander went back to reviewing a document with another officer.

A thank you wouldn't hurt either, she thought as she steered her steps toward the big desk in the corner of the room next to the communications station. She put the papers down on the desk and pretended to sort them for a few seconds as she was trying to find the correct logbook in the pile on the desk.

There it was, 11th April 1982 to 16th April 1982. That would have both change orders in it. Rather than trying to hide what she was doing, which would look odd if anyone bothered to look her way, she flicked the book wide open on the table. She went through the pages and pretended to be comparing them to the papers she had brought, running her finger down both of them. *There it is.* The change of operational area for the submarine, along with the supporting order that was used as a basis for the message. The supporting order she had forged and walked into this very room with, without these morons noticing.

Her hands were shaking now, and she didn't dare to look around in case she would catch someone's eye. It was probably in her head, but she had a feeling anyone looking her in the eye would see how nervous she was. The background noise in the room was still high but would die down soon as the relieved watch left. She would have to act now.

Quickly, she coughed and ripped the entire page out of the book. Out of the corner of her eye, she could see the signal officer look over his shoulder briefly, but he never turned around. She turned a few more pages and found the reversal of the first order.

The signal officer had now sat down next to her, and it would be hard to cover this with another cough. She threw a couple of her pages on the floor next to him. He caught it out of the corner of his eye, and as he pulled his chair back to get up and help her, she quickly turned and pulled the second page.

"Oh, I'm so sorry, lieutenant."

"No problem, here you go."

She smiled at the lieutenant and grabbed the papers out of his hand. Quickly, she spun around, stacked all papers in one pile, and put the logbook back where it belonged. Trying her best to look normal, which was difficult with her pulse throbbing through her temples, she started to walk back through the room. Once at the door, she turned around.

"I'll get you that coffee now, Commander."

The commander didn't look up from what he was doing, and she just turned and left the room.

Outside, she had to force herself to walk slowly. *Stay calm now. Stay calm. The worst is done. Just do not mess this up by trying to run from the base and raise any suspicion.* She looked at her watch. About three hours left of her day. Those three hours would be among the longest in her life.

Chapter 30 – Blame

Berga Naval Base, April 27ᵗʰ, 1000hrs

L indberg was walking along the almost infinite benchtop at the storage facility of Berga Naval base. He was wearing civilian clothing and all his military gear was packed in two big Navy canvas bags. On arrival at the storage facility, he dumped all the content in what looked like a supermarket shopping cart. He started the long process of walking along the facility and returning the right gear to the right station.

He wasn't sure what to feel in this situation. The ordeal of the encounter at sea had been dreadful but not as rough as the treatment he was put through afterward. Once he was able to sleep better and was back to some level or normal function, he could follow how the military needed to know what had happened out there. To push their own people through what they called debriefing and what a war crime court would call torture had still been unexpected.

As soon as they closed the debriefing and that awful lady left, everyone changed their demeanor entirely. They all took good care of him through the next couple of days he spent in that place, wherever that place was.

Yesterday back at Berga, there had even been a small ceremony at Berga Castle. He was told to put on his dress uniform, simply referred to as the Donald Duck uniform in the Swedish Navy, and he was escorted to the castle in the early afternoon. Once there, he received a decoration directly from the supreme commander of the Swedish Armed Forces, Fredrik Rosenfeldt. He had pinned it to Lindberg's uniform and assured him he had served his country well.

After the ceremony, which lifted his spirits some, came the more serious formalities of exit. Given combat stress and the tough debriefing that followed, he was entitled to compensation from the Navy, which they would deposit to his regular account with his final Navy pay. The piece of paper he signed said one hundred thousand crowns. This was a minor fortune for Lindberg and would make for a good start in civilian life. They also agreed to cut his service short. He still had almost nine months to serve but was told he could return his gear and leave immediately. The catch that made him shiver was the non-disclosure agreement he had to sign before they were done.

He would never speak to anyone about this. What he had seen or heard at sea or what had happened to him afterward would never be talked about with anyone, anywhere. Breaking this would be treated as treason and was punishable by life imprisonment. The very idea of this scared the hell out of him, but as he walked up toward the storage facility, with the sun on his face, things started to look a lot better.

He would walk out the gates a rich man, at least by his standards. He would be able to start life after service and see where it took him. He knew it would take him home to Jenny first. He had been away for a long time, and it wasn't like they were in a stable relationship, but he hoped they would be able to pick this up where they left off in some way. A trip, maybe.

Lindberg continued along the line and threw his gear across the bench as he went on. Socks, shirts, shoes, rain gear. All went into different buckets on the other side. The staff was lazily observing him as he walked around, apparently not being very concerned whether he returned it all or if he had happened to keep some stuff in his civilian bag left outside on the ground.

He thought about Sandberg and wondered whether he was put through a similar treatment because of his involvement in the encounter and the attempts they made to analyze it afterward.

It still wasn't clear to Lindberg. It could be a Soviet submarine, but not even Sandberg had been able to tell for sure.

End of the line. He chucked his Donald Duck shirt into the bin and parked the cart on the side. Because he was exiting the military outside the regular rhythm, the storage building was almost empty. Not like when he started and hundreds of recruits were handed their gear on the same day.

As he walked down the hill, past the exercise field and the canteen on his left, he turned around and took one last look at Berga Naval Base. That was it. He had done what was expected of him. Now he would catch a bus into Västerhaninge, and from there could carry on back to Stockholm.

Little did he know, he wasn't done with this. For as long as he lived, he would never be done with this.

* * *

Muskö Naval Base, April 28th, 1300hrs

Löfgren left lunch headed back to his office. Things were going well. The shooting was unfortunate, but the interrogator and her crew were sure nobody would find any evidence of what happened there. The Swedish submarine was tied up at the pier, and the crew was debriefed and sent home. All items in the Navy archive that could suggest this wasn't a Soviet submarine were cleaned out, and the contractor crew had bagged all the materials from the investigator's locker.

He didn't know where the materials were at this time. That had to change. They would need to be destroyed or put somewhere under his control. As the Swedish submarine was safe now, what he had agreed to do was really no major thing. He simply highlighted the sighting to the Navy and then the Defense ministry. He was handsomely paid for it, and there was a promotion in the works for him. The Navy was getting the budget they needed to be a force to be reckoned with in the Baltic Sea region. All in all, a good outcome.

He turned the corner toward the entrance to his office and walked up the stairs to the yellow brick building. Inside, he made a left and waved to the receptionist, who let him in without showing his ID. That was the end of the great day he was having.

Walking into his office, a man was sitting in his visitor's chair. He was wearing plain clothes, jeans, and a short sports jacket over a shirt that had seen too many wash cycles. Löfgren walked into the office and sat down in his own chair.

"Can I help you?"

"Yes, Commander. You will have to come with me."

Löfgren laughed, "What are you on about? I don't need to follow you anywhere."

"Yes, you do. I work with the Swedish Security Police, and we have reason to believe you have been engaging in unlawful activity here. You best come with me so we can sort this out." Löfgren's laughter immediately shifted to rage.

"I'm a first-degree commander in military intelligence. What we do here is highly classified, and I doubt you have any authority to barge in here and demand anything. Now get the hell out of my office, or I'll call base security."

"Well, if I read your sleeve right"—the man nodded toward Löfgren's uniform—"you're not a commander of the first degree just yet, are you?" The man stood up, stepped around the desk, and grabbed Löfgren by the arm. "Now stop wasting both of our time and let's go."

Furious, Löfgren stood up and yanked his left arm free from the man's grip. With what seemed like a reflex, he spun around to the left and delivered a straight right to the man's face. He hit him cleanly on the nose, and the man toppled over backward, hit his back and head on the wall, and fell toward the side.

He wasn't unconscious but remained on the floor, trying to get to terms with the rattling of his brain. Löfgren stood over him, hesitating on what to do next. He didn't have to think for long, as two more plain-clothed men burst through the door at the same time, weapons kept low along their sides.

Unsteadily, the first man got to his feet, holding his nose. Surprisingly, he smiled at

Löfgren. "That's what I get for trying to be nice, is it?" He gestured toward the other two men, who were standing still in the entrance to the room. "My friends and I will need you to come with us. You can quietly come with us, or we can hurt you so bad you'll wish you were dead. I got my nose as an alibi of you resisting. Your choice, Commander. I'm indifferent and would quite frankly enjoy the opportunity to return the favor."

There was nowhere to run from the office unless he wanted to fight with the two men blocking the entrance. As opposed to their superior, who remained surprisingly calm, both men in the doorway were looking at him like they would really enjoy the opportunity as well. Löfgren threw his palms out in front of him and shrugged his shoulders. "Where are we going?"

"Not of your concern, Commander."

* * *

Unknown Location, April 29th, 1500hrs
Rosenfeldt walked in through the doors of a basement in the northern suburbs of Stockholm. He didn't know this part of town very well but had been driven here by a member of the security police outfit that had detained Ola Löfgren.

"It's an old bomb shelter. We use it for various purposes when things are, let's say, less public in nature."

Rosenfeldt, dressed in civilian clothing that wouldn't draw attention, followed the man down through a dark and damp set of concrete stairs. At the bottom was a heavy-set door, like the one you would expect to see in an underground bomb shelter, but this one had a few different and shiny locking mechanisms on it.

The police officer spent some time working the door before slowly opening it. It was dark inside and completely silent. *Like an old tomb*, Rosenfeldt thought and shook off an oncoming feeling of discomfort.

The security police inspector came to greet him and motioned him into a small room with a camping-style table and a few chairs. The man had a band-aide across his nose and the area below his left eye was discolored.

"Anything?"

"Not much yet. He claims all he did was highlight the sighting to make sure the Navy took it seriously. That's not a crime, of course."

"No, it's not, but this time he called the Ministry of Defense directly. Not to mention all these other things. Once you add them all together, that's when it stops making sense and starts to smell like treason."

"Yes, the other things. In terms of the intelligence order for the submarine, he claims

Nylund told him to plant those in the order file of the submarine. We are looking into the accuracy of that statement."

"The head of the Navy would have told him to plant made-up orders in the archive? Interesting. Can you verify that in any other way than simply asking Nylund himself?"

"Not really. It will be Löfgren's word against Nylund's unless there is some other track record of this instruction."

"Yes, so maybe we leave Nylund out of this for now. The admiral will have some other matters to attend to."

That was true. He was going to attend to his own retirement, and Rosenfeldt didn't want him involved in this. It was best to get Löfgren out of the way. The supreme commander casually looked around the room. Maybe, Commander of the First Degree Ola Löfgren could simply stay in here?

He turned his attention back to the man in front of him. "So, what else can you tell me?"

"The requisition form to get ahold of a small craft and four uniforms. He claims he never saw it before."

"But it is, in fact, his signature, isn't it?"

"According to our experts, yes it is. Now, a signature is difficult to fake, but it isn't impossible. I'm sure he has signed hundreds of documents, so there's also a possibility he was asked to sign something he doesn't remember. He wouldn't be the first person to sign something without knowing what it is."

Rosenfeldt thought about the number of times his secretary asked him to sign something, where he would simply do so without even looking. No, Löfgren wouldn't be the first person to do that. Very unfortunate circumstances to have it happen. Very unfortunate.

The man across from him looked down at a piece of paper. "For the bits on stealing evidence, he says he was ordered to do that too."

"Ordered by Nylund?"

"No, by you, General."

Fredrik Rosenfeldt smiled and leaned back in his seat. "Poor bastard. He has completely lost it. I take it he has some excuse about why there is no order like that."

"Verbal order only, according to him. We will, of course, follow up on all items, but as far as I'm concerned, Commander First-Degree Löfgren is neck-deep in the shit. Neck-deep and unlikely to get out of it. Unless we come across a paper trail that proves some of his claims. I would think that is unlikely, though?"

"Yes, I would think that is very unlikely," Rosenfeldt responded. He looked around the room again

"Can I talk to him? Privately, I mean."

The supreme commander got a nod of understanding around the likelihood to prove any of Löfgren's claims. The inspector got up and gestured for Rosenfeldt to follow him.

"Right this way, general."

They walked through a narrow corridor before the man stopped in front of a heavy door and pulled some keys from his pocket.

"He's cuffed to the wall. The chain is long enough for him to move around, but there's a line on the floor the indicates how far he can go. I'll be out here if there is anything."

"No recording devices?"

The man shook his head. "What we do here is better kept off any records."

Rosenfeldt walked into the room and closed the door behind him. Löfgren sat on a simple chair in front of a desk. Very similar to how police interrogation rooms were depicted on television. *So there's some truth to that then*, Rosenfeldt thought as he sat down on a chair pushed back behind a white line that ran in an arch on the floor. They were probably used to people more prone to violence than Löfgren, even if the inspector's nose told a different story.

Löfgren had a black eye as well, and he sat slumped in the chair as if other parts of his body were hurting as well. Apparently, the agents apprehending him had made sure he paid the price for assaulting them.

"How are you doing, Ola?"

"How the fuck do you think I'm doing, you piece of shit. I was ordered to do every single thing I have done. Every single fucking thing."

"Ordered to release craft and uniforms to people that hijacked the tapes?"

"You don't believe that for real, do you? That I signed for materials to be used against the Navy. That's ridiculous."

"I don't know what to believe anymore. It seems you've been busy making changes to every archive and leaking information like a sieve. Frankly, it smells like you have been playing spy and done it poorly. And when you get caught, you use some sort of blanket excuse of being ordered to do everything. Does that include meetings with a yet-to-be-identified individual who is suspected of having something to do with this?

Löfgren tried to stand up but fell back in his chair again, wincing in pain.

"So they did mess up more than your eye, did they?"

He got a grunt as a reply while Löfgren tried to get comfortable on the chair again.

"Treason is a serious charge, you know. Serious enough to get you decades behind bars. That is, of course, if we involve the regular criminal courts."

"I'll kill you, you piece of shit." Löfgren hissed through his teeth.

"No, you won't, Löfgren. You won't. You will never get out of here again. Goodbye, Ola. I'll see you later, on the other side of a seventy-year confidentiality stamp."

* * *

Police Depot, April 30th, 1130hrs

The technicians watched as the tow truck reversed into the hall and stopped. The driver jumped out and quickly released the vehicle before gently reversing it off the forklike hydraulic arm that held it in place during transport. He waved at the technicians before he jumped back in his truck and disappeared as fast as he had shown up.

They looked at the vehicle and then at the big clock on the wall. One hour to lunch break. With a bit of focus they could probably knock this off before then. The paperwork said there was a missing person related to the vehicle, but with no current suspicion of a crime. That would call for a first run-through of the vehicle to see if there was anything of interest in it, but not for a complete forensic analysis.

"Well, let's have a look then," the head technician said and picked up a set of plastic bags and a clipboard. He threw the clipboard to his colleague and reached into the car on the driver's side to pull the lever to the hood.

"Volvo 142, black, registered to one Frida Maria Wikström." Leaning under the hood, he read out the chassis number and other notable observations that could be useful later.

"Looks like it may have been in an accident but has been fixed. Screws around the engine seem to have shifted slightly from the impact."

They went on to open all the doors of the Volvo as well as the trunk.

"Let's see. Nothing interesting in the trunk. Towing line, Jump cables. There's a white jacket here. Looks female and probably female size as well."

He held up the jacket in front of him. "Yes, definitely female."

Most of the other things in the trunk were perfectly ordinary. A warning triangle to put on the road in case of a breakdown. A first aid kit with a logo on it, probably where she had her insurance.

His colleague was busy looking underneath the seats with a small flashlight. It was amazing what you could find under car seats that would tell you a lot about the owner. They didn't find one single thing. That told them something about the owner as well.

It could be timing. Maybe she just cleaned her car. He looked around again. No, he had a feeling it always looked like this. No children, that's for sure. Those little monsters would wreck a car in no time, and this one had been running for quite a while. Probably used mainly for shorter distances.

"It's spotless," his assistant said.

"Yes, very clean. Almost too clean. Like a work tool. You know the other people that have clean cars like this all the time? German taxi drivers. It's their workplace. They want it clean. Among the cleanest cars I've ever seen."

"So you are saying the owner is likely a German taxi driver?"

"shut up idiot, I am saying this person may spend a lot of time in their car."

His colleague was about to rise from the floor when he let out a loud whistle.

"What? What is it?"

"One black holster, taped in place underneath the steering wheel."

"Holster, like for a gun, you mean?"

"Hold on." His colleague picked up a camera and took a picture of it before carefully removing it from its place. He put it in a plastic bag and held it up in the light. "Leather holster, black, the size would suggest something like a Walther, I would say. We should check if she had a license for something like that. I can't find any trace of the gun, though."

With renewed interest, both of them went to

work, re-examining the interior of the car. After half an hour and with no other exciting finds to show for it, they both lost energy and started looking at the clock to see if lunch was approaching. It was getting close. The head technician started to look through the form they were filling out to ensure it was all bagged and tagged correctly. His colleague was still looking at something inside the car.

"Not even a note in the owner's manual. Who doesn't write down what the correct air pressure is for the tyres? I forget that every time I check it, and I work with cars. Hold on, there's a cassette in here."

He stood up and walked over to the workbench, put the cassette in a player, and pressed play. A low rumbling sound filled the room.

"I'm not sure what that is, but it isn't music. That's for sure."

The two men looked at each other, shrugging.

"How would you describe that?"

"I don't know."

They both stood there and listened to the tape for another thirty seconds.

"You know what, I'll put that down as unidentified noise. Bag the tape and let's go for lunch."

Chapter 31 – Regrets

Russian Embassy, May 2ⁿᵈ, 1982, 1300hrs

Markovski walked across the yard and met up with the other two gentlemen from the embassy staff. Two men with the same experience as him, just to a varying extent. One was his predecessor, and the other one, the young one, his successor. The weather was brilliant for an afternoon in May, and the sun gently warmed the three Russians as they sat down in the garden. They were waiting for some drinks to be delivered.

"So, we're done now?" Markovski's successor asked.

"Just about, Alexei. Just about. We'll have to see what happens now and let it play out. These things take on a life of their own once they're out of the box. It's like a tree. Planting it is the most important bit, but it will need careful gardening for a while to grow well."

"And you think this will grow well?"

"Well, their defense department is announcing us as the villain, while the admiral has different ideas. Different ideas that he suddenly retracts. The rumor has it the head of the Army still thinks it's a stunt from the Navy to steal his budget. Trust me, with the right care, this will grow well."

"I'm not sure I understand what we are trying to achieve. It seems confusing to me too."

Markovski laughed heartily and smiled at his successor. "That's right, comrade. Confusion. Confusion is our friend, Alexei."

He took on a more sinister tone as he continued. "You know as well as I do, comrade. Not all is well back home. The Rodina is suffering. Our economy is stagnating since some time now. We have to get our grain from the US, for crying out loud. With developments in technology and the fighting ongoing in Afghanistan, some are afraid we're in a race we can no longer win."

The gaze of his successor fell to the ground as he contemplated the bleak future of the motherland. Who knew for how long Brezhnev would be around, and the divide around the defense spending was getting more significant by the day. The future was indeed uncertain.

Markovski continued. "We have known for some time that we would lose a conventional war in Europe against NATO. When a pure matchup of force isn't an option, other means and measures become necessary. Then, by chance, the *S-363* runs aground in Swedish waters. The effects were surprising, even to our campaign planners."

Markovski rested his face toward the sun for a few seconds with his eyes closed. "The point is that superior military power is only of use if you can determine where to decisively use it. This is the way of the future, Alexei. When *S-363* ran aground, the Swedish military and its government argued for months, engaging in internal battles completely unrelated to us. They argued with several NATO countries, effectively drawing everyone's attention away from what was important. Instead, they all spent their time coming up with theories about what happened and why. Complete and utter confusion, Alexei. It couldn't have gone any better had we planned for it to happen."

"So, one sighting of a Soviet submarine in Swedish waters and NATO's focus goes out the window. That's what you mean?"

"Something like that, Alexei, something like that. Politics has been helpful too. Once they officially blamed us, their generals and politicians had no choice but to stick to their statements. It would be too hard politically to reverse, no matter what happened. There are numerous doubts with them now. Probably enough to keep them going for decades on this."

Drinks arrived, and the three men greedily helped themselves to both the tea and the stronger options placed on the table in front of them. As the staff member turned and disappeared back toward the embassy building, Markovski continued his explanation. "Trust me, comrade. You're looking at uncertainty and debate that will keep Sweden occupied for many years to come. The current government is likely to lose the election. The new one will have a hard time being effective with our countries now being enemies. They will launch a commission to find out what happened, and they are doubtful to find anything decisive. Their archives will be full of inconsistencies and items that have been lost. The outcome will probably say it was us still, but there will be no certainty. I would say they will need several commissions over the next decade."

The three men laughed as Markovski used the word *decade*. Ten years was a long time to argue without getting to any conclusion. Could something as simple as this really make enough waves to last for years?

"But won't they increase funding to their Navy and be a bigger threat?"

"Let them. We don't give a damn about Sweden, comrade."

"And Skaggerack? The American Polaris boats. How do we threaten them with a strong Swedish Navy in the way?"

"Our intelligence is telling us with certainty that the Polaris range will allow them to fire from anywhere along Norway's coastline by the end of the year. Skaggerack isn't important. It's nothing but a local puddle. And trust me, comrade. Once Sweden has built its Navy and they realize they have no enemy to fight, what do you think will happen?"

Alexei nodded slowly as he tried to make sense of the explanation he was hearing. After a few seconds, he verbalized his conclusions. "When a country that hasn't seen war in 200 years is spending too much on its military instead of on its healthcare system and its pensions, then the reaction will be aggressive. The build-up will be temporary, but the decline will go on for a long time."

"Exactly, Alexei. Uncertainty and internal fighting, uncertainty and internal fighting. Over and over again."

"And what about when the effect wears off?"

"What do you think, comrade? Then we do it again. How does 2014 sit with you?"

All three men laughed again at the random year that Markovski had picked, more than thirty years into the future.

"Maybe you, Alexei, will be around to see it happen. Old Viktor here and myself—probably not."

Old Viktor raised a glass of vodka to his two colleagues. "To confusion, comrades. To lots of confusion for many decades to come."

They toasted and emptied their glasses. Clouds covered the sun now and though it was a fine spring day, they could feel there was still time before summer would arrive. As Alexei stretched out for the bottle to provide them all with a second round, he curiously asked the more practical question. "The submarine—where did it go after the encounter with the Swedish Navy?"

Markovski looked at him and smiled. "What submarine, comrade?"

Alexei leaned back in his chair and took a sip of his second drink. "Maybe it was a West German boat then, and we will never be the wiser?"

"Something like that," Markovski stated. He also took a sip of his drink before he continued. "Of course, we'll send Mr. Nordin a letter about this, stating that we're open to an international inquiry. We'll willingly put all of our official archives on the table if they do the same. They'll never go through with it, of course. Too many inconsistencies in their archives."

"How do we know that?"

"Let's say we've had a solid information source close to the archives for some time now. Until recently, that is."

"What happened?"

"She walked out of work one day and never returned. But not to worry. We would have known through other sources if she had been caught. She probably just executed her own exit plan. Smart woman. I doubt NATO will ever find her."

"What about us?"

"Us? Oh, we'll find her eventually. It may take a while, but we *will* find her."

The younger man looked down at his glass for a long time. Finding her could only end one way for her. He then stated, more to his glass than to the other men, "So Sweden is a pilot study?"

Markovski and Victor looked at each other. He was a bright young man, Alexei. Victor leaned forward in his chair to catch Alexei's eye. "Tell us, comrade. What are you thinking?"

Alexei seemed hesitant at first, as he was called out based on a comment he'd made without thinking. He then regained his focus and shrugged his shoulders. "Seems to me like the maskirovka carries significantly less risk than trying to beat our enemies in a measure of military might. Why not attack them all?"

* * *

Stockholm, August 11th, 1982, 2000hrs
Nylund was sitting on the couch. On the table in front of him was a letter of retirement from the Navy. Next to it, a box with a symbolic additional star that would go onto his uniform. As a young and ambitious lieutenant, he had dreamed about this

day. The day when he would be a full admiral of the Swedish Navy. Not a rear-admiral or a vice-admiral. Plain and simple: an admiral.

It had been a long path to get there, and he had enjoyed a lot of it. Command at sea was always his preference, even if it meant a lot of time away from the family. Christina always understood, while his daughter, to this day, was probably unsure why her father didn't seem interested in spending more time with her. His career in the Navy had cost him a marriage and the relationship with his only child. Here he was at the very top of the Navy chain of command, a brief moment of achievement before the Navy was taken away from him by a single signature.

He stood up and walked over to his bar cabinet. What would be more suitable than a glass of rum to celebrate? He poured himself a generous serving and contemplated a walk to the freezer for some ice but decided to walk straight back to the couch. He put his glass down on his letter of retirement. As he lifted it again to take a sip, a wet ring had formed on the piece of paper. He read the sentence running through the middle of it. *The Navy is grateful for more than four decades of distinguished service.*

He wasn't sure what had become of his Navy. Through the sightings that occurred the last few years, he had felt the Navy swinging from one extreme to the other. Men and women on the Navy vessels performed their duties as they were trained. And most of the time they did an exemplary job. On the other hand, politics and bureaucracy had muddled the waters within the Navy and created a complex environment that he struggled to cope with. All bark and no teeth. He struggled to the point where he had sought some outside help.

Löfgren had something to do with this. He wasn't sure how or why, but he did have something to do with it for sure. The Navy coroner had called him a few days ago. Nylund had all but forgotten about the plan he and Wikström derived. Spread out information and be selective about who knows about it. He had asked the Navy coroner to put the file on one Michael Wozniak under HC58d in the archive.

Apparently, the coroner forgot all about the file as well, but when he suddenly remembered, he checked the location and called Nylund. The file was gone. It was gone, and the only person who was told about its location was Commander Ola Löfgren. Löfgren was the leak. Nylund had tried to reach him, but he had disappeared from the face of the earth. It was too late now.

Wikström. What happened to her? He felt an icy ball in his stomach telling him he would never know. She was a tough girl who could take care of herself . . . but to be gone for this long. Would the

Swedish government really have stretched into the territory of murder to keep their cover-up a secret? Lying came easy to politicians, but hopefully, murder did not. Either way, Wikström was no longer here, and if she had been killed, he might as well have done it himself. He brought her into this, and she paid the price.

Sometimes he had pictured Frida Wikström as Cecilia's older, stronger sister. Cecilia did well in her bank job in London. She was tough and could take the enormous pressure they put on her in that awful workplace. She could endure anything they threw her way.

Wikström, on the other hand, was more aggressive in nature. She simply wouldn't put up with some banker putting undue pressure on her. He couldn't help but smile as he pictured Wikström tearing into one of Cecilia's bosses. She would have been a great older sister. She would probably have done a better job raising Cecilia than he ever did.

Admiral Klas Nylund walked up the stairs with heavy steps. The rum had done its bit, and he used his hand to steady himself against the wall. In his bedroom, he laid out his parade uniform on the bed and started to undress. Once in his full uniform, he took a minute to shine his shoes before he walked over to his desk and pulled out the wedding picture—the one he had knocked over a while back. It didn't have a frame anymore, so he pinched it in one corner to protect it while walking downstairs again.

He laid out the four things in a straight line in front of him on the table. A glass of rum, a final admiral's star, a retirement letter, and his wedding photography. He looked behind him. The back of the couch was facing a concrete wall. That was unlikely to be a problem.

He looked at the row of items again. It was missing something to remind him of Wikström and his failure to keep her safe. It was too late to do something about that. After pulling the revolver from his pocket, he inspected his uniform. In two quick movements, he cocked the weapon and brought it up to his forehead. He took a deep breath, and without further hesitation, pulled the trigger.

* * *

Stockholm, August 13th, 1982, 1300hrs

Nordin felt better than he in a long while. His party was still enjoying some benefits from the debacle, and a new wave of anti-Soviet sentiments was sweeping the nation. The number of Swedes that considered the Soviet union a real threat had risen by almost fifty percentage points, to peak somewhere around the eighty mark. Eighty percent. That is one scared country.

At the same time, his party promised significant funds to the Navy and the military in general. *We might give the socialists a run for their money after all,* he thought. The 19th of September would tell them the answer to that question. Until then, Nordin held on to a small hope to make the socialists stay in opposition.

A knock on his door brought him out of thought, and he shouted out a simple "Yes" to the unknown person on the other side. One of his closest aides walked in with a worried look on his face and a few pieces of paper in his hand.

"What could possibly be that bad?" Nordin asked him. "You have another month before you're officially out of a job." He chuckled at his own cynicism.

His aide rolled his eyes at the bad joke but then shook his head and nodded toward the papers in his hand. He dropped them on Nordin's desk. "The official response from the Soviets regarding our protest."

"And they say they didn't do it, I take it?"

"Worse than that. They have put their suggestion of an international inquiry in formal communication. They are officially challenging us to put all of our evidence on the table."

Nordin sat up straight in his chair. That was bad news indeed. Löfgren had cleaned the archives, so there should be no information to state otherwise, but it also didn't hold any hard evidence supporting the claims they made. He picked up the letter to read it.

"They're bluffing."

His aide continued to shake his head. "I thought so too, but this is no longer a background conversation between diplomats. This is an official signed letter from the President of the Soviet Union. There is a risk they will wave this letter around, in which case we will be in a precarious situation."

Nordin took a deep breath and prepared to speak, but his aide beat him to it.

"We could get a commission of our own together as soon as we can and have them start the work of investigating what happened. That would show how seriously we are to get to the bottom of it without inviting international diplomats to our archives."

Nordin shook his head. "There will be no commission into this. We know who it was, and we have told it straight to the Swedish public. It will look more like we are second-guessing ourselves, which won't be helpful a month out from the election. If anything, we need to think about how we avoid the socialists digging into this in case there is a change of government."

"I don't think we can do that."

"Why not?"

"This is official communications. An unwillingness to answer from our side will likely make them go public with this. Then what?"

"Then the socialists can launch their own investigation. They won't find it to be very useful. We know what it was, and there's no information to contradict us. If we stick to our guns, this matter will never really be clarified, and we win. No resolution is in our favor. Besides, militarily speaking it doesn't matter who was here, but from a political point of view, it makes all the difference."

* * *

Stockholm, August 16th, 1982, 1030hrs

Defense Minister Thomas Nordin gave the supreme commander a hard look.

"You've got to be kidding? We're about to tone this down, and now this. First, the damn Soviets formally tell us we need to put our evidence in the light of the world to see...and now this."

"Believe me, I wish I was joking, but there is no doubt. He was found on his couch in his parade uniform. Single gunshot wound to the head. Death would have been immediate."

"God, what a mess. It won't look good for us if this comes out. He was just retired with honors, and things were calming down. This will cause a new shit storm."

"I agree. Despite the press conference, the media and the public are well aware of the discussions that happened within the Navy about the sighting. It won't look good once this goes public."

"Does it have to go public?" Nordin gave the supreme commander a questioning look.

"Well, he used to be married and has one daughter. We can't simply not tell them."

"I know, but could we perhaps avoid the details of what happened and perhaps pull it off as, let's say, a heart attack. The man has been under considerable stress. We could keep this hero thing going, you know. The admiral, who chased the Soviet Navy away, not once, but twice. The Admiral who build a powerful Swedish Navy. He essentially sacrificed his life to defend his country. Something like that."

"Who found him by the way?"

"A Navy driver that was delivering some items from his office. The enlisted man saw his feet through the window, and as he failed to get any response at the door, he called the watch officer at Muskö. They called the ambulance service when they couldn't raise him on the phone."

"So, how many people saw the mess?"

"The enlisted man only saw his feet, nothing else. The police officers that broke the door and the ambulance crew, four people, I would think."

"What do you think? Doable?"

Rosenfeldt had lost count of how many questioning looks he had received.

"Definitely. We can contact the people and go through this with them. The man was a hero and should remain one in the memory of his country. Something like that."

"So the matter is settled then."

"Yes, settled."

* * *

Lake Orlången, August 24th, 1983, 0830hrs

Police cadet Mats Svensson walked around the area. He had just used the blue and white tape for the first time to seal off an area around a dead body. Now, they were canvassing the forest for anything that could be related to the death.

Three hours went by, but nobody could find anything that would suggest this was anything else than an accidental drowning. A young man had taken a boat out on the lake and returned. His girlfriend, who was supposed to meet him this morning, had arrived finding only an empty tent and dinner still on its plate.

Walking around the area looking for him, she made the horrible discovery of her boyfriend, face down in the knee-deep water close to shore. It had taken the emergency services operator several minutes to calm her down to a level where she made any sense. Finally, they got her name and a location. Both police and paramedics were dispatched, but they could do nothing but confirm the young man's death. They assumed it was drowning, but the autopsy would need to verify that.

Mats was exhausted. He was on the force since only a month, and dragging a dead body out of the water was enough of a stressor on him for one day. Searching the forest was easy work, physically, but it did nothing to help him shut the first pictures of the scene out of his mind. A young man, not far from his own age, face down in the water. He had started to tug on the body, unsure of what to do, when a paramedic had thrown herself at the body, turned it over, and checked for vital signs. There were none to be found.

One of the senior inspectors walked by, "No sign of violence to the body. No sign of struggle. I would assume this is an unfortunate, probably intoxicated man, that made an awful decision. We'll have to wait and see what they make of it when they open him up."

Mats subdued a shiver when there was talk about opening the man up. While that work was done by people with a stomach for that stuff, he would be typing up the report and ensuring parents or guardians were notified. He looked down on his pad. Fredrik Wikingsson, age twenty-one.

Police cadet Svensson looked up from his notepad again. "But walking away with the tent open and dinner ready?"

"What's your point?" the inspector stated arrogantly.

"Just odd, cooking dinner on a camping stove, and once you're done, you stand up and go rowing around on the lake."

"Cadet Svensson, is it?"

"Yes"

"Well then, cadet Svensson, why don't you take that pad and pencil of yours and get back to the station to type this up."

* * *

The *Kakariki*, Leaving Gothenburg Harbor, August 26th, 1983, 1400hrs

The *Kakariki* had just left Gothenburg Harbor an hour earlier. She was loaded to the brim with cars destined for the northern island of New Zealand. The Volvo might be seen as a standard car in Sweden, but it was considered a luxury vehicle in large parts of the southern hemisphere. In combination with its well-marketed focus on safety, it was increasing in popularity on the streets of Auckland.

The captain had seen the passenger come on

board, but he'd been too busy casting off to ask his first mate about it.

"Who's the passenger?"

"Someone who needed to get out of Sweden without any questions asked. Paid well, and a former sailor apparently. I think he could prove useful. It's a long trip, and we're short-handed as it is."

"So he's not going to cause us any trouble, is he?"

"Doubt it, and he's already paid. So if he does, we can just throw him overboard."

Both men laughed about the prospect of chucking the Swede over the side.

"You think he'll hack it? It's a very long trip."

"I have twenty-five thousand Swedish crowns in my cabin. That's something I know for sure. He looks fit for work, so we'll feed him as long as he shows up in the galley on time and we get him to do the simpler maintenance. I think he'll mind his own business. He seems a bit . . ."

"A bit what?"

"I don't know, a bit unpredictable."

The captain looked his first mate straight in the eye. "Unpredictable?"

"Ah, you know what I mean. The people who try to get away like this are hardly doing so for the fun of it. I'm sure he is harmless."

"If not, it'll be you going over the side. You

can quote me on that."

"So you don't want your cut?" The first mate grinned.

The captain laughed. "I'll take all of it once you're both shark food in the Indian Ocean."

Both men laughed.

"Jokes aside, I think we can use him. He works for food, and we make some extra profit on this voyage. Should work out well."

"Does he have a name?"

"His name is Carl. That's all I got out of him."

"Well, get Carl some overalls then. We have lots of maintenance that needs doing."

* * *

Sandsjön, December 14th, 1983, 1300hrs

The two men stepped out of the vehicle and cautiously closed the doors. Few people realized how the sound of a slammed car door carried across the woods up here. Especially on a day like this. The sun was setting, and the trees threw long shadows across the corner of the road. Thirty more minutes and dusk would be taking over.

"We're early."

"I know. Just a bit of daylight left, but I don't want to freeze my butt off, so let's have a look."

"He should be alone, right?"

"Yes, he should be alone. As far as I've been

403

told, we're looking at one man. There is more than likely a hunting rifle or two lying around, but I doubt we need to assume he is armed and dangerous."

The two men slowly walked down a narrow path that led them to what would have been the shore of a lake in the summertime. Now it was frozen solid, with a thin layer of fine snow on top. They frequently stopped and listened for any sound that would give away what was happening in the woods around them.

As they drew closer, they could hear the light chopping of an ax, but between strikes, the afternoon lay perfectly still. It was a cold day, and their breath formed a cloud in front of them as they kept walking toward the noise. If it was possible to make it look like an accident, that would be preferable. If not, that would work too. It just meant extra work to tidy up.

Both men stopped dead in their tracks as they heard the sound.

"Shit, that's a fucking dog."

"That's bad news. The worse news is, he's not supposed to have a dog. Maybe someone else is nearby."

"Okay, we need to be careful now. The dog could become a major problem if it's not tied up. I say we skip the accident and go for silent efficiency instead."

The other man nodded and opened his jacket to pull out his weapon, a PB-silenced pistol they were equipped with specifically for this operation. The first man did the same, and they slowly continued along the side of the frozen lake, weapons at their sides. They probably wouldn't need them, and they didn't want to look obviously hostile if anyone saw them.

Moving among the pine trees, they reached a small cabin, right by the water. They stood perfectly still for a full minute. The chopping sound of the ax had stopped, and there were no other sounds other than a slight breeze occasionally moving the trees around them. There were tracks on the lake. Someone had been getting around on a snowmobile, or maybe a dog sled.

They both moved up to the house, careful to keep low and out of sight from the windows. Moving extremely slowly, making sure each footstep was calculated, they entered the decking area by the front door. The snow gave off a low creak under their feet—like the creak of a door but without the high-pitched notes.

There was a rumble from inside, like someone stumbling on something, and the men didn't hesitate any longer. The lead quickly gestured for his colleague to go around the back before he delivered a powerful kick to the door. The door broke but didn't open completely.

As he took aim for his next kick, a shot rang out. It missed them both but tore a big piece of the railing between them. They both dove for cover as they tried to locate the shooter. A rifle would have a superior range to their silenced pistols, but they quickly realized this would not be a big problem. The man with the rifle crouched behind a rock only thirty meters from them, clearly struggling with the bolt action in the cold. Both men took aim and opened fire on the man, who disappeared behind the rock.

The man probably had no military training. He had put himself behind a single rock in the open, and the two of them would easily flank him. Their pistols only held eight rounds, but they were a good team and carried enough ammunition to handle this. A bolt action rifle would be slow and clumsy at short range. The Siberian husky was barking like mad again, but his chain was attached to a tree twenty meters up the hill. He would do them no harm.

Still lying on the deck by the busted door, the lead looked around and got ready to stand up. They needed to close the distance and take this man out as soon as possible. As he got to his knees, he heard a creak from the door and could sense more than see a movement behind him.

Edward Sandberg brought the ax down across the back of the man's neck. With gravity's help, the heavy ax struck with enough force to break the man's collar bone and tear his trapezius muscle clean off its attachment. The man dropped onto his stomach without making a sound, only to start screaming a second later as the pain signals forced their way through to his brain. Sandberg kept standing over the man as blood began to color the snow on the deck.

His colleague spun around and was now caught choosing between Sandberg and the man behind the rock. As he could see no firearm on Sandberg, he turned again and took aim at the old man, now visible and ready to fire his rifle again. Both men squeezed the trigger of their weapons, and both men fell backward a second later.

Sandberg managed to move again and ended the screaming of the man in front of him with a stomp to his head. He then threw himself on the deck, trying to pick up the silenced pistol. Time slowed, and in his head, it took him ages to get a good grip on it in the cold and get it trained on the second man. After a few seconds, he realized there was no need to do anything else. The second intruder wasn't moving.

As he held the weapon in front of him, his brain caught up with what was happening, and his hands started shaking uncontrollably. He dropped the pistol on the deck. Standing on all fours, Sandberg struggled to get enough air into his lungs to calm his senses.

There was movement to his right and he started to look for the pistol again before he realized it was his neighbor. Carrying his rifle on his left shoulder, he was holding his right arm tight to his torso.

"You're hurt."

"Silenced crap. I've been hurt worse than this working on the house."

His neighbor then looked at the blood dripping down his hand and added, "I do think you'll have to patch me up before you go. Clearly, you're not safe here."

Epilogue

Stockholm, May 12th, 1997, 0900hrs

Police Inspector Mats Svensson walked through the hallway of the homicide section. He grabbed a cup of coffee from the pot to have with him in the briefing in case it took longer than anticipated. As he walked through the doors of the meeting room five minutes late, he looked across the room and judged that most of the colleagues were present. He dropped the file on the table in front of him and fired up the projector.

"Okay, everyone. Listen up. You have heard about the find in the woods north of the city about two weeks back. A guy walks his dog. Dog scratches around in the dirt. Dog finds what looks like the part of a human hand. Guy calls the police. I hope everyone can follow me so far?"

He could see the smiles of his colleagues, which was a good sign for a Monday morning and at the start of a new and seemingly puzzling case. The worse the case, the more positivity was needed in the beginning. Despite the one-hour TV shows replete with sexy sleuthing, real police work was a long, slow, and grueling process. Not to mention frustrating, given the number of dead ends any major investigation would run into.

"The technicians have been working on the site and have uncovered the remains of a person. Identification has taken a while, but dental work along with pre-existing injuries have eventually led to a positive identification of what seems to be a murder victim."

He clicked on the computer to get the picture up on the screen behind him.

"Frida Wikström, Inspector Frida Wikström. Born in 1946. One of Stockholm's finest from 1969 to 1978. Considered a brilliant investigator. It was before my time, but some of you may have met her back then."

There was no more smiling, and all he got was a grunt from one of the older men in the corner who acknowledged he had, in fact, met Frida Wikström.

"She went missing on 23rd of April 1982 and has been missing since. Some investigation went into her disappearance back then, but it's been a cold case since the middle of that year."

He clicked the computer again to switch pictures. Behind him were human remains on a stainless steel, autopsy-style table. Two red arrows on the image pointed to the chest and to the left leg.

"Cause of death, shot twice by a heavy

handheld weapon, likely a high-caliber rifle of some sort. One bullet hole to her sternum along with damage to the left femur. Technicians have determined that both shots would have been fatal by themselves. Sternum shot immediately; leg shot would likely have ripped the femoral artery, which will cause a person to bleed out in minutes.

This is still guesswork, but a current working assumption is that she was shot in the leg from behind, potentially running away from something. Then, she was shot in the sternum from the front, based on the angle almost certainly while on the ground."

"They believe this isn't where she was shot but that she was transported to this location and buried after her death. They're still looking into materials and fibers found on and around the body that could help determine how she was moved. I don't think we should expect too much of that. Most likely, they'll just tell us she was transported in a tarp or blanket or something similar."

Another click on the computer. "This is the location where her car was found back in 1982. Parked in front of an entrance to a construction site. The construction crew reported it to the police in the morning as it blocked their heavy crane from entering. The same morning, a break-in was reported at a warehouse turned self-storage facility over here, about one kilometer from her car. The

411

break-in remains unsolved as well."

"The two incidents are suspected to be linked since Frida had a storage locker at this warehouse under the name of Maria Wennergren, a name she has reportedly used in conjunction with an official-looking Police ID. There is a report of her showing it to several witnesses in a submarine sighting investigation in 1982, just a few weeks before her disappearance. The head of the Navy at this time, Admiral Klas Nylund, reportedly hired her to investigate the truthfulness of these sightings. Nylund himself died from a heart attack on, let's see, 11th August 1982."

"When searched by police, her locker was empty. Whether anything was in there in the first place is unknown."

He looked at his notes. "This is one of ours, people. We need this solved. There are some materials in storage from the missing person investigation, I believe. The car has been disposed of, but the search protocol and items should still be around. Let's go. Let's get all the old stuff back on the table and see what we have to work with."

As people stood up to go about their work, Svensson packed up his materials and started his walk back to his office. On the way out the door, he realized his coffee cup was still on the desk, and he turned around to pick it up. He leaned over to grab it as he suddenly froze mid-step. Something about this had been gnawing at him for days. Navy. Submarines. Early eighties. He shivered as he pictured the young former Navy submariner face down in the water. The one he had tried to pull to shore on his first or second month on the force.

He quickly snatched his cup and walked through the corridor. The archives would still hold the files on that case too.

* * *

Stockholm, May 14th, 1997, 1430hrs

"This is ancient history. It'll be a tough one to solve now," one of the investigators said while attempting to open an old evidence box covered in dust. He grimaced as he moved the box and dust hit him in the face.

"Yeah, amazing that the technicians even managed to identify her at all. Stefan in forensic said that injuries from the line of duty were the determining factor."

"The injuries Mats was talking about?"

"Yes, apparently some creep punched her in the face way back and broke her cheekbone. Then she broke her ankle from being pushed down some stairs. Tough girl. Both injuries were on duty, so they were reported and well-documented. Along with the dental work, they're sure it's her."

The first colleague managed to get the box

open and started to read from a list of contents from her car.

"Towing line, jump cables, motor oil, warning triangle, blanket, a white winter jacket. Nothing very interesting here. Oh, wait. Holster for handgun taped in place underneath the steering wheel, no gun in it, though. What the hell was she up to?"

He held up a plastic bag against the light and looked at the black holster.

"That's what we're here to find out, idiot. What else?"

He held up another plastic bag. "One tape found in the tape recorder containing unidentified noise."

"Unidentified noise? What the hell kind of protocol comment is that? That isn't the name of a band, is it?"

"How should I know? Play it and see."

The colleague looked around. Tape recorders were less frequent these days, and he had to run around the floor to find a portable unit to play the tape. Once back in the room, he put the unit down on the table and pressed play. The three investigators could do nothing but give each other questioning looks.

"What on God's green Earth is that?"

"I've never heard anything like it, but it sure as hell isn't music. Go get Mats."

Made in the USA
Coppell, TX
08 June 2023